THE
UNDERGROUND
WOMAN

BOOKS BY KAY BOYLE

Novels

THE UNDERGROUND WOMAN

GENERATION WITHOUT FAREWELL

THE SEAGULL ON THE STEP

HIS HUMAN MAJESTY

"1939"

A FRENCHMAN MUST DIE

AVALANCHE

PRIMER FOR COMBAT

MONDAY NIGHT

DEATH OF A MAN

MY NEXT BRIDE

GENTLEMEN, I ADDRESS YOU
PRIVATELY

YEAR BEFORE LAST

PLAGUED BY THE NIGHTINGALE

Stories and Novelettes

NOTHING EVER BREAKS EXCEPT
THE HEART

THREE SHORT NOVELS

THE SMOKING MOUNTAIN

THE CRAZY HUNTER

THE WHITE HORSES OF VIENNA

THE FIRST LOVER

WEDDING DAY

THIRTY STORIES

Poetry

TESTAMENT FOR MY STUDENTS

COLLECTED POEMS

A GLAD DAY

AMERICAN CITIZEN

For Children

THE YOUNGEST CAMEL

PINKY, THE CAT WHO LIKED TO
SLEEP

PINKY IN PERSIA

Memoirs

THE AUTOBIOGRAPHY OF
EMANUEL CARNEVALI
*Compiled and Edited
by Kay Boyle*

BEING GENIUSES TOGETHER
*Revised and Supplemented
by Kay Boyle*

Essays

THE LONG WALK AT SAN FRANCISCO STATE

THE
UNDERGROUND
WOMAN

Kay Boyle

Doubleday & Company, Inc.
Garden City, New York
1975

"A portion of this novel first appeared as excerpts in *Icarbs* and a portion appeared under the title "Nolo Contendere" in *Antaeus,* Copyright © 1974 by Antaeus.

Library of Congress Cataloging in Publication Data

Boyle, Kay, 1903–
    The underground woman.

    I. Title.
PZ3.B69796Un   813'.5'2
ISBN 0-385-07047-0
Library of Congress Catalog Card Number 72–186008

This book is for
Bessie Breuer,
great writer and beloved friend.

THE
UNDERGROUND
WOMAN

I

THERE WERE FIFTEEN PEOPLE seated in the patrol wagon that had not yet begun to move, and one young man sitting in the lotus position in the center of the aisle. The sturdy men in blue had carried him in and deposited him there, inflexible as if carved out of stone. There he sat at the feet of the other demonstrators, a Buddha in a woven yellow cloak, his shaved skull as well modeled as a Donatello. Even at the moment of arrest, when he had instantly begun to keen his prayers aloud, his voice wailing high and fervently, the cops, the fuzz, the pigs, had not told him to knock it off. They had not so much as taken the trouble to split his lip before carrying him in from the steps of the Induction Center, nor had they cracked his skull when they placed him, ornamental as a vase, on the paddy wagon floor. This time those they had taken into custody might have been bodiless wraiths they accompanied to the ten or twelve waiting vehicles, and slammed the doors on, and locked in. The mace, the boots in the groin, the swinging nightsticks, were held in reserve for the others, the recognizably criminal, who would strike and run. For they could identify as enemy those who advanced carrying lids of garbage cans as shields, wearing motorcycle helmets, who would let the air out of the tires of police cars, and who overturned others in order to halt the buses bringing draftees to the security of uniforms and serial numbers and the probability of death in a country ten thousand miles away.

The California sun had been yellow as the cloak of the young Buddha on the city building and streets, but in the bleak, black wagon everything was in shadow as Athena looked at the faces of these strangers, and tentatively smiled. The young man sitting at her feet she called Siddhartha, wanting names to be exact because her own suited her so badly. She put her hand out and touched his shoulder, and he turned his head at once in bright friendliness.

"Your monk's robe is beautiful," she said in a low voice.

"It's the cloak of the ascetic," he said, and she saw how eloquent his eyes were in his shaven skull, serene and translucent as mountain lakes, and the lashes like dark fern at the edge. "It has a cowl. I got it in India last year."

At the far end of the van, sitting side by side as it straddled the San Andreas Fault, were two other young men, students it might be, one of them short-nosed as a skeleton, with a length of black and purple wampum binding his fair locks, the other bearded, wearing a torn, short-sleeved russet shirt, with tassels of black hair showing at the neck of it, his muscular forearms overgrown by a matted jungle of hair. Athena remembered a psychologist saying that when a man bares his forearms it is as much a sexual invitation as when a woman bares her thighs.

On this side of the two young men sat a distinguished, elderly gentleman, his patient, silvery locks parted in the middle, his pince-nez attached by a black ribbon to the lapel of his tweed jacket; and next to him his partner, wearing steel-rimmed spectacles, her rosy flesh packed solidly into a crisp blue linen dress. From the genteel look of her, she should have been sitting at a bridge table instead of where she now found herself; and Athena saluted her in silence for the good humor with which she brought all she had been born to, and discarded, to this unusual place. The white-haired gentleman and the lady held each other's hands.

Opposite these two tossed a young woman larger in bulk and length of limb than any of the others, nursing a pair of crutches, like a machine gun, on her hip. The left leg of her blue jeans was hacked off at the knee to accommodate an outsized plaster cast with three peace signs inked on the soiled and battered crust. It encased her leg and foot but allowed the bare, bloodless toes to hang free. Her head was as compact and tough as a prize-fighter's fist, the sandy hair on it clipped short, her ears the tight-lobed signature of those who are mean with money and mean with love. Her face was full and sallow, her round chin deeply cleft. Here was hostility to deal with as best one could, thought Athena; here was the unhappy ego screaming in silence, I, I, I, I! Sullenly, endlessly, it was muttering: Not you, my friend, but me, me, me! Athena looked at the naked toes, curved like the sallow claws of a bear, as they hung out of the plaster cradle, and she knew that one whack of the crutches could fell either friend or foe.

(And how do I myself appear to these strangers? Athena asked herself quickly; how can I explain to them that the hollowness of the cheeks and the sober look of the mouth took over without my knowing what was taking place? What in the world happened to the rounded throat and the exquisite brilliance of the eyes, I cannot tell you. Perhaps they were presented as gifts to my daughters: the smooth skin, the limpid orbs, given to them in an unguarded moment of helpless love. The widow's peak on my forehead is less pointed now, and this is because the hair is going gray around the shipwrecked face. The belly is no longer concave, there being no more glaciers to cross, no more mountain refuges to climb to, for these are things you do not do alone. Why did all this happen, and how did it happen, and does it matter that it happened? And yet it must matter as long as I sit here questioning the right of an alien history to hack and hollow its record on my flesh. If I had the whole treasure trove back again, the flashing sapphire eyes, the unfurrowed brow, the marble bosom with its rose-petal fastenings, would I be able to take action without suffering this inner drama of division? Would I accept them back as my natural right, my heritage, and cease asking myself in moments like this why the outside describes so badly what the inside has always sought to be?) And now Athena, forty-two years old and the mother of three, looked at the young people in the van and remembered the exact words she had written her father when she had left home, and never gone back, and never laid eyes on him again. "I've known since the moment I was born, drank it in with my mother's milk," she had written, "that you named me Athena in the expectation of shaping me into the answer to some question you were asking of life. And I couldn't be the answer. I was not the protectress of cities, for I do not like cities, and I was also the wrong one to be designated as the goddess of war."

Next to the young woman with the crutches at her hip and the plaster leg sat a girl of delicate coloring, who before a mirror at dawn that day must have given herself courage by weaving the strands of vermilion wool in and out of her glossy chestnut braids. She wore a thigh-short tan Mexican dress, and nail-studded sandals laced her prim, scrupulously clean feet. A daughter, Athena thought, seeing her fragile bones that all mothers would wish to protect from onslaught, and her eyes shy with respect for the older people there. Beside her sat a young woman dark as a gypsy, whose black hair fell in long straight curtains across her temples and eyebrows. She was thin as a lath, and had that distinction of face and figure that the French call *du chien.* Perhaps in awareness of this she was dressed like a French poet of another century in a flowered silk shirt and a waistcoat of yellow and gold, with yellow twill breeches tight on her boyish rump and tapering legs. Next to her was a woman whom Athena accepted in gratitude as probably her own age; and after a moment of blind imperception, she reproached herself for not having seen this woman first, before all the others. There was gray in the dark braids that were coiled in a modest crown above the woman's small, square brow, and her eyes between the charcoal lashes were a vivid, gentian blue. Her mouth, well shaped and without malice, and with no red painted on it, was twitching to smile, to speak. (I could make her laugh, Athena thought. I could tell her I am not the one who slew the Gorgon, because I would have been afraid of being turned to stone. I could tell her that the building of warships cannot be attributed to me, and she would say, "nor are you the goddess of war-horses," and she would commiserate with me with humor and wisdom because I had been misnamed.)

There was no blacks in the paddy wagon, their crimes being more desperate and despairing than that of sitting in on the steps of an Induction Center, crimes committed at the extreme of hope, expecting no reprieve. Those in the van had sat hour after hour courting arrest, convinced that if man believed deeply enough, and acted on that belief, he generated a power that no law could subvert. The blacks, or the poor of any color, had good reason to know this was a lie. Two inductees had slid down from a second-story window of the Center to come and sit in passive protest with them, and a black draftee had talked for over an hour with them before finally going in, saying: "This is a way for me to have some money coming in every month, maybe to get training for a profession, if they keep their promises; maybe to have a future in this society, maybe to send my kids, when they're born, to college, get them a higher education"; squatting there, talking gravely and eagerly to whitey, whose body blocking the Induction Center was saying that here was still another place where he wasn't allowed to go.

In place of the missing blacks were three boys, Chicano children with light golden skins and Indian hair; and the woman wearing the crown of braids leaned forward in her green suit (fine-ribbed corduroy, it was, or velveteen), and Athena saw the small green stones shining in her ears as she asked them, her mouth half smiling, how old they were. The woman's voice was low-pitched, tentative, as if in deference to everyone alive. "You were perhaps just walking by, on your way home from school,"

she was saying to the Chicano boys, "and you suddenly decided . . ." Athena listened to her speak, and she thought of
Calliope, the muse of eloquence and poetry, and she gave the
woman in her emerald suit that mythical name. The boys said
that one of them, José Jesus, had a brother fighting in Vietnam,
and they wanted him to come home, so that was why they had
sat down. They told Calliope they were cousins, and it was clear
they shared a family shrewdness, for they said that when they
got to the jail, and it was seen that they were juveniles, they'd be
able to telephone the drugstore at the corner of the block where
they lived. "They'll let you have one telephone call," they told
Calliope, talking eagerly to her. "You gotta make up your mind
before you get there if you want to call your lawyer or call home."
Because their families had no telephones, the drugstore owner
would go and tell their mothers or their sisters (the way he'd
done before, they might have been saying), and in the evening,
when their fathers got home from work, they'd come and get
them out. "My older brother, he once had a public defender,"
one of them said. "They'll give you a public defender if you
can't pay for a lawyer." And another of them said that maybe
he'd have a public defender some day, but now they were
juveniles, and they couldn't hold them in the city jail. "That's
the law," they said. "So it pays to be a juvenile," Calliope
said, and she repeated after them the musical sounds of the
names their families had given them: Encarnación, José Jesus,
and Anatario. Of all those in the paddy wagon, thought
Athena, only the three golden-skinned cousins had traveled
this way before and would travel it again after the genteel
had returned to their gentility.

There were others: a young minister with downy cheeks and
boldly troubled eyes; a man perhaps in his fifties with a neat
gray Vandyke, whom Athena remembered as a professor from
the college campus, and who leaned forward now and nodded to
her, smiling in triumph because the act had finally been found
that spoke for the belief. There was also a middle-aged poet of

some renown, decked out for incarceration in a tailcoat of Victorian cut, a shirt with a high winged collar, a polka-dotted foulard, cream color on brown, holding between his knees a cane with a silver duck's head as handle, an arm of defense the cops had somehow neglected to take away. A bowler hat, dark brown as well, was jammed down on the poet's ears as protection for his skull. His wiry sideburns and his bushy brows should have denoted great alacrity, but somehow they did not. It may have been a sign of what the cops thought of the lot of them that they had not taken the trouble to seize the silver-headed cane.

Athena saw that whenever Calliope looked at the girl beside her, at the gypsy face, narrow as a panel between the straight black curtains of hair, her eyes dispensed with their curiosity and became abruptly humble. The paddy wagon had shifted into gear now and begun to advance, and Calliope put her hand quickly on the girl's knee and looked at the side of her face with shameless love. The girl, as if taking the movement of the van as signaling the moment when courage might falter, turned almost in shyness to face the two rows of her fellow prisoners, and began to sing.

"Show me the prison, show me the jail," she sang, at first quite softly, but the clear voice gaining power as the van advanced. "Show me the prisoner whose life has gone stale," the voice ringing out bell-like, as if across water. "And I'll show you a young man with so many reasons why . . ." But the song and the paddy wagon had scarcely got under way when both of them came abruptly to a stop.

"Probably a demonstrator who's flung himself down in front of us," said the young man whose brow was bound with wampum.

"Why 'himself'?" demanded the young woman with the plaster leg, and she shifted her crutches in impatience on her hip. "Why not 'herself,' or wouldn't that enter your calculations?"

"More likely a group who has linked arms, men and women together," said the bearded young man, stroking the hirsute growth on his forearms from elbow to wrist as he talked. "I've seen it happen before, and nobody was ever hurt," he said, speaking in manly authority to them. For a moment his teeth showed white in the dense forest that enwrapped his face. "They were just herded into the next paddy wagon," he said.

And now the young woman got a better grip on her crutches, and leaned forward to look the young man in his quailing eye. "Aided by just a touch of mace," she said coldly, savagely. "With a couple of cracks on the cranium from those mothers." She turned now to the girl with the strands of vermilion wool in her braids, who had, without warning, begun silently to cry. "Save your tears," she said. "You'll need them later. You'll need them for those where we're going who stopped crying a long time ago."

Calliope was holding the hand of the girl beside her, who had ceased to sing, and Athena saw with a start that their hands were alike, nervous, nimble-fingered, gypsy hands, not strumming music out of guitars or jangling it out of tambourines for the moment, but holding to each other with love. And because of her own daughters, Athena suddenly knew. They were far, far from the touch of her hand, and in her weakness she wanted them there; and in weakness and silence she spoke their names. Sybil, Paula, Melanie, she said. The black wagon had been shoved into gear again, and was rolling on, and the mother and daughter opposite Athena held to each other's dark, elusive fingers as the girl said:

"Perhaps we'll have better luck this time."

"Save your luck," said the young woman with the crutches. "You'll need it to pass out to them where we're going."

"Be not too hard, for life is short," the girl sang behind the black silk curtains of her hair; and as the van sped on, Siddhartha, sitting in his yellow robe in the aisle, turned his shaven head from his meditations to face her, as all the others did. Listening to the incredibly untroubled voice, Athena named the girl Callisto, seeing her as the nymph whom Zeus had loved.

(Oh, God, Athena thought, Zeus certainly got around! He was my father, and he swallowed his wife whole when she was pregnant. And I, I had to come into the world by means of an ax which split his head open. I came out of his head, not out of his heart, remember that; not out of his heart because an oracle had warned him that his children might be stronger than he was, and his heart shriveled up like a raisin in the sun. Oh, Father, oh, Zeus! she cried out to him now. Is that the simple truth you were not able to accept—that one's children are always stronger than one is?) "Be not too hard when he blindly dies," Callisto sang as easily and simply as breathing, "fighting for things he does not own . . . ," the sound of it purer than an echo out of a mountain cave, as clear as a high, unfading star.

But abruptly again the motion of the paddy wagon and the singing were brought to a stop, and Siddhartha lowered his head and keened his prayer of exhortation as the motor died. At once, the double door at the rear of the van was unlocked and pulled open, and the prisoners saw they were in the paved, clean catacomb of what must be a garage set beneath the city jail. One after another, as directed, they stepped down into the electric glare, and, one after another, followed where their uniformed escorts, broad-beamed and thick of neck and shoulder, led them to the position chalked on the garage wall. One by one, they took their places behind the orderly row of stabled patrol wagons, and each was photographed side by side with his or her arresting officer, and thus coupled for life with him, and perhaps even beyond, in the irreversible memoranda of this sterile place. Only Gautama Siddhartha, still folded like a lotus flower, remained behind on the floor of the empty van, his eyes lowered, waiting in a vacuum of quiet until they would come and deal with him. As the prisoners walked through the barred door from the garage into the lower regions of the jail, Calliope feigned surprise, and gave a quick, formal bow to Athena.

"Enter, Noble Etruscan!" she said.

"No, that can't be right," said Athena, looking in wonder at her. "They were enemies of the Greeks, you know, and my name's Greek, Athena. . . ."

"But your head, it's like the ones in profile on the sides of the black, bucchero pottery."

"Move along! Get going!" the guard ordered the lot of them, and Callisto, her thin shoulders a little stooped, her teeth pure white in her dark face, paused hesitant, before him.

"I just wanted to ask," she said, whether guilelessly or not, "if we could get copies of the shots they took of us. If the pictures happened to turn out well, they might be fine for Christmas cards, both for your families and ours," she said. "Fellow Americans caught in a bind. . . ."

II

THAT EVENING, forty-two women crowded into the wide dormitory that had been cleared of regular prisoners to accommodate this fine catch of war protesters. There were not enough bunk beds to sleep them all, so the policewomen, smart as whips in their navy blue, their hair tinted auburn or brass and stiffly lacquered, with outsized rings of keys clamoring for keyholes at their belts, brought in mattresses flatter than pancakes, and flung them down on the bare, dusty floor. Each prisoner was allowed a gray or navy blanket, and issued a thin slab of soap, a small, faded towel, and a toothbrush which, it was rumored, would instantly dissolve if rammed down your own or anyone else's throat. No sheets were provided for the overnight stay, but the other properties they had been given the women held onto for reassurance; for the soap, the towel, the toothbrush, and even the soiled blankets, were evidence that one still had possessions, and thus, in some measure, an identity. Handbags, earrings, rings and bracelets, had been taken from them. The deputies had, in their line of duty, even removed the lengths of red wool from the shining, supple braids of the girl in her Mexican mini-dress.

Among the rumors that ran from lip to ear in the locked and bolted dormitory was the one that a streetwalker had died the night before in that lower bunk bed just over there, died from an overdose of whatever it was she had shot into her veins.

"Not on that same mattress?" one of the women murmured. And the young woman armed with her plaster leg leaned on one crutch and fixed her fellow demonstrator with a combative eye.

"Yes, oh, yes, indeed!" she said in elegant scorn. "One of the black kids passing in the hall when they brought us in said she helped to clean up after they'd hauled the poor bitch out, the corpse wrapped in a blanket like . . ."

"Do you know if the blanket was blue or gray?" Calliope asked as she folded hers over to serve as a cushion on which to sit. (And what gift has this singular woman got, Athena asked herself, that she can speak in the same breath both tragically and comically?)

"Not specified," said the young woman, her right palm firm on the padded handrest of her crutch. "They told the black kids just to turn the mattress over and shake the blanket out in the hall."

"That's one way to dispose of death," Calliope said, her voice quite low.

Athena lay down now in her black wool skirt and black jacket on one of the mattresses that had been tossed onto the boards between the bunk beds. As she shifted to avoid the map of what might have been New Zealand engraved in long-dried blood on the ticking, she saw that the cuffs of her white shirt were already ringed with dirt. (Except it doesn't matter for an instant, she thought; or at least not the way it matters that one has to go to the bathroom in front of everyone, on either of those two white thrones in the corner over there.) And the delicate-boned girl in the Mexican dress came shyly to the edge of Athena's mattress, and sat down, her smooth legs folded under her, her gentle eyes fixed in respect on Athena's face.

"My name is Ann," she said, speaking even her name in apology. "You know, I've never seen a dead person. I've never seen the place where a person died."

"Well, now you have, Ann," said the young woman who hovered above them on her crutches. "She died right on that bunk over there." She jerked her plump chin toward the bed that nobody wanted to see. "You've had quite a lot of exposure to reality so far today, haven't you, Ann?" she said, her voice savage as a knife blade held between her teeth.

"I have a daughter who's about your age, Ann," Athena quickly interrupted the sound of it. *Don't let the blade so much as nick you,* she wanted to caution Ann, but instead she reached out and touched with the tips of her fingers the girl's braid that was glossy as a chestnut's hide. "Her hair is long like yours," she said, "only not the same color. She's very blond."

"I was twenty yesterday," Ann said, her face alight.

"Melanie not until December. That's pretty close," Athena said, and her fingers faltered on the girl's soft hair.

Moment by moment now, the prisoners in the dormitory could be seen taking on the two inevitable womanly roles, the third role held in abeyance until relationships had intensified. The choice now was between mother and daughter, and at times the women changed from one role to the other with disturbing facility. It had nothing to do with youth and age, the choice that was made, but simply that at certain moments, thought Athena, some asked the questions while others sought to find the answers by which they all might live. She and her own daughters, Sybil, and Paula, and Melanie, still persisted in this classical exchange, and perhaps even more since the three daughters had married and taken on their own authority. And there was Callisto now propped on one elbow on the top tier of a bunk bed, stretched slender-legged in her canary yellow breeches and her poet's golden waistcoat and flowered shirt, the famed young folk singer, taking on the role of mother for those demonstrators who had swung up the iron bed-frame to where she was. It was perhaps some temporary caveat that daughter Callisto served on mother Calliope, laughing at times, or else not laughing, advising the college girls who clustered around her as a mother might on the questions about anger and the chastening of it, and about the new non-violent good in men that could turn away the old, wearisome violence, and about the Christian counterfeits that had taken on the name of love.

"When I wake up in the morning, I usually feel like cracking a few heads because of the state the world is in," Callisto was saying, her teeth pure white as she laughed. "So I have to go to school to better people than I am to learn how to handle that." And the people she named were Eric Simon, who had also been arrested that day, and Gandhi, who was dead, and Ronald Sampson, who lived in Somerset, England. "Make a pilgrimage to see him," she said. Once Eric was walking down Market Street in San Francisco at night, she said, and at a dark corner someone put a knife against his gut. "The guy wanted his wristwatch, and his wallet, and whatever else he had. But a half hour later the two of them were having dinner at the Hilton instead"; and the demonstrators gathered on the bunk bed laughed uneasily, knowing this miracle that identified love as the lack of fear was alien to all they had been taught to recognize as love.

But then Callisto became bored with being the prophet, and she began an imitation of Bob Dylan for them, her voice his voice as she took the guitar from him, and twisted his arm, and forced from him the lonely, nasally recounted story of his life.

"'Hey, Mr. Tambourine Man,'" she twanged out the words, "'I'm not sleepy and there is no place I'm going to. . . .'" The young women, college students or whatever they were, listened to this telling of their own brief histories and his as Callisto sang about answers blowing in the wind, and England's Empire returning into sand. "'Oh, mothers and fathers throughout the land,'" she sang, squeezing her clear voice almost to extinction in a resemblance of Dylan's, "'then don't criticize what you can't understand! Your sons and your daughters are beyond your command, for the times they are a-changin' . . .'"

Calliope sat erect on her neatly folded blanket on the floor, one of a group of women in their good street clothes seated as casually there as if in easy chairs in a hotel lobby. She was ab-

sorbed for the moment in speaking into the ear trumpet of one
of the seated ladies, who carried it on an elegant length of black
satin cord around her neck. The trumpet was shaped like a
morning glory, and the old lady proffered it first in one direction
and then in another to catch the major and minor notes of the
murmur of women's voices that she could barely hear. Calliope's
words, shouted into the trumpet's throat, could be heard halfway across the dormitory, saying that although their ordinary
apparel would be certainly taken from them once they reached
their permanent quarters after sentencing, she was sure eye-
glasses and ear trumpets would not be taken away.

"We'll probably all be handsomely outfitted!" she whooped
into the morning glory's cornet. "We may be given a choice of a
Dior or a Fabiani or a Capucci! We must think of our new life
in the county prison constructively! No decisions to take, no
conflicts! We'll all be sisters in equality!"

The old lady looked in pleasure and astonishment into the
depths of the plastic trumpet flower she held, and in her old, un-
steady voice, with the deep echo of deafness in it, she said that
her home in Sonoma was just such a place of true community.

"Based on Tolstoy's beliefs," she said. "Everyone who comes
there is strengthened and purified by working from sunup to
sundown in our fields and vineyards." And Calliope shouted with
great gentleness and serenity into the trumpet that this was the
way their permanent place of confinement would be.

The women were still strangers to one another, their names,
their professions still unknown, but in time they would be identified as schoolteachers, housewives, librarians, and one among
them as a portrait painter, another as a nun who had set her
habit aside for this act of devotion, one a medical doctor, one a
psychiatrist. The iron-curled lady, still packed buxomly into her
linen dress, sat there on the floor among the others, bereft now
of her silvery-haired mate. He and his pince-nez were taking the
rap in another section of the city jail. The truth was that whatever males had journeyed with them in the official vehicles

might as well never have been mentioned, for the women were not to be exposed to them again. They were to hear their voices briefly the next morning when what must have been the whole male contingent sang in unison as they marched past the women's holding cell. "We shall overcome," they sang, and the forty-odd women contained in the airless, windowless cubicle, with its photographic eye fixed on them, waited hour after hour for the door that opened into the courtroom to be unlocked and the hearing to begin. And as they waited, the men's voices were to rise in such volume in the bleak corridor that it seemed the walls would have to draw back upon themselves so that the great torrent of sound might go, unimpeded, roaring and cascading past. "I ain't goin' to study war no more!" the men shouted, and they proclaimed with fervor that they were like trees standing by the water, which, in the circumstances, seemed inaccurate. As they passed, Athena listened for the high keening of Gautama Siddhartha's complaint to soar above the forthright affirmations of the others, but she did not hear it. The women were to glimpse their male concomitants for the one last time as they all awaited sentencing in the courtroom (Siddhartha no longer a lotus flower, but standing upright in his yellow robe among the rest of them), the men segregated by the near hysteria of prison regulations from the touch of any woman's hand and even from the compassion of her eye.

In the dormitory, it was now the turn of the buxom lady, her scalp showing pink through her gray curls, her blue dress a little wilted, to shout out her answers to Mother Morning Glory. Within five minutes the other prisoners had learned that her husband was a professor of ornithology, that they had organized an active peace group in the university town where they lived, and that they had no children without wings; and at this she shook with marvelous good humor in her blue dress.

"We have a pigeon who moved in with us three years ago," she shouted gaily, a pigeon they called Daughter, who made their two Chesapeake Bay retrievers toe the line. For a moment,

Athena saw them balancing on their webbed feet on a high wire stretched from pillar to post, until the lady went on saying that Daughter was black as jet, with a rose-colored beak, and with that beak and rosy claws she kept the retrievers from getting up on the beds, or on the sofas, and chairs. Six times a year, as regular as clockwork, the story roared on, Daughter came and asked for bits and pieces of whatever was available to make a nest. "She even pulls a long white hair or two out of my husband's head!" the pigeon's mother shouted into Mother Morning Glory's convolvular horn. "Making a nest, although she's never seen a male, and sitting for twenty-one days, six times a year, on eggs she hasn't got!" It seemed that Daughter doted on the professor, and she would sit on his shoulder for hours, and at mating time she would preen herself in the mirrors of his pince-nez. So loudly and clearly was the portrait drawn that Athena could see the black svelte head of the pigeon there in the dormitory with them, turning this way and that in unavailing vanity. "Daughter's going to miss my husband while we're locked up," the gray-curled lady shouted, and this seemed to her to be one of the funniest things that had ever been said.

Husbands, thought Athena, for now Calliope was being questioned about hers. He conducted an orchestra, the entire dormitory learned, for Calliope had to repeat it even more loudly, as Mother Morning Glory had failed the first time round to hear. Mother Morning Glory looked for a moment in rebuke into the trumpet's depths, her head, with its white bang cut straight across her wrinkled forehead, lowered, and white strands of hair combed neatly down to the big lobes of her ears. Then she gave the trumpet one more chance, and she extended it toward Calliope again.

"My husband," Calliope shouted, "is being taken care of by my elder daughter while the two of us are in this home away from home!"

In this community of women demonstrators, four maidens in Levi's and sandals had come to sit at the foot of Athena's mattress, and begun to talk about college courses; while the girl named Ann still sat close as a lost child to her, listening with shy respect to all that was being said. I shall not mislead you by saying that you can learn much from any course, she wanted to say to them, but she thought of the look of dilemma that would come into Ann's grave eyes, and she could not say the words. Instead, she said tentatively to the four college girls: "I believe if you keep your imagination alive enough, probably one course will be able to do one thing for you, and another course will do something else, although none of the things may be at all what you expected." Above them, the plaster leg hung over the mattress in menace, thrust forward like a flying buttress; and in five minutes, thought Athena, she will offer it to us as a gift if only we will acknowledge her, and listen to her speak, if only we will give her the homage (and this is perhaps her true sorrow) she knows she has no right to claim. If anyone had told Athena then that the young woman who inspired no homage would play a part in their next incarceration, she would have answered impatiently that, in the first place, there would not be a second arrest, that the gesture once made had to stand or fail on its own merits; and, secondly, that this woman with her plaster cast opened no vistas of any kind because she was forever in prison, and that no talk, no act, no book laid open before her and the pages marked, no music, no dancers, no stretches of wide open land or sky, would ever be bail or parole enough to get her out. "Sometimes students forget that it's better to bring as much to the course as they hope to get from it," Athena finished a little lamely.

"If it's of any interest to anyone," said the young woman leaning above them, "I'm doing graduate work in Asian languages. I'm on a full scholarship at Berkeley. Languages," she said, making them at once her exclusive property, "because if you're halfway honest you know that's the only solution. It means being able to talk with people, all kinds of people, about their agriculture, for instance, and the birds in their fields, and the fish in their waters. That's what people want to talk about. To hell with the mind," she said.

The girls sitting at the foot of the mattress gave no sign that they had heard her speak, and this was a greater outrage to her than a slap across the face. One of them asked Athena what the reading list for her course in Greek mythology included, and the young woman braced on her crutches gave a savage growl of fury in her throat.

"The books vary. They have to," Athena said. "At times, I suggest different books to different students, but the list is never exactly the same from year to year. I like them to learn about the deities who seem to have no story worth telling, and about those others who appear like shooting stars for an instant—the way so many poets have—and suddenly are gone. I'm more drawn to the gods whose names are not very familiar, the obscure ones who were worshiped almost privately," she said, "not the glamorous ones who lived in high style on Olympus, feasting on nectar and ambrosia—"

"Isn't that like going slumming? Isn't that what you're advocating?" asked the young woman, ready to smite Athena with one crutch and then the other if only she could maintain her balance on her plaster leg. "Isn't that saying you're only interested in failures? And isn't that a pretty negative way to teach?"

"Perhaps it is," Athena said, "but, you see, I'm new to teaching. Just because I'd written two books on myths, and one on Irish fairy tales, I got into the academic world by the back door. As I have to make a living, I can't afford to get out again."

"And you don't like what you're doing?" the young woman said, her eye narrowing, her cleft chin jutting triumphantly. Athena fixed her gaze on the three peace signs inked on the plaster cast.

"I like talking about books with students," she said. "At this moment, I might say to them, try reading an Irish writer called George Moore—for one thing, because he wrote about communes, and this has great meaning for us now. He's written about people who are panic-stricken, frantic, stumbling this way and that if they can't submit to another's vision, another's will, and who cling together under a common roof. . . ." And then the strange, faltering thing happened to her voice, happened again, as it always did whenever she thought of Melanie. "Or I might ask them to read 'The Grand Inquisitor,' " she said, and for a long moment she didn't say any more.

(Melanie is twenty years old, or will be in December, and already two babies, which is just one of the ways that the lives of daughters transcribe their mothers' lives. It was that way with Sybil and Paula, though not so early, and now I am the grandmother of six. There are some who would call Melanie a witch, as one boyfriend did who rode a motorcycle to his death, a witch who had done nothing more evil than give her will and her conscience into the bondage of idolatry. In olden days it might have been said that she made a bargain with the devil, but she has sinned a different but equally ancient sin in submitting her life to one of the endless saviors of the lost, believing him to be the true redeemer come to live on earth again. "For the Buddha and I have come to inhabit this planet at the same moment in history," this redeemer said, or wrote, or cried aloud to all who would listen, and to those who would not as well. "Rejoice, rejoice, we are come together in our omnipotence to unite all men!" was what he cried from the housetops; and at another time he declared that he was the great erection come to fecundate a world that was already in the throes of impotency and death. "The throes of impotency" evoked the spectacle of a dance so convoluted that Athena could scarcely bear the writhing vision of it. At still another time, the redeemer confessed that he had studied all the Eastern philosophies, and discovered they were shit. "I warn you to avoid every occult science you've ever heard of!" he exhorted his followers, "for mysticism will destroy you! You can learn more from me than from any so-called reincarnation and so-called karma. Don't go down the unholy road of the fucking Eastern philosophers! Stay with me, and with Abraham Lincoln, Thomas Jefferson, Clarence Darrow, and Edward Kennedy"—these names, Athena thought, perhaps merely because of their astrological signs— "for we are the true exponents of religion. We are MEN!" She could hear Melanie's voice reading aloud his words, these actual words, and see her face, fresh as a jonquil, high on the long stalk of her neck, so startling in its beauty that people would stop in the street to marvel as she walked by. Her long, long hair swung to her waist, and babies blond as Saxons clung to her breast and held to her flowing skirts. Athena could go back far enough in time to see Melanie pushing her doll carriage through a dime store, no one knowing that she ripped off lipsticks and hair curlers from the counters, tucking them under the doll's blanket with the purse-size flacons of French perfume from somewhere else, and no one suspecting, not even if they were to see her hand actually selecting what she wanted, because of her saintly beauty, the total ethereal innocence of her face.)

"George Moore," Athena, the professor, went on saying to the college students who sat at the foot of her mattress, "wrote about communities of nearly two thousand years ago, religious orders or wandering groups who believed that all property was common to all men. The communes of our time relate to that." (One of my daughters lives in such a commune, she could not say aloud.) "But some orders, the Essenes, for instance, believed that in stealing from the rich to help the poor you do not deprive the rich man, but you harm the society in which you live. They accepted everything that was given them without question, and without gratitude, but they did not steal because they believed that a society no longer has value if it becomes a community of thieves. In one book of Moore's, a disciple complains that money has been their trouble ever since Jesus drew them together, for the disciples wished to live without money, but like the commune children of our time, they could not find the way."

She was thinking of Melanie and the babies and the others (with the exception of the redeemer, who had solved the question by using what money came in for his own needs), who lived off the vegetables, the fruit, the packaged cakes, the three-or-four-day-old bread that supermarkets threw away. The men of the commune retrieved at midnight, before the garbage trucks passed, this discarded bounty of a nation run amok on its own extravagance, and in the end the madness of the redeemer appeared no more irrational than that of a mighty chain store paving its back alley with cupcakes and stale raisin bread.

One of the girls in Levi's said she had never heard of George Moore, and another of them, sitting cross-legged, wanted to know what Athena's requirements were if one took her course.

"Do you ask that papers be handed in, or can one just sit and rap with you?" she said.

"Good God!" cried the young woman with the cement leg, unable to bear any more of it. "Where the hell is real life in all this crap? Look, my name's Lou, and my old man's a pilot in the harbor out there, and I can tell you what he's doing over at Port Chicago in Suisun Bay tonight! He's piloting cargo ships out loaded with napalm, Thanksgiving presents for the mothers and kids in Vietnam! Ironic, isn't it, me here, and my dad out there? Ironic, but certainly not literary!" she cried out, and she flung the crutches into her armpits, and swung off across the dormitory.

And now Calliope left the older women and made her way in her dark emerald suit, on her soft, glove-leather, emerald-colored shoes, to Athena's mattress. The curious, bemused smile was on her lips, but she did not speak at once, but sat down on the ticking. She had never been so close before, and Athena saw now how narrow her wrists were, and her ankles, and in the dark tan of Calliope's face she saw there were fine white lines around her eyes, lines as delicate as threads and bleached like the roots of young grass, perhaps from squinting season after season into the California sun.

"The prisoners down the hall are asking for more music," Calliope said in a low voice across the mattress to Athena. "Oh, God, only music. We're pretty grasping compared to that."

But how the messages and rumors managed to reach them behind the locked prison doors, no one could say. The black prisoners who had passed them in the hall as they filed in, or whom they had caught sight of in the deputies' offices when the booking and fingerprinting took place, had developed quicker ears, and eyes, and tongues, and the demonstrators were the dullwitted there. None of them could even speculate on how the black prisoners managed to slide the information they collected under the bolted doors and around the massive hinges, speeding it accurately through keyholes, both good and evil tidings spreading from dormitory to dormitory, cell to solitary cell, ear to desperately harking ear. It was perhaps nothing to wonder about, Athena told herself, inasmuch as the black prisoners were the prison itself, the many-tongued, many-eyed body of the prison, and the demonstrators with their principles, and their handy quotations, and their respected professions, were merely visiting the place.

When the supper wagons were wheeled in (tea in a paper cup, pressed ham between two slabs of bread, and exactly forty-two cookies for the forty-two women), another piece of information was silently transmitted to them. Word had gone out over the radio, the rumor went, that more than a hundred and fifty demonstrators had been arrested that day and the city jail was full to overflowing. The identities of some of those arrested had been broadcast: five college professors, four ministers, the owner of a bookstore, were among those named, as well as a folk singer and her mother; a poet, a portrait painter, and a teacher of modern dance.

Just before the lights of the dormitory were dimmed, the confirmation of this was spoken from the battleship gray of the ceiling: a policewoman's husky voice addressed them with the authority of Zeus himself from somewhere above their heads.

"A—then—ah Gregory," the voice said, "someone's downstairs with bail for you. Are you taking bail? Just answer yes or no."

Athena could not place the center from which the words came, for the voice had the power and the mobility to reverberate throughout the wide, low, hermetically sealed room. She sat upright on the mattress, and raised her eyes, searching for the god or deputy who had pronounced her name.

"No," she said. "I'm staying here," and she was shocked to hear the little scattering of applause from these women who were strangers to her still.

"Would that be a frantic husband?" one of the demonstrators called out, making it funny, and Athena looked in the direction of her fellow prisoner and stretched a foolish grin on her own face as she shook her head.

When the lights were lowered, she took off her black knit jacket and rolled it up as a pillow, as the two of them had done when they slept in the forests and fields of Europe together, only this time she had a prison towel to spread across it as pillow slip. All about her on the bunk beds in the half dark, the women lay prostrate, and on the mattresses that had been flung down on the floor. Mother Morning Glory slept with her ear trumpet suspended at the head of her bed, and the quavering cadenza of her snoring already began to shudder and grind through the dormitory. Ann, her hair unbraided for the night, was breathing quietly on a mattress just beyond; and Callisto, her thin back turned to them all, laughed her muffled laughter on the broken mattress where she lay, until Calliope reached down from the lower tier of the bunk bed and took her hand.

And then the wooing of sleep began. It was always the figure of a meek woman in biblical dress who was first brought to life, a madonna-like emblem whom Athena made use of at night to shame the underground woman hidden in her flesh. This gentle figure had given shelter to a stray lamb, and she carried it in her arms through the blue, untroubled dusk, climbing slowly up the flowering fields to where the sheep would be descending before dark from higher grazing land. The sheep would begin coming tentatively and singly down the slope, and then come faster and faster, herded by manic dogs, one sheep behind the other's matted woolen tail, and they would leap the weathered crossbars into the fold. Faster and faster they came, and Athena would try to count them as they leaped, counting hopelessly, helplessly, night after night, seeking the mother of the lamb she held. And always, without warning, the sheep would turn into running children, running naked, their mouths stretched wide in soundless screaming, and Athena clutched the lamb in her arms and counted, counting one hundred and two, one hundred and three, counting and failing to count the running, leaping children whose terrible cries could not be heard as they fled down a shell-pocked highway straight toward the camera, straight into the unsleeping iris of the eye, with napalm running like quicksilver at their heels and streaming down their flesh.

III

In MIDAFTERNOON of the second day, the bus ride to the Rehabilitation Center began. The morning had been spent in one of the airless holding cells that the forty-two women had been packed into, with the official, unblinking eye of a gyrating camera fixed on them. During the hours that they waited, Callisto bopped a few dance figures before it, and once she asked the camera for word of Eric Simon. She said: "Eric is not strong physically. His spirit has worn him so thin that his bones show through. Give him a good bed to sleep on. Give him orange juice, if you can." It might have been a mother broadcasting in determined hope to the kidnappers of her child, saying: "Please give Eric the medicine he needs. He must have it in order to live." And when she leaned over the drinking fountain set in one corner of the cramped, windowless place, she said to the nickel pipe from which the arch of icy water sprang: "Eric, wherever you are, answer me if you can. They can't give you the medicine you need because they haven't got it. They haven't got the barbiturate called love of the other guy." And Lou, the harbor pilot's daughter, said in fierce scorn: "So that's how you define it?" And Callisto said: "Sure. It deadens the pain of life for a little while."

Callisto's lawyer had requested that two or three of the women be allowed to address the court before sentence was pronounced, and this was granted. But long before the women spoke, their fate had been decided and the sentence already entered in the register. The judge had a weary look in his eye when a lady librarian stated to the court that theirs had been a symbolic act, and that it was therefore not punishable by law; nor did he tremble in his outworn skin when Callisto said in a clear, boylike voice (somehow less compassionate than the voice that sang) that there comes a time, or at least there came a time for her, when she had to make her feelings more public.

"So what I wanted to do by committing civil disobedience," she said, "was to make an appeal for the young men, to ask what we can do about them, who are for the most part young boys. . . ."

"Address your comments to me, not to the audience," the judge said in his old, old voice.

"I didn't want to tell anybody anything," Callisto went on, turning toward him, "because I am tired of telling. It was rather to ask, to make an appeal. I wanted to appeal. I wanted to appeal by this act to policemen, mothers, presidents, newspapers in this country and in the world, because I believe there is something drastically wrong, truly, something drastically wrong with the use of arms in trying to solve our problems. . . . That's all. Thank you."

The judge gave short shrift to Athena's statement that for years she had believed that the American people had the power, if they would only choose to use it, to stop this war.

"To this end, I did everything I possibly could," she said, trying to find the judge's spent eyes. "I signed petitions, wrote to the various presidents of our country, called on Mr. Stevenson to act for us as a peace candidate, and met with nothing but frustration."

"I don't want to cut anyone off," the judge said, "but there are other cases on the calendar."

"Your honor, I am proud to be able to tell you why I took part in this demonstration," Athena said, her heart trembling. "I now believe the most effective way to end the present war is to back up those young Americans who are refusing to fight in Vietnam. I think that the act of older people and professional people, such as we are, putting our liberty in jeopardy, is an important thing. We must all, every American, commit civil disobedience until the war in Vietnam has been brought to an end. Thank you."

What fine ladies they were, with their "please, your honor's" and "thank you, your honor's," and as a reward for their gentility they were all, men and women alike, sentenced to ten days at the county Rehabilitation Center, twenty-four hours of which had already been served in the city jail; and Athena wished she and the others had saved their rhetoric and their breath. Before leaving on their journey, their handbags and rings and earrings and make-up kits had been returned to them, and for a few hours they gave the appearance of being the same women who had entered the jail the night before, but they were not the same. They were very good imitations of themselves, but how long they were going to be able to play these roles they did not know.

Lou had been the only one not to plead nolo contendere and thus get out on bail. She looked at none of them as she swung on her crutches out of the press of people in the courtroom, but the story of all Lou was or was not had not yet come to an end. She was writing her own scenario over and over, composing it with a curious blending of brashness and wiliness and caution, the opening night of the production to take place some weeks ahead. Had Athena known then that she would again at Christmastime be facing Lou's ire, she would have cried out impatiently that it could not possibly be. One of the college students in Levi's said now that Lou had broken her leg in a motorcycle crash, swerving so as not to hit a child; but the psychiatrist demonstrator reported that Lou's story to her the night before had been that she had broken her leg in a rock-scaling incident in the Yosemite Valley, when she had climbed six hours in order to bring an inexperienced hiker down. As the buses drew out of the underground garage, the prisoners made the V sign with two fingers lifted to their supporters who stood on the pavement, bearing picket signs on high; and a sense of almost unbearable grief because of the helplessness of them all before the outrage of war swept over Athena, a grief that pledged and bound her to them, even to Lou, beyond personal cavil or individual name.

"You're about the only one I haven't got acquainted with yet," said Mother Morning Glory, riding beside Athena in the bus as it moved off with the others, a convoy of rhinoceros-like vehicles proceeding cumbersomely, nose to tail, tail to nose. "How's your husband going to make out while you're away?" she asked, not offering her trumpet to receive the answer, but going on saying in a voice so deep that it seemed to speak already from the grave: "That's another beautiful thing about living as I do in a community of saints. Each one who comes to share my fields, my vineyards, my house, is responsible to his brothers, and responsible for their lives as well as his own. Now that I'm to be ten days away, nothing will suffer, neither the relationships nor the chickens and geese. The horses will be fed and watered, the garden attended to, the berries picked, and my chair will stand empty at the table until I go back. They will keep it there as a sign that my spirit is with them still, even though my body has been put in jail. It is not a household of isolated couples, but of men and women who form a warm and loving community." As the buses of women moved through the city streets, Mother Morning Glory turned her head under its straight white shingle of hair toward Athena, and her ancient gaze fixed itself on the side of Athena's face. Her eyes were golden in color, and her pale lashes as long as a mountain goat's, and there was such a look of grief and yearning in them that Athena believed they were not only turned outward on the community of love, but inward as well on the vista of her endlessly long life. People it, people it so as to give it meaning, the sepulchral voice did not say aloud. "When we are out again, you and your husband must come and see how we live, and perhaps you will want to stay with us. There is always work for everyone. My name is Lydia," she said, and Athena called into the smooth horn of the trumpet her own ambiguous name. "Athena was supposed to have invented the plow," Lydia said. "Are you fond of plowing?" she asked. "You and your husband . . ." she was going on with it, and Athena could think of nothing but the man who was the last person in the world to be dead.

The buses were moving out into the country now, and into the beginning of the California dusk, and through the glazed window pane Athena watched the headlights of cars that came toward them, blooming palely in the last hour before evening. The memory of Rory smote her with the same pang of despair that had changed the sound of people's voices, and the length of the hall, and the dimensions of the stairway, when they had telephoned her at the college. She had not been ready to know then, and would never be ready, for if the invasion of the Aleutians had not killed him, or the parachute drops into Occupied France, then what authority had this other enemy to follow him, unperceived and in absolute silence, from country to country until the shuddering, gasping end? It was not from wounds he had died, or from anything the war had done to him, but from cancer reaching, long-armed as an octopus, through the labyrinth of his veins; it was the little serpent of smoke he drew so quickly in that had slithered from lung to brain.

Rory was the last person in the world to be dead anywhere at any time, and certainly not at forty-four in an army hospital; for he could take a wasp in the deep hard ditch of his hand, and talk to it as it stepped with its probing feet across his heart line, and with the tip of his finger stroke its head and alter the direction it explored until, under the stiff little cape of its gauze wings, it followed the curve of his life line down to the crease of his wrist. He was a tall man, with a good singing voice and a loud, happy laugh, and in wartime, in California (where Sybil was born) it had been the seals in the saltwater inlets that he had pleased with questions about their lives, questions put to them in their own tongue, and the barking and chortling of their replies made a clamor that even the native fishermen stopped to hear.

That war was done with, or so it was said, in 1945; and then it was the Mediterranean gulls in the South of France (where Paula was born) that Rory wooed out of the steep cliffs the screaming birds used as fortress, and out of the green caves of the waves that arched in across the sand. Those seabirds, vicious as jackals, Athena could not bring herself to trust any farther than the length of their coarse-feathered wings, but Rory entranced and cajoled them until the savagely-beaked-and-clawed laid down the scimitars of their voices on the beach in temporary surrender, and came to eat the slugs he had carried from the garden, and fresh almonds from the orchard, whose pastel coverings he split open with the square nail of his thumb. And at night in the woods he would answer whatever quavering voice of owl might have waked them as they slept on a pliant bed of moss and viscid leaves, with her jacket as pillow under their heads. He spoke with owls this way in the gothic forests of Germany, allaying and lulling their complaints about the scarcity of nightingales; and in the olive groves of Italy he talked with snow-white owls about the shrewdness of frogs who camouflaged their succulent bodies with the green of lily pads, for no other reason except that they wanted to live; and Rory talked with snakes at noon, commending them for their litheness and elegance as he carried them gently in his strong, broad hands out of the gloom of rocks into the sun.

After that war, he had become a Foreign Service Officer, and in this incongruous role he had committed himself to eight or ten hours of work a day, six days of the week (avoiding the cocktail parties and the tennis clubs), and kept the evenings and Sundays free for the beasts and the birds and the lonely places of every country where they lived. In Germany (where Melanie was born), he had taken to walking the woods at night with the Hessian forester, in order to save, or put to death, what game survived the random shooting by GI's from their darkened army jeeps. They were recruits fresh from the States, these young men, trusting nothing that moved on foreign soil, and by Saturday night too drunk to know doe from roebuck, or to care, and too careless or fearful to follow the beasts they had wounded through the forest to deal the coup de grâce.

One clear blue evening, such as comes only on mountain heights or in the water-cress-growing valleys of Germany, Rory brought home in the car four terror-stricken piglets, the boar sow having been shot with the five others (machine-gunned, tommy-gunned, it may have been) in the wild flowering of the forest ditch. And almost at once the young boar had understood the stories Rory told them as he wrapped them in the blanket from the PX that he had cut into four squares, and gave them doll bottles of warm milk. He told them their mother had put the nine of them behind her, and defended them with her own body until she dropped before the guns. She did not abandon you, he said; she stood like a Valkyrie before the onslaught, and when she went down, the four of you who were still alive jumped up like popcorn in the pan. *She did not abandon you*, he said; and the piglets squealed with delight at the knowledge that she had not fled, as they had feared in their panic, but had died for love of them; and as they sucked the milk into their small dark snouts, they looked at Rory with sleepy amber eyes.

All the doomed beasts in their fur coats or birds in their feathers, or insects in their split shells, all, all understood the explanations Rory gave them about the shortness of life upon the earth they knew. And after supper, he would turn the endless speech of their hooting, or barking, or whistling, or buzzing, or neighing, or snorting, or warbling, into stories for Sybil, and Paula, and Melanie. He told them a chapter nearly every evening, and Sybil (born five months after they were married) would sit in his lap because she had known him the longest, and Paula would sit on the rug near his feet in his embroidered, ski-hut slippers (that the German hunting dog brought him when he came home from work, glistening with her slobber), Paula holding Melanie on her lap and combing, combing, combing, Melanie's pale, silky hair. When Rory stopped talking for a moment and reached for his drink, Sybil would take his left hand and open it wide, and trace the deep scar of his life line with one finger, as the wasp had traced it on its striped, bowed legs; and when Sybil came to his wrist she would say in her cold, prophetic child's voice: "You're never going to die."

"But that's my left hand," Rory would say. "So it doesn't count. I was only *intended* to live forever. You have to look at the right hand to know."

"Go on with the story," Sybil always said.

But there were others besides Rory, others not even allowed their forty years, who would have to die in the sweet time of their youth. There was one who had been born in a California internment camp, a Japanese who had been permitted to grow up for the sole purpose, it would seem, of going to Vietnam. He lay in the intensive care ward of the army hospital where Rory lay, his body naked to the waist, lying there week after week that August, with plastic tubes in his nostrils, and glucose dripping topaz drop by drop into his punctured vein. He lay on a high, hard bed to the right of the door as you went in, his back and one shoulder (for they had turned him on his side) like creamy satin, his eyelids as if stitched closed so that he need not see death taking shape ahead. Two or three times a day, Athena walked past him on her way to Rory's bed, seeing his brows as black and fine as the pointed hairs of watercolor brushes above the sealed caverns of his eyes. In that long summer, Athena came to believe that wars went on because men cannot bear to die alone, just as they cannot bear to live alone, and in army hospitals the young could meet death together, like children who had lost their way, and could travel the final distance hand in hand.

The wives who waited in the long hall outside had the illusion as well that company can divide the nearly unbearable burden, somehow mitigate the granite gaze of tragedy. One of these was the Japanese wife who waited in spurious hope the same weeks that Athena waited, and although they did not speak, they were sisters for a while because behind the closed doors of the same ward the hearts of their husbands beat ever more slowly in their broken breasts. They were sisters as well in that each of their men would have a flag-shrouded coffin, and the long lament of farewell taps would unwind for each of them upon the sunlit air. But, God damn it, no! Athena had tried to tell the absolute silence. It's not going to happen that way! I am not going to let it happen! But they were to learn that death has no need of acceptance, and in the long hours that Athena and the Japanese wife sat side by side, they had not looked at each other, but straight into the chasm of fear and loneliness and self-flagellation, and neither gave any sign of what she had seen. They might have been statues of women, stricken from flesh into stone. Why did I not, as woman, save him from this, they may have asked themselves, but never for an instant were they permitted to glimpse the infinite gray wasteland their men were beginning to cross together, drugged, confused, groping through darkness to find the lonely way.

In that last week when they both died, Major Fletcher came out from the ward, still wearing his green operating dress, the green cap on his sandy hair, and sat down—a young man still, with deep gashes that may once have been dimples of merriment in his narrow cheeks—sat on the varnished bench beside the Japanese wife in her pink wool suit. The pupils of her eyes were tilted pieces of jet, and from their bituminous substance no tears, it seemed, could ever fall. Major Fletcher never even took Sundays off, and Athena believed this was because he had to be there to call the anesthetized back from their long dreams. She had seen him day after day when the newly operated would be wheeled in, his quick, golden-haired hand on the shoulder or wrist or knee of the deeply sleeping, knuckles knocking at the closed door of their somnolence until they opened it to let the living in. "I want you to come out of it now, Bob [or Hank or Tom or Al]," he would say in a voice so steady, so earnest, that even the obtuse must sense that he was asking for something as crucial as their lives. "It's morning, Jim [or George or Ted or Jack]," he would say. "This is Major Fletcher talking to you. I want you to think about having breakfast. I want you to answer me, Jim. Jim, this is Major Fletcher asking you to come back."

Having heard his voice and seen the urgency with which he moved, only the dull of wit could fail to visualize, and recoil from, as from a painting by Bosch, the demons which struggled in darkness to possess forever the flesh and spirit of the sleeping, wounded men. Major Fletcher would call them by name and sometimes they roused and answered and sometimes they did not, could not, answer again; but the orderlies, and the men who had already returned, were witnesses to the violent truth that sometimes men did not come back from the confusion of limbo or Judgment Day simply because no voice summoned them loudly enough and over and over from the alien regions where they were. The thread that was each man's life might have slipped away forever if Major Fletcher had not been there to hold fast to it, entwining it around his clean-nailed fingers as he called out to each of them, urgently, eagerly, the magic injunction of their own familiar names. They might be lying flat on their bellies under the smoothly folded sheets, or on their sides, or on their backs, some wearing turbans of bandages, some swathed like mummies, with white tubes writhing from their nostrils, while he leaned above them, touching them with the hand of life, saying:

"Come back, Hank [or Jack or Bob or Al]. This is Major Fletcher asking you. I want you to answer me."

The afternoon he spoke to the little Japanese wife outside in the hall, his eyes seemed to have faded, and under the green operating dress the electric energy that informed his flesh appeared exhausted, the circuit from mind to body gone suddenly dead.

"We've done everything we could," he was saying. "I'd like you to come in and just take his hand before he goes."

And now, riding in the bus with the other women through the California evening, Athena finally answered Lydia. She picked up the ear trumpet on its black silk cord and shouted into it:

"My husband died five years ago!"

IV

THE REHABILITATION CENTER spread in a complex of long low
barracks across the countryside, with here and there (as far as
the women could make out in the blue-white road lights) a
tilted, shingled roof or a dark web of ivy around a doorway to
give the bleak buildings the look of home. But the avenues lined
with cyclone fences and hedged with entanglements of barbed
wire said something else entirely. Inside the bowling-alley-like
structure of the women's quarters, the demonstrators were locked
temporarily inside the steel-meshed cage of the visiting gallery
that ran half the length of the entrance hall. In the density of
women, the young nun she had not yet spoken with now stood
close to Athena, close because she could not do otherwise,
withdrawn from them all in her brown wool dress and her shabby
moccasins, her eyes lowered, her face small and tight and freck-
led like a child's under her neat, coffee-colored cap of hair. She
could not be said to appear modest or shy, but more that the
flesh and its concerns had been, by uninterrupted habit, deliberately effaced. (St. Theresa is said to have willed all
worldly emotion within her to perish, thought Athena; but if
this descendant of hers could exchange a prayer or a poem or a
piece of music with me, then no idle remarks about the strangeness of this place, or the sandwiches the deputy is bringing at
this moment to the cage door, would have to be spoken; or if
either she or I had Callisto's voice and simply sang, flesh and

blood and assurance would be restored to her, and St. Theresa would be visible among us.)

Although the sandwiches had little to do with food (each square thick with a slab of plastic cheese and a slice of baloney) the women ate greedily. Only Callisto, her face sallow under the high, unshaded light bulb, could not eat. She leaned against the wall with a piece of cheese cupped in her palm as mirror as she slapped a flexible slice of bread like a powder puff against her cheeks and chin. The women who were pressed close to her in the crowded cage laughed almost to the point of tears at this, relieved for an instant from their uneasiness for what lay ahead; and Athena looked from one face to another, seeking Calliope. A rumor had begun to dart and flicker among the women as they ate, but where the documentation came from, nobody knew. The story was that rivers of blood had flowed in the streets of Oakland that day, that protesters had fought with bricks and rakes and whatever they could lay their hands on, as they met the ferocious assault of the police. Parked cars were overturned, it was said, and the approaches to the Induction Center blocked, while all day the city wept with tear gas. The emergency rooms of hospitals were swamped, the rumor went, for this had been the day of the guerrilla fighters, the day of the flea, who strikes and leaps away to strike again. The demonstrators of the day before had seen only one act of violence, that moment when the mother of a draftee, with her son in tow, had sought to stampede her way and his across the women and men seated on the Induction Center steps. She had trampled in fury over their legs, over their backs and shoulders as they doubled over, dragging her son behind her in her savage advance.

"In spite of the lot of you, he's going in!" she shouted. "He's going to fight for his country! He could wipe out you bunch of Commies with one hand, do you hear me, with one hand!"

"They've locked the doors from the inside now," the well-known poet had said bleakly from where he lay underfoot, his bowler hat pulled low on his sideburns and his ears. "You may have to take him around the corner to the basement entrance. That's where they're delivering them today." But she did not desist, a big woman titubating on whatever pieces of anatomy happened to be on the steps, continuing to smash her one free fist over and over against the plate glass of the door.

That day of passive resistance, of the lotus position of devotion, of an unfrocked nun who had discarded her earthly flesh, of knitting wool woven in innocence into the glossy braids of a girl's hair—all this was done with and would be forgotten. "In placing our bodies between the draft system and the young conscript," the order of the day had read, "we must seek to persuade others through the non-violent power of reason. In our contact with the police, we must remain courteous and understanding. May our love of justice, and the expression of that love, bring an end to involuntary servitude." Ho, hum, sighed Athena; but as the mythical giver of the olive tree, and the inventor of the flute, she wanted the spirit of that day to prevail. Yet she knew it was the chapters of panting terror and streaming eyes, the tales of men and women clubbed and dragged through the streets, of kicked genitals, and handcuffs locked behind the back, of piercing outcry, that would be remembered in the history of their time. The non-violent, the peacemakers, could not wholly envisage, and thus were not prepared to meet, death in the streets, and on rooftops, death drenching the grass of college campuses, that was to come.

"Did you hear that one cop took off his jacket?" the women would ask one another as they ate, having heard the second or third or maybe fourth-hand account of what had taken place. "They say he laid it down on the curb, and set his helmet on top of it, and said, 'I'm quitting. If this is what I'm asked to do, I've had enough.'"

Through the baloney and the plastic cheese that gummed their mouths, the women, packed cheek by jowl in the visiting cage, talked of this good omen, and of still another that came winging in from the wide night of the California countryside.

"There was a student in a wheelchair, a Vietnam veteran," the story went, "who rolled his wheelchair into the doorway of the Induction Center, and sat there handing out leaflets to the men going in. And the cops refused to arrest him. They took the anti-war leaflets away, but they refused to put him in the paddy wagon, although he wheeled himself right up to where it was."

Aren't these things a sign of something changing, the women were saying to one another in different ways as they swallowed the last of the limp crusts. Maybe even the cops, the fuzz, the pigs, every one of them, will lay jacket and club and medals for bravery down in the thoroughfares of the cities for the people to see that they have finally understood. But none of the women foresaw what lay ahead, what lay, in fact, on the other side of the stained plaster wall that Callisto leaned against. Had there been the place to lie down on the floor, she would have done so, but because of the crowded, standing women there was no room. All her beauty was gone for the moment, and she looked gaunt as a hunger marcher in a country stricken with famine, leaning there incongruously dressed in her tight yellow breeches and her brightly flowered shirt.

"What we need is a little optimism around here, if we're going to make it!" an eager voice cried out from among the women.

"No, no!" said Callisto, shaking her head, the dark curtains of hair falling across her face. "No." Perhaps something of all that was present behind the wall she leaned against had suddenly been communicated to her, and now she held in her trembling hand the words of a terrible message just received. "We are going in there to be with other kinds of prisoners, women whose lives have not been like ours," she said, speaking scarcely aloud. "I don't know if we're ready to go in with them. I think we have to try now to believe that our separate lives are really of no importance. For now, anyway, they are of no importance. I think we have to prepare ourselves to accept this—"

And Athena thought in sudden panic that if Calliope didn't materialize from wherever she was and get to Callisto in time, Callisto might slide down, unconscious, to the floor. "I don't know if we're going to be able to see these other women's lives, so different from—" she was saying, and Athena wanted to stand beside her, for now Callisto and Melanie had become interchangeable to her, but she could not force a way through the mass of librarians, housewives, teachers, students, packed into the visiting cage. She wanted to stand close to Callisto in acknowledgment of the dilemma of daughters and mothers alive in this time, or in any time, but she could not get through the mass of women to where Callisto stood alone, her eyes closed now, leaning against the wall. "The thing about counting on words is that they may not be the right ones," Callisto said, speaking scarcely above a whisper. "So we have to go in there with something else, maybe with our hearts, but anyway without judgment, because words—"

And words, thought Athena, still hearing a voice on a tape that had never ceased playing, hearing the fearful, delirious words repeated, repeated, and repeated, until the end. *What words?* the memory of them demanded of her. *What words? Or are you afraid to listen to them again or face the meaning of them?*

(Well, it was like this, she began telling herself as she stood there silent among the murmuring women; it was one evening when I dropped in at the commune, if you can picture a parent dropping in on dropouts, but I was invited for dinner, if you can believe it, as had happened often enough in the three years since Melanie joined the order. Whenever I was in that city, I'd telephone Melanie, and ask her if it was all right if I came up, and she'd say, "I want to see you, woman." She'd call me "woman," and she'd ask me to come as quickly as I could, and I'd sit down before the fire in that cold wintry city, and sometimes brush the grandchildren's hair, or cut their toenails, or maybe read to them, making sounds like twenty wind instruments, one foghorn, and two ambulance sirens, and the redeemer would be in another part of the commune, in another of the redeemed houses they had. He would never be there when I came. And on this one night after the children were put to bed, Melanie said, "I'll play a tape for you while I'm getting the mashed potatoes mashed. It will make you laugh." Ha, ha, I said, ha, ha, ha, already delighted, always ready to make the best of any situation, that's me all over; so I settled back in the armchair Melanie had salvaged from the Goodwill, handsomely upholstered in mustard velvet by Melanie's own quick, still childish hands, and the voice began speaking from the tape recorder, a young girl's voice speaking in strange, bubbling delirium, and even if you only half listened you heard latent in each separate word a long, far, not quite uttered scream. The girl was talking with two men, at least it seemed there must be two, for at times her voice bubbled up out of the morass with the names Lucky and Pete, and maybe my hearty laughter died on my lips by that time, because Pete is the redeemer's name. The little ribbon of tape unwound, unwound, and the girl was telling them some kind of story in which she thought she was a principal character, but neither heads nor tails could be made of what was going on, for whenever her voice began soaring and crying out in ecstacy about being the Hell's Angel in the tale, the two men would titter or snicker on the tape, not laugh outright like honest men, but cackle and laugh up their sleeves, and Pete the Redeemer would say with a quip and a sneer, "You can't be a Hell's Angel, honey; you're a beautiful golden girl"; and then her voice would take flight, would scud, and spiral, and mount the air, and at these moments the lurking scream could almost be heard, and the other man's voice, Lucky's voice, would say with a supercilious twit and jeer, "You're the girl in the story. Don't you remember, you're the girl?" And then the scream would come even closer to being uttered, but not quite, and the girl's voice would cry, "But the girl's burned up! The girl has to die!" So she wanted to be the Hell's Angel instead, and her voice rising higher and higher on the witness stand testified in somebody else's vocabulary, "You see, we was hired by this crazy-looking cat with long yellow hair and long kinda, you know, side-whiskers, and we was to sit on the platform, that was what we was hired to do, we was just to sit on the kinda like the front of the platform while the Rolling Stones and like the other rock groups would be playing, and we was to drink beer all afternoon, that was part of the deal, we'd like sit there on the front of, you know, the platform, and keep people from like climbing up when the groups was playing, and we was to take care of the situation, like that was the order, to sit to the front and see nobody tried climbing up where the bands was playing, and we was being paid with beer, like all the beer you wanted, and we wasn't asking for no trouble with nobody.

("Our bikes was parked around by the side like where the crowd couldn't get to them, but one Angel, you know, he'd parked his bike right there like out front where he could watch it, like to see nothing happened to it, and then the people, there was maybe two thousand of them, they started shoving up close, real close, and they kept pushing a girl up onto the platform, and we had to stop drinking beer and start pushing the girl back down because we was hired for that, to keep anyone like from getting up there, that's what we was doing up on the platform, even between the groups playing we was to keep people from getting up there, and you know if you say you'll do a thing, well, that's a contract, it's like you got to do it, and they kept pushing this girl up. . . ." And then Pete the Redeemer would say on the tape, "You're the girl, honey, you're the beautiful girl," and the girl's voice, drenched with crying, would beg him to let her be the Hell's Angel instead. "Oh, Pete, Pete, don't make me be the girl!" she'd cry out. "The girl has to die!" And even with half an ear you could hear the two men cackling. "This trip, you're the girl. You're the girl," Pete the Redeemer would say to the accompaniment of Lucky the Disciple's snickering and tittering. But maybe her own will wasn't quite gone yet, not quite broken, or maybe it was because the Hell's Angel had moved completely inside her skin and there wasn't room for both of them there, that she could still defy them. Whichever way it was, her voice went stubbornly on with the incessant story.

("They kept pushing this girl up, and almost all her clothes was tore off her," the testimony went in a vocabulary that had nothing to do with whoever she was. "And like a lot of people was pushing her up on the platform, but she was stoned or something and she couldn't stand, and then they, you know, then they started pushing this Angel's bike around, the one that was up to the front, and that was like the end of everything, like we had to save the bike. I tell you, I'm not violent or nothing like that, but you know what, you touch my bike and you've had it. I'll kill you, I'll kill anyone lays a finger on my bike, like my bike's my life, you know, it's my life, and everything on that bike is mine, like my eyes and hands and anything else I was born with is mine. I mean, if you touch my bike, shit, you're a dead man right there, you got to understand that, you're dead because I put my life into that bike, and you touch it and you're like cutting my heart out, and that's what happened. If it was like one Angel knocking that girl back down off the platform, when that was what we was being paid to do, it wouldn't of turned out like it did, any rioting would of been over quick, but it was maybe twenty–fifty people pushing her up right over the bike, and like the Angels pushing her back down, and then what they do is start ripping out the clutch cable, and pulling the fuel lines loose, and then they got knives out, and they was cutting the saddle into strips, and what I mean is, you touch an Angel's bike and you're finished, man. You should of seen what some of these here Angels looked like, they was crying right in front of maybe two thousand people, they was crying like babies when the bike started burning, because that's what happened, the crowd, they opened up the carburetor valves, and they set fire to it, and when it exploded, that girl had to go with it, she had to go with the bike, like there wasn't no way to stop it. I tell you, lay a finger on an Angel's bike and I don't care who the shit you are, you've had it. The crowd was the ones that done it all. We was just hired to sit up on the platform and drink beer, and we wasn't doing nothing. It had to end like that, because them two thousand people made it end like that. If they hadn't of laid their hands on that bike, or like on that girl they kept pushing up on us, nothing would of happened, and the bike wouldn't of had to go."

(The tape came to an end now, and Melanie, her hair hanging straight and pale to her waist, her cheeks and throat like flower petals, came in from the kitchen with the potato masher in her hand. "So what did you think of it?" she asked. "How did you like it?" And I said, "She seemed to be in an awful lot of trouble, that girl." A look of amazement came into Melanie's wide, green, marvelously fearless eyes. "Trouble?" she said. "That wasn't trouble. She was just finding out who she was. Pete and Lucky were guiding her on a trip. Pete says everyone has to have three trips in a lifetime, that is, if he or she's honest enough to want to know who he or she really is." And I said, "You don't believe that, do you?" And Melanie, as beautiful as Venus riding on the wave, stood there with the potato masher hanging from her hand. "If you haven't studied about drugs, you haven't the right to talk about their effects," she said. "Like I've never studied the Greek myths the way you have, so I wouldn't presume to talk about them. Pete uses these trips like an initiation rite," she went on saying hurriedly, hurriedly, as if knowing already that the time between us was running out. "But he doesn't advise more than three, except in very stubborn cases," she said. "Leary gave his people around two hundred and fifty micrograms of LSD, while Pete gives a thousand, or even twelve hundred. You heard how he keeps it under perfect control." Good God, I wanted to say, this is the Grand Inquisitor's definition of the three powers that alone can conquer the impotent rebels: miracle, mystery, and authority; but I couldn't say anything, I couldn't speak. Melanie went back into the kitchen, and after a little while her voice said, "I've just got to put the steaks on, and then everything will be ready. I'll make them rare." Her voice was less exalted now, and my mind kept on saying, Good God, Good God, and I wanted to get some kind of answer from her, not knowing that once I had been answered, the room would no longer be a room with a lamp lit on the table in one corner of it, and a fire barely burning on the chipped bricks of the hearth, but that it would become in a clap of thunder, a tunnel, a cave, a shapeless, blind, interminable darkness in which I would crawl on my hands and knees, groping to find my way. "That girl on the tape, whatever became of her?" I asked, and Melanie said from the kitchen, "Woman, that girl on the tape was me. Lucky was taping it. That was my second trip." She might have been speaking of a jaunt to Mexico or a weekend on the Cape as she turned the steaks. "I still have one more trip to go," she said.)

V

AT FIFTEEN-MINUTE INTERVALS, the women prisoners were taken two by two from the cage and escorted the length of the bare reception hall, and there they passed around a high varnished counter and were lost to view. And as the crowd of women diminished, Calliope, with her modest crown of graying braids on her small head, could finally make her way through the others to where Callisto still leaned against the wall.

"Believe that our separate lives are of no importance?" she said, repeating Callisto's words. "Is anybody ever prepared for that? Isn't that the thing they always forgot to make convincing in church or school or whenever we asked for advice?"

The door of the visiting gallery was being unlocked, and over the heads of the demonstrators the women deputies could be seen, square-shouldered in their navy blue and braid, taking two of the prisoners out, then turning the key in the lock again.

"At this rate, it's going to take five hours to book us all!" cried out one of those who still waited. "I'm an accountant! As I figure it, we'll be here until eleven o'clock tonight, so we have time to plot our future strategy!"

Some of the women laughed at this, and others groaned aloud in mock despair, trapped as they were in the inflexibility of prison time. It was only Callisto who had recognized the dimensions of all that would be asked of them, and who had sought to give it a simple name; and now she slid inch by inch in her foolish yellow breeches down against the wall until she was finally seated limply on the floor. Calliope stood meekly beside her, her lips twitching to speak, to smile, but saying nothing more. There was no need for her to explain that if her daughter had a pain in her gut, and if Callisto's eyes were closed because of that pain, her own eyes, even faded and weary now, could serve for both of them, and her presence serve as custodian for two instead of one.

Near to Athena, St. Theresa waited still, her grave, gray eyes under slightly bulging brows moving with anxious deliberation from the steel wire of the enclosure to the door, and then to the backs of her own hands, wishing neither to see nor be seen. (I had a great-aunt who was a Carmelite, Athena remembered, a poet, born blind; and in my childhood I believed that all nuns were poets, and all born blind, and that all nuns could put their hands through the grating of their impoundment and touch the eyelids and hair of their visitors, as my great-aunt touched mine, and cry out in wonder at the color they sensed in their fingertips; and I believed that all nuns could type, for she typed her poems and the letters to her brother, my grandfather, without making a single error; and I believed that all nuns would say to me, as she said once through the grating, that clothes are a vocabulary that express to others what one is, and that the habit nuns wear can be a language so foreign that others cannot decipher what is being said. "And do you type, dear Sister Theresa," Athena jingled as she waited, "and could you tell in your fingertips the color of my hair?")

Ann moved through the women now to come closer to Athena, and St. Theresa extinguished herself even further to let Ann pass. Once beside her, Ann slipped her arm through Athena's in desperate haste, and began talking quickly, in a voice so low that no one else could hear the words. She was saying that she was here under false pretenses, that is, here for the wrong reasons, speaking nervously and rapidly, saying she was not like the other prisoners, not like all the rest who had "acted out of purity."

"I have such terrible reasons for being here," she said, holding tightly to Athena's arm, "and I am so ashamed about not having convictions, or anyway not acting on convictions, and I should have got up in the courtroom this morning, the way you did, and told the judge and told everyone, the lawyers, and all the other demonstrators, that I have no principles, because I really came here out of anger, only I have never been angry with any-one, or anyway not let it out—"

But it was Lydia now, her ear trumpet hanging askew on the braided cord around her neck, her white shingled hair pressed as smooth as vaseline on her skull, who took the center of the stage. She was trying to untie the laces of her sneakers, but her fingers were thickened and slowed by arthritis; and when Athena slipped out of Ann's grasp and sat down beside her on the bare boards, Lydia turned her manlike, granite face to her in grati-tude. Her mask of intricate wrinkles was white as a clown's as she watched Athena undo the laces and pull the sneakers from her swollen feet.

"They have to take all our things from us. Those are the rules," Lydia said, the echo of deafness in her voice as cavernous as if the words were halloo-ed through cupped hands. "They take away our shoes as well, I've heard, so before we go in, I want to share with everyone here the messages from Tolstoy and Gandhi that I brought in."

She slipped the folded, ruled pages out of the sneakers, where they had served as inner soles for a day and a night and again for this long day, cramping her feet, crowding her humpbacked toes, and now with her heavy, crippled hands she flattened out the papers on the floor, pages not for a moment written by men who were strangers to her, but personal letters the two gentlemen had had delivered to her by special messenger from their graves. She took a pair of steel-rimmed spectacles from her worn leather handbag, and hooked their spindly loops behind her ears.

"Leo Tolstoy wrote this," she said, her unquavering voice strong as a man's as she began reading aloud to the thirty prisoners who were left. " 'I received a letter from a gentleman in Colorado, who asked me to send him a few words or thoughts expressive of my feelings with regard to the noble work of the American nation, and heroism of its soldiers and sailors. This gentleman, together with an overwhelming majority of the American people, feels perfectly confident that the work of the Americans—the killing of several thousands of almost unarmed men (for, in comparison with the equipment of the Americans, the Spaniards are almost without arms)—was beyond doubt a "noble work" . . .' "

Athena was standing again, and Ann had again taken her arm and was clinging to her as if to life itself; and Athena thought, as had happened before from time to time with her girl students, how demeaning both for woman and girl, for teacher and student, to be drawn into this unnatural, this almost shocking, position of dependency. *Oh, be worthy of your looks!* Athena wanted to cry out, thinking how foreign was the cool delicacy of Ann's coloring, and the careful workmanship of her bones, to the chaos and incoherence of her total helplessness. Although the story Ann told in a low, hurried voice at the same time that Lydia read aloud was an uproarious story, it was one that could not be laughed at, for it had taken her from her home, and brought her to this place, and she herself looked on it as tragedy. Ann was saying that she respected her father for all he was, an army officer who controlled them all: her mother, herself, her brother (three years older, and finishing college now), and the dogs they had as well. The dogs sat when her father told them to, ate when he gave them the word to eat.

"He gave us standards," Ann said, speaking quickly and barely aloud. "I know that sounds crazy, but that's the way I really feel about him. I really, really do. You see, I can't discipline myself, I haven't any convictions. I'm just a mess," she said, the tears of self-pity glazing her childlike eyes. It was because of her mother that she had come to the Induction Center, she was saying, the words, the thoughts behind them, jumbled like the pieces of a jigsaw puzzle that she kept trying, first one way and then the other, to fit together. "It wasn't *for* my mother that I came here, but *against* her, terribly against her," she said, while Lydia's voice read deeply from the tomb Tolstoy's words concerning the men who rule mankind.

" 'On entering this army, you will cease to be men with wills of your own; you will simply do what we require of you. But what we wish, above all else, is to exercise dominion; the means by which we dominate is killing, therefore we will instruct you to kill.' "

And then her mother had suddenly inherited a great deal of money, Ann said; that was two years ago, and at once the money took over, and the authority ceased to be the father's.

"It was like this," Ann said, clinging to Athena. "My father's hair was beginning to get thin on the top, and my mother had it—his hair—transplanted from the back of his neck and put on top. They can do that kind of thing now, you know. Perhaps she had wanted to have that done for a long time, and there were other things: she had his teeth capped, all of them, and then he wasn't able to whistle for the dogs anymore. My mother inherited all this money," she whispered, "and the money took over, it really did, and my father stopped telling us what to do. He allowed—he accepted—the operation on my brother's ears. They stuck out a little from his head, and my mother had them put back flat. She may have been thinking about that too for a long time. We had three Cadillacs, and I was sent away to study in Switzerland for a year," she said, as if confessing to some act of shame. "And my mother, she had—she had her breasts lifted, things like that. And all the time I couldn't stop crying; I cried at least an hour every day, because I could see my father was afraid of the money, and he would do whatever it told him to, and before that I didn't think he could ever be afraid—"

"'A pacifism which can see only the cruelties of occasional warfare, and is blind to the continuous cruelties of our social system is worthless,'" Lydia read, offering Gandhi's words steadily, tirelessly, to the silent, weary, slowly diminishing group of women, some of whom had fallen asleep now on the boards of the floor. "'The idea of accommodating oneself to imprisonment is a novel thing for us,'" she read. "'We will try to assimilate it . . .'" And she told them that by December 1921, twenty thousand Indians had been jailed for civil disobedience; and the little nun returned from the far place where she had been, perhaps in search of cloister and sanctification, and smiled at the irony of their own small number. In January, ten thousand more were jailed for political offenses, Lydia said in her deep, deaf voice, and by that time whenever Gandhi heard of a friend or colleague who had been arrested, he telegraphed congratulations to him. In the courtroom, before being sentenced, Gandhi had stood before the bench, she told them, and called out to men and women throughout the world to overcome their "excessive dread of prisons." He said that "imprisonments are now to be courted because we consider it wrong to be free under a government we hold to be wholly bad . . ."

But there was still one more thing that Ann was trying to tell Athena, if only she could get the words of it out.

"My getting arrested, could it make my father—I don't really know—could it make him the way he was before?" she asked; and Athena, feeling light-headed with fatigue, tried not to visualize the army officer going bald again, and the hair restored to the back of his neck, and his teeth miraculously uncapped, enabling the whistle for the dogs to pierce the air again. "Do you think it could make him strong enough, or angry enough to tell me—you see what a mess I am?—I think strong enough just to tell me I'm wrong," Ann whispered to Athena in something as absurd as hope.

Hour after hour, Lydia read, and when she came to the end of the closely typed pages, she would begin over again. Her voice was little more now than a dark croaking, and her thick, big-knuckled fingers shook, but still she read on until after ten o'clock, when the deputies unlocked the cage door and called hers and Ann's names. Then she folded the typewritten pages over, smoothing them carefully in a gesture of farewell, and put them in the bulging handbag, and removed the steel-rimmed glasses from her nose. She reached for her sneakers and pulled them on, and did not stop to lace them, and Athena took her hands and helped her to her feet. Ann had walked alone to the cage door, and she waited docilely there, her head lifted almost in pride, as if she carried with her now a portion of the message that Lydia's unwavering voice had read aloud. It might have been nothing more that she remembered than Gandhi's gentle chiding to the uncertain that men in the end become what they believe themselves to be.

Even after Lydia was gone, the laces of her sneakers trailing, she and Ann flanked by the deputies, even after they had walked the length of the entrance hall and disappeared from sight, the echo of the old voice could still be heard. The fragments of the letters written personally to her were still captive there within the confines of the visitors' cage, so that when future prisoners were held there they would hear Gandhi saying forever that: "A violent man's activity is most visible while it lasts . . . but it is always transitory . . ."; or hear Tolstoy crying out: "I wish now, this moment, without delay or hesitation, to the very utmost of my strength, neither waiting for anyone nor counting the cost, to do that which alone is clearly demanded by Him who sent me into the world; and on no account, and under no conditions, do I wish to, or can I, act otherwise—for herein lies my only possibility for a rational and unharassed life."

It was half-past ten, and the accountant had been right, for there were only four women left in the cage: Callisto sleeping, a tall, slender, long-haired child, her head in the green velveteen of Calliope's lap; Athena lying with her jacket rolled under her head, as it had been in the forests of other countries so many times before; and St. Theresa sitting with her legs crossed under her, withdrawn in her cassock-like dress in deliberate, considered penance for all that life offered so heedlessly. For a moment it seemed to Athena that the roles of daughter and mother had been abandoned, and that they were four potential lovers waiting there, each waiting for the other to reach out a tender and compassionate hand. But that moment passed, and almost at once Calliope and Callisto were summoned, and the cage door was locked again, and they went, their beauty almost extinguished, down the endlessly long hall.

Half in sleep, Athena wondered what St. Theresa, who was left here with her, would make of Blake's view of God the Father as symbol of ruthless, relentless tyranny, the highest instrument for the breaking of man's will, and of Christ as the living figure of all that is searching and fallible in man. For Athena did not yet know that they had come to the end of their vocabulary, to the end of all the quotations by which they lived, and that another language must be found, one by means of which the poor could speak to the rich, the rich to the poor, the illiterate to the literate, the fearful to the unafraid. A new and violent place lay at the end of the hall, and she did not know that when she entered it, whatever had been before, whatever had served as experience, would not be able to serve again.

Before the deputies came for the last time, Athena kept herself awake by singing words that Blake had written, telling herself that if Callisto had been there, she would not have dared to sing. She sang the lines of Blake's that Rory had put to music a long time ago (over twenty years now), and sung to Sybil when she was three and four months old in Glenwood Springs, in the cold heart of that Colorado winter and the cold heart of the war. Rory would come down at night from the army ski camp above Leadville, down the long winding road through frozen drifts, past the unending tiers of high moonlit crests and curving valleys, all somberly glowing with snow; down, down, past the black of the forests to the warm lights of the wintry town. And after a drink in the shabby hotel room, while the radiator hissed in anger near the frosted windows, the taste of the cold would be wiped from Rory's mouth, and the blood would move like summer through his veins. He would take Sybil out of the basket where she slept, and hold her, asleep still, over his shoulder in the khaki tunic, his eyes deathless and bright with love. He would pat her on her tiny back, steadily, rhythmically, and when he stopped laughing he would begin to sing. And Athena sang the same words softly now, feeling the weak tears gathering behind her lids.

> *Was Jesus Humble? or did he*
> *Give any proofs of Humility?*
> *Boast of high Things with Humble tone,*
> *And give with Charity a Stone?*

It had become such a part of her life to draw strength (to draw identity even) from words that had been written in other times, music composed in other centuries, that it seemed to Athena the lines of Blake's poem had stirred a response in St. Theresa. Through her blurred lashes, Athena believed she could see the living flesh restored to the little nun's bones, the small cheeks beginning to fill out, as if a painter were shaping them in with oils. For the first time, St. Theresa's lips parted, and her shoulders in the brown wool dress sloped gently and vulnerably. It was only her square hands, the short fingers slightly convexed, as though from long years curved in prayer, that appeared to resist. And Athena sang a little louder now, so that the hands too would change.

> *When but a Child he ran away*
> *And left his Parents in dismay.*
> *When they had wandered three days long*
> *These were the words upon his tongue:*
> *"No Earthly Parents I confess:*
> *I am doing my Father's business."*

When the deputies came down the hall, St. Theresa stood up and smoothed her brown dress with her flattened palms. Then she walked in her scuffed moccasins to where Athena lay, and she held out one open, and unexpectedly palpable hand to her, and helped to pull her to her feet. She stood there, shorter than Athena, not looking at her as Athena picked up the jacket that had served as pillow and put it on, not like a nun at all, but like a student, her brow puzzling over some difficult text. Then she said very quietly, her eyes averted:

"I'm doing my Father's business," and the two of them went with the deputies down the hall.

VI

IN EACH OF THE two main dormitories of the women's section of the Rehabilitation Center were fifty iron cots, twenty on one side of each of the two long narrow rooms, the barracks-trim formation of cots divided in mid-center by an archway that gave access to the toilets, sinks, and showers; thirty along the opposite walls, where no archways intervened. The dormitory on the west side of the building ran parallel with the bleak entrance hall and the visiting cage, and thus had no windows. The dormitory on the east side had a row of windows in its outer wall, old-fashioned sash windows, with cracked ancient shades that pulled up and down, pleasant and even homelike to the eye except for the presence of iron bars fixed to the outside sills. By daylight, the demonstrators would be able to see from these windows a ragged stretch of grass bordered by overgrown beds of iris plants, their sabers rusted and split from long neglect. There were also three or four dejected plum trees, and a solid maple that leaned in weariness against the south corner of the fence, its trunk girded with a spiked chastity belt so that it could not serve as avenue of escape. Unpruned rose bushes, their lean arms gesticulating wildly in the breeze, almost reached the tangle of barbed wire that topped the eight-foot barrier standing between the prisoners and the countryside. Above all this soared the wide, ever changing California sky.

But none of it—not the lock-up wards, or the iron-barred

massive doors to the solitary cells, or the view of the garden—
were the demonstrators able to see that night. By the time the
processing and fingerprinting were done, it was close to midnight, and the women groped their separate ways down the
aisles between the rows of cots where the regular prisoners lay
sleeping in the half dark. Their possessions had again been
taken from them, this time their clothing as well, and now they
wore the prison-issue nightgowns and sneakers that had been
given them after their showers. Over their arms, each carried a
towel, a washrag, two sheets, and a gray dress for daytime wear,
and each held a cake of soap in her hand. They had been
directed to take whatever unoccupied beds they found, designated by a blanket folded over at the foot, and when they had
found them they laid their towels and washrags on the night
tables that stood between the cots, placed their soap in the
night table drawers, and folded the gray dresses for morning
across the iron head bars. They spread the coarse, patched
sheets over mattresses no thicker than their hands, and, like
obedient children, arranged their sneakers under the night tables,
and slipped off the threadbare, prison-issue underpants. Then
each of them lay down in the deeply breathing strangeness of
this place, drew the navy or khaki blanket over her, and sought
to sleep.

That was the first night, and before there had been the time
to dream, the lights came on, and a woman's voice spoke sharply.

"Time to get up, ladies," the woman said, and the prisoners
got silently from their cots. "Stand at the foot of your bed until
count has been taken," said the deputy, neat as a pin in the
dormitory aisle. In her left hand she held a clipboard with the
typed list of their names, black, white, and Chicano, fixed to it,
and the angular fingers of her right hand drummed on the wood.
She was haggard-cheeked and long of jaw, and each separate
name she pronounced might have been a fruit pit she spat out,
the taste of it as bitter as gall. When she was done with the lot
of them, she instructed them to wash and dress. "Do not line

up for breakfast until you have washed and opened your beds for airing," she said, her eyes sharp on the watch at her wrist.

Some of the regular prisoners were already making for the showers, running on bare feet down the dormitory in their flannel gowns, their towels slung over their shoulders, carrying with them their sneakers and dresses; black women, and Chicano women among them, pushing one another aside in their haste, needing this moment of triumph over others, even over their own kind, in order to bear the defeats of the day. They might have been children running eagerly, for the nightgowns, cream-colored and ruffled at the neck and wrists, had an innocence and charm to them, like the nightgowns of little girls, and Athena wanted to hold hers fast to her heart. Obediently and modestly, she dressed beside her cot, pulling the prison underpants and the shapeless gray dress on under the gown, and then slipping it off over her head.

"They didn't give us any combs," one of the college girls called out from two cots away; and another voice warbled from the far end of the dormitory: "Madame Deputy, what about toothbrushes?"

In time they were all to learn that this slat-legged, lean, and easily rattled keeper of order feigned an absorption in things of greater moment whenever a question was put to her. She was not deaf, but she could not afford to hear, for a direct response to a question would have unmasked her, an argument shattered her. Thus her single weapon was her ability to convince them that their questions went unanswered because they had not been heard, and not been heard because for her their voices had no sound. Her iron eye advised them that their faces had been rubbed out, their bodies obliterated without trace, her exclusion of them from life permitting them only one reality: that of their names on the typewritten list she held. Any other claim they made to existence was no more than a hallucination of their own disordered minds.

"You have six minutes," she said, her jaw moving up and then down, then up again, as if insecurely wired to her skull.

Corporal Anxiety, Calliope was to name her in one of those hours when any words, whether funny or not, seemed better than no words at all. And now Corporal Anxiety was joined by another deputy, who came in from the eastern dormitory, clipboard in hand, she too having summoned prisoners from their beds. She was statuesque, by which Athena meant she was larger than life-size and handsomely made, almost Grecian in allure despite the navy blue turtleneck sweater worn over the white shirt and the uniform's navy skirt. Her legs in tan nylons were muscular as a dancer's, and drawn in tight at the ankles in unexpected delicacy. She alone in the room seemed without tension as she leaned against the footrail of an empty cot, her hair coiled into a smooth golden bun at the nape of her neck and held in a filet there. Athena hastened past them both toward the washrooms, but in that last instant of quiet she did not reach the doorway before the screams came, rising higher and higher from the showers, and the clatter and crash of flung objects, the slap of flesh on flesh, the shattering of glass, turned them all to stone.

All, that is, except one; for the Grecian deputy at once threw the clipboard she held onto the cot behind her, and sprang forward on her dancer's legs. She crossed the dormitory with such speed that she and the naked black girl collided as, shining with water, gleaming with blood, the girl exploded through the doorway. Behind her came a second girl in pursuit, tall, and handsomely proportioned, with fine, high, blue-nippled breasts, her head turbaned in a towel. Her black flesh was wet and glittering, and there was an animal splendor about her as she let fly the battered and blood-stained metal wastebasket that she swung above her head. But with one hand, the Grecian deputy caught it in midair while with the other she pushed out of the orbit of attack the girl crouched low behind her on the floor, who slipped and toppled now in the slime of her own blood.

Then the deputy seized the pursuer by the wrist, but held her only for the instant it took for the soapy flesh to escape her, and the tall girl went dancing off again. The deputy had flung the wastebasket aside, and now she had the girl's slick shoulders in her strong white hands, but the shoulders too writhed, eel-like, from her grasp.

"Get a sheet around Prudence," the Grecian deputy said without turning her head, knowing, although she did not see it taking place, that her long-jawed colleague and the white prisoners would be standing there as if bound hand and foot, handcuffed and manacled by their own uncertainty. It was the black inmates who wrapped their fallen, panting sister in a sheet, and lifted her to a cot, and pressed their towels upon her wounds. "Get the key to the medical supply room," the deputy directed Corporal Anxiety, her voice low, unperturbed, still not turning her head; for now the eyes of the tall black girl and hers had met, and the precise *pas de deux* was engaged, to be danced warily and shrewdly to its end.

"She said she'd get me! She's been waitin' to get me!" Prudence cried from the cot, the words wrung from her in separate, convulsive sobs. She lay shuddering like a night-moth with a pin transfixing its soft, trembling, dying body while the handmaidens stanched her blood. "She come back here to get me!" Prudence screamed out. "She come back with murder in her heart!"

The arms and breasts of the deputy were as firm as stone in her turtleneck sweater as she stood with the sovereignty of a statue before the dancing black girl who spun forward, armed now with a drawer wrenched from a night table, the contents of it scattering as she raised it in blazing fury over her head. The deputy moved serenely in the measure of the dance, reached for the drawer and without apparent effort jerked it from the girl's hands. She did not turn her head as she set it down behind her, as she had the wastebasket with its traceries of bright blood; these awkward weapons she could deal with, but when she sashayed forward to join hands with her partner, the girl slithered away. It was a stylized gavotte that now proceeded, two steps to one side, three to the other, with no music playing, but the breathing of the two women who danced whispering a soft, staccato rhythm on the hushed air. The deputy held the girl's gaze in hers, her arms not yet around her, her eyes alone drawing her closer and closer into the final embrace. If the girl resisted, it was only because the contest was not, had never been, with the deputy, but with Prudence, who lay on the cot beyond. For the third role was neither that of mother nor daughter, and the drama was now between lover and lover, with the deputy usurping a place in the triangle by virtue of her illicit authority.

"That two-timin' bitch, she done me in," the tall girl whispered, dancing still. "Done me in, done me in."

The deputy moved from side to side as the girl moved, seeming to follow but actually leading her in the figure of the waltz; and step by step, breath by breath, she narrowed the distance between them, guiding the girl by nothing more than her unfaltering gaze. Then, without warning, the deputy leaped forward and caught the girl fast in her arms, gripping her just above the high, black, cushioned hips, pinning the girl's arms to her sides. The strong, impervious hands were locked like a steel trap in the small of the girl's back, and in the same instant that she clasped her, the deputy forced one of her dancer's fine muscular legs around the girl's black, gleaming, left leg, and held her rooted there.

"Cool it, baby," the deputy said through her teeth. "Cool it, Marvella," the vise of her hands not breaking, the girl's pear-shaped breasts pressed, soft and giving, against the turtleneck sweater's navy wool.

Even before two more uniformed women moved in battleship formation the length of the dormitory, the girl had surrendered, her rage spent, defeated perhaps by something as unexpected as the deputy's gentle pronouncing of her name. "Marvella," the Grecian deputy had said, and not in admonition, in a place where gentleness was allowed no gesture, authorized no speech.

Another of the deputies ripped a blanket from a cot to fling over Marvella's nakedness, and her companion grasped Marvella's upper arm; and Marvella went with them, majestic in the blanket's folds, her turbaned head not lowered, her eyes fixed blankly on the familiar outline of what waited at the end of the long hall.

"Don't let Marvella keep the towel!" the Grecian deputy called after them, cautioning them as she jerked her turtleneck sweater into place, and with the palm of one broad, steady hand smoothed the filet that still held the gold coil of her hair. And then she turned to Prudence on the cot. "Get into chow line," she directed the prisoners quietly. She sat down on the sagging edge of the mattress, and her square-tipped, blunt-nailed fingers set the matted strands of Prudence's hair back from the deepest of the lacerations, scarlet velvet or plush, it seemed to be, hanging over her right eye. She did not so much as glance at Corporal Anxiety, who stood hesitantly there, her long jaw swinging, a bottle of iodine and a tin container of Band-Aids in her uncertain hand. "You'll have to have some stitches, baby," the Grecian deputy said. "It's not going to hurt. They'll freeze it insensible." It did not seem permissible, not acceptable, somehow, that she should hold Prudence like a small child in her arms, but this is what took place. Carefully, carefully, she held and tended Prudence, touching her delicately so as not to harm her in any way, cradling her, wiping the tears from the girl's small, dark, lacerated face, pressing the towel to the jagged slash across her breasts. "You won't feel anything, baby," she was crooning to Prudence, and the girl clung to her and no longer wept. "We'll get you to the hospital right away."

Now that the routine had been disrupted, all was in a state of panic. The day was twelve minutes behind schedule, the prisoners were told, and the hysteria this generated in the figures of authority silenced the speech on every tongue. The pace of activity was so quickened that Athena saw herself and the others as those ludicrous, darting shapes with flailing limbs that flash across the screen when a movie film is accelerated. Breakfast was cut from fifteen minutes to seven, and then the inmates flew to make their beds, were counted again with the swiftness of lightning, and rapidly divided into three work groups. One contingent was dispatched to the laundry, under guard, another began the scraping and waxing of the endless halls, and the third battalion was rushed by deputies to the annex where the sewing and ironing rooms were housed. The walled courtyard that lay between this annex and the women's dormitories was an area that perhaps threatened sexual confrontation, for it was rumored that the men's quarters lay beyond the western wall. It was even said that from the narrow windows, those just over there, the men could look down through the unrelenting bars and covet the women as they crossed the paved yard—the men who were not even voices in the distance, on whom no woman's eye was authorized to rest.

In the sewing and ironing space the demonstrators learned that the long-term prisoners wore blue dresses with smart white collars and cuffs, trim enough for a beauty parlor operator to have selected, while those with shorter sentences must wear the grieving, shapeless garments of steel gray. In this unfamiliar dress that hung almost to her ankles, Athena worked at an ironing board, the sneakers on her feet a size too large and contoured still with the outline of other women's bunions and other women's toes. The ironing board swayed unsteadily as she pressed shirts that reached their denim arms across the scorched padding, empty male arms stretching out for every woman there.

Lydia and Calliope had been assigned a closetful of blankets to sort and fold and stack in two piles. On the left of the closet door were to be placed those which could still be darned or patched and put into service again; on the right, those that were beyond repair. A record of the long durance and endurance of the prisoners was written into the faded khaki or navy wool of these blankets, depositions made in the cacography of dried vomit and the hieroglyphics of blackened blood. But, soiled or not, they were to be spread out on the center sewing table so that the black girls might cut them in half, or even into thirds, working not only heedless of the white faces suddenly there in such profusion, but working as if they, the permanent black prisoners, were contained in a separate world that no one could enter by any of the simple ways that people customarily enter one another's lives. Calliope and Lydia would carry the ailing blankets to them, and four of the black girls would hold the four corners of each blanket, while a fifth girl cut expertly from one side to the other of it with outsized shears. And then Calliope, the bemused half smile on her lips, small-boned and modest in her sad gray dress, would carry the salvaged sections to the women busy at the machines, and they would piece them together, making whole blankets of them again.

Once, when she passed Athena at the ironing board, Calliope paused a moment with the bisected blankets in her arms.

"I've been brought up to believe," she murmured, "that a woman is never happier than when ironing for her loved ones." And another time she stopped long enough to say that Callisto was waxing a dormitory floor. "She's going to be such a help around the house when we get home," she said.

St. Theresa worked at a table apart from the other demonstrators, replacing buttons, repairing pockets, setting neat patches in the seats and the knees of the coarse, white coveralls for men they had never seen and were never to see. Her small, tense, puzzled face with its swollen brows, looked strangely anemic to Athena, actually drained of pigmentation, white as death itself among the black faces and throats and arms of the girls who worked beside her and across from her, and who talked among themselves, but by no word or glance acknowledged her bleached presence there. Perhaps the God to whom St. Theresa had humbly dedicated her life was now beginning to fail her, and so the others were uneasy with her; but however it was, it was only to Calliope that the black prisoners turned, as if she were neither white nor stranger to them. Their Afros were neatly trimmed, and their flesh as smooth as ebony, but their faces were not in any way alike. The white college girls and the white librarians, Athena reflected as she ironed, were scarcely distinguishable one from the other, and this might be because white women were shaped despite themselves and their convictions by the rigid molds of the timeless traditions they upheld. But the look in the black girls' eyes filled Athena with fierce grief. No human being had the right to examine others with such cold, high censure, or with such detached and grudging curiosity; and while Athena raged within herself at all that had brought this about, it was Calliope who won them, for she knew exactly what to do with a sewing machine. She could make it come to humming life, like the sound of a hive of bees, as the needle sprang back and forth, embroidering the names of the girls who pressed around her. In the hours of that first long morning, she began making deeper hems in the trailing gray dresses that the demonstrators wore. And "Love," she stitched quickly inside the man's underpants they had just patched, and "Peace" inside the cuff of a denim shirt. The two deputies at the far end of the room perceived nothing but the diligence of the women at their work, and at that distance they did not hear the voices saying:

"Me, I come here for a rest. I bin in an outta jail so many years, I don' try to count 'em anymore. This time I took the rap for my kid sister, but none of us, we don' go roun' makin' announcements 'bout why we're here. At firs', a long time back, I use go roun' askin' who done what. But after a while it jus' don' interes' nobody, 'cause everybody done jus' 'bout the same. I'm twenny-five, and jail's bin my life since way back. But it ain't bad, not here it ain't. You got a bed with sheets, and no hustlin', and the meals all cooked up fine. I come back, an I know all the deputies, and who'll be like my mama to me, and the other ones who won't. Here is jus' somewhere you come back to rest up in 'fore you go back out and git busted over again."

Or saying to Calliope: "They's two things I knows a lot about. One's dope and one's women. I guess I knows a little about men, too, but when you're in here you get to likin' women, an that's cool. You ever make it with a broad?" Or saying: "You in here for your reasons like I'se in here for mine. We both believes in them jus' as strong. Soon as I git out, I go back, do my thing, an you go back out an do yours. . . ."

It was a woman called Tallulah who first spoke of children, not to Athena and not to Calliope, but to the other black prisoners. Tallulah sat at the head of St. Theresa's table, a woman so large that she might have been two women contrived to look like one, stretched as if at ease in her chair, but she was not at ease, for her shoulders were bowed like an old woman's under the nearly unbearable burden of mountainous flesh they bore. The buttons of her blue and white prison dress (which may have been two dresses stitched together to contain her) were strained to the bursting point across her belly and her ballooning breasts. She had stretched her enormous legs out under the sewing table, and the skin of them above the white socks was burnished to mahogany. Her forearms, heavy as any other woman's thighs, lay idle in her lap, resting from the weariness of merely being alive, and Athena saw that the sleeves of her dress had been slit above the elbows so that they would not throttle her flesh like tourniquets. Her neck was short and as solid as a bull's, and above the three thick layers of her chin swelled the dark stoical face, its placid grief crowned with a multitude of tiny braids that lay close to her skull.

"They keeps me here acause they don' want me doin' for my kids," she was saying. "Tha's the reason for it. Six months ago when I come out, my boyfriend ask me if I wanna go firs' see the kids or firs' have a fix, an I says I take the fix, acause what happen is, sometime you scared to see the kids right off, sometime you gotta kinda collec' yo'self. So now they put the kids in forster homes, all six of 'em, an when I get outta here, I gotta go lookin' for 'em, like they was los' dogs or cats, mebbe fin' 'em at the SPCA."

"Tallulah," they'd say as her three hundred pounds of dark flesh shook with laughter, "Tallulah, pass the scissors up this way," or "Tallulah, quit integratin' the black an white sewin' cotton you holdin' onto down there," or "Tallulah, you lookin' for a fix, the way you keepin' them needles down there under yo' auspices?" And Tallulah, her rosy-palmed hands lying empty in her lap, would talk about the children again.

"My Auntie, she tol' me when she come out Sunday, the twins is callin' that forster mother 'Mama,' an I told her that ain't right. Tha's what the prison system do, take away yo' kids an make 'em think back on you like you was dead. Tha's what the power structure doin' to me an my life," she said, and for a while she didn't laugh any more.

VII

ATHENA BELIEVED it was still night when she was awakened by a hand touching her shoulder, and in the cold beam of a flashlight's single eye she saw the blue of the uniform, the mannish shirt collar, and the Grecian deputy's face close to her own.

"You're on kitchen detail, Athena," she said in a low voice. "Get dressed. Martha will tell you what to do when you get there."

"What time is it?" Athena whispered. "Is it some kind of an emergency?"

"Four forty-five. Everything in prison is an emergency," the deputy said in quiet irony, and the beam of her flashight moved off down the aisle.

In the kitchen, Athena looked quickly and uncertainly at the others working there, and then she took a long blue denim apron from the pile of them on the larder shelf, and knotted the strings of it around her waist. She saw the others wore canvas caps covering their hair, and she put one on; and Martha, who was white, did not look in her direction as she asked Athena to be so kind as to stir the deep metal vat of oatmeal that stood gasping on the electric range. Athena felt herself as nameless and faceless now as the prison willed them all to be, one of a crew of half a dozen working quickly under the glare of the fluorescent lights. She watched the others and did as Martha bid, filling the glass sugar containers and the salt and pepper shakers and setting these at each end of the long tables in the dining hall. She slivered the great blocks of butter into pats and laid them in orderly rows on sheets of waxed paper (*all thumbs, all thumbs,* she rebuked herself as one pat fell to the floor; *how did I ever manage to invent the bridle and the flute?*). And the black girls hid their hilarity behind each other's shoulders at the sight of her doing so awkwardly what they did rapidly and well. Martha, seeing without appearing to see, spoke in her defense, taking on, Athena learned of her that first morning, the collective, impersonal defense of all the maligned and all the justly or unjustly condemned.

"No one on the face of this earth can learn anything in two minutes and a half," she said, a trace of a brogue in her voice, speaking to herself it might be, as she laid the limp slices of bread, one by one, on the hot grill.

She was a woman of perhaps fifty, plump as a partridge and quick on her small feet, her face veined ruddy with the daily and nightly history of all that had taken place in her life before coming here. She was the flawed mother-figure behind the zinc top of the kitchen counter, mistress over the separate cauldrons of pulsing farina, of eggs bobbing, ten deep, in scarcely bubbling water. Her brown, lidless eyes, hard as two little beads, appeared to be fixed on the work under her hands, but saw, without giving any sign, the failures and the accomplishments and the frailties of them all. She saw the Chicano woman, thin as a snipe, the outsized white canvas cap like a balloon above her sallow face, retiring behind the refrigerator door to take deep, furtive swallows from the can of grapefruit juice reserved for the lady lieutenant and her deputies; and she saw the black girls, the many-tongued, many-eyed substance of the prison, who were on kitchen detail as well, their backs turned to her as they spooned raspberry jelly they had no right to out of the glass onto their velvet tongues.

There were over two hundred women to feed three times a day, seven days a week, and Martha so deft, so expert in the kitchen that it was always in her mind, she told Athena, that this was the reason they kept picking her up off the street, or wherever she happened to be, and bringing her back, and putting her into the blue and white dress of those who would have a long time to stay. It was not on Athena's first morning in the kitchen, and perhaps not even on the second, but on the days that immediately followed Athena learned they needed her only to listen to them speak. What she had been in the real world, or even why she was here, was of no interest to them, for their hearts were filled to overflowing with the torment of the deception of their own lives.

"Over and over, picking me up and bringing me back here," Martha said to Athena, and she kept on wiping the zinc top of the counter clean, the muscle taut in her bare white forearm, with the little red knob of her elbow shining at the end of it. "Bringing me back for no good reason on the face of this earth," she said, "unless having a drop too much is good enough reason for them, and the whole lot of them, Mr. and Mrs. America, drunk as lords every day of the week, and Sunday the worst of all. Two years ago I spent a year to the day here," she went on saying, her eyes appearing to see nothing, yet seeing everything as she stirred the cauldron of cream of wheat. "The law is, they can't keep you over a year in this place, so I'm out for three months, and I'm maybe doing my shopping, when what do they do but pick me up again. I tell you there's something behind it all. One night a couple of officers comes up the front porch and into the house just before my husband gets home from the railroad yard, and they ask me what about a can of beer, and I get the cans out, nice and cold off the ice for them, and we all have a nice refreshing drink, like friends, you know, and then one of them says to me, like passing the time of day, you're on probation, aren't you, Martha, and with that we have another beer around, and when my husband walks in, tired and all, we have another one after that, and then they leave, after shaking hands with us, and the next day I get a summons to come to court. They charge me with violation of parole, and they give me three months for that.

"Here's my word, if it's anything to you, and may the saints be my witness," Martha said, "the last time it was the officer himself who tripped me up and laid me flat on the floor of the liquor store where I'd just finished buying a fifth of Ripple for me and my husband to drink with supper, as if there was any harm in that. And the bottle breaks in the paper sack when I go down, so he apprehends me for being a public nuisance, and when I start crying and carrying on and saying I can't go back, that I haven't the courage left to go back, he adds on to it 'resisting arrest,' and I get six months. That was September, that was one month ago," she said. "I tell you it's some kind of conspiracy. The lieutenant, she likes the way I do the bacon, crisp and all, and the way the kitchen's run, quiet and clean as a whistle, when I'm here. She says she can't drink the coffee they make after I'm let out, and the scrambled eggs dry as sawdust. That's what she says. So maybe that's why my life's the way it is."

The inmates in lock-up, who wouldn't be coming into the dining hall when the others came, were always somewhere in Martha's mind, and now she jerked the spatula under the squares of toast and lifted them onto a tin platter she had heating on the stove.

"Cover them over as quick as you can," she said to Athena. "God knows I try to serve it up hot to them, but the girls don't push the carts as fast as they ought to, and everything gets cold on the way up the halls."

The Chicano woman's name was Isabelita, Athena learned on that first morning in the kitchen, and she was certainly the puniest, most bedraggled hen in the barnyard, skidding this way and that, with her thin, rigid neck stuck out, trying to grab up whatever she could from under the beaks and talons of the other fowl. But either she managed to get nothing, or else her haste and her eagerness reduced to nothing whatever she snapped into her avid craw. When she set the sugar containers on the tables, she would turn her back to Martha at the stove and pour sugar out of each of them into the cupped palm of her hand, and lick it up, tense and sly and hungrier in her sallow, threadbare skin, than anyone alive. There was not enough food in the entire world to satiate the gnawing famine of her needs.

"Soon as you're lookin' the other way," the black girl tall as an African queen would say to Martha, "that Spic's rippin' off cocoa powder an' my-naise an' spoonin' lard right outta the can. She's slier than a weasel, that fox," she'd say, and tip her canvas cap forward over her eyebrows, over her nose, and go bopping with her flexible behind across the kitchen to the open larder door, snapping her fingers as she went, her head tilted back on her strong round neck in order to see.

"There's nothing missing," Martha would say, her eyes on the cereal bowls she was setting in the oven to warm so that the oatmeal or the cream of wheat or the farina would hold the heat as the wagons moved up the halls. "Maybe you'd get me some jelly out, as long as you're there," she'd say.

And when the black girls were out of earshot, Isabelita would finally speak, the words coming rapidly as machine-gun fire under her breath to Martha:

"They got tins of sardines in the pockets of their uniforms now, them spades. I seen them taking more in there right now."

Martha would spoon the eggs out of the boiling water in the vat, and arrange them symmetrically on a metal tray on the counter, and say in an abstracted voice:

"I didn't see anyone taking anything, and that's God's truth. Maybe you wouldn't mind setting out more cups, so things will be ready when the lot of them come."

It was not that first morning, but perhaps the second, that Isabelita told Athena about the seamen on the waterfront, with their tattooed chests and forearms, who were her living, and the four children she had that her mother took care of in San Mateo. That was the way it had always been, her mother and her, without any man to cause them trouble. Monday mornings she'd take the money over to them, going by bus from San Francisco or Oakland, Monday because business was better on weekends, and she'd sleep like the dead in the cemetery the first three days of the week, and then go back to the waterfront again. But all, all these things she spoke of were reduced in the final telling to nothing, for neither the children, nor the mother, nor the seamen, were the requisite provender, not the sustenance she scratched so frantically for, her black feathers in disarray, under the claws and beaks of the multi-bodied menace of humanity.

At eight o'clock, you had to be back in the dormitory for bed count, and at nine, after washing the cups and tin trays and the cutlery with the others, and wiping the tables off, and mopping the dining hall and the kitchen floors, you stayed with Martha, who was finishing cleaning out the vats and scouring the grill. You stayed with her to help prepare the soup for lunch and the vegetables for supper, although she did not ask this of you. She simply sat down before the basins of raw carrots and potatoes and celery, a ragged dishcloth laid across her lap, and began scraping, not with a paring knife, but with the slit-mouthed, saw-toothed gadget that regulations authorized; and Athena sat down on a chair beside her, and took up a like gadget, and began to scrape.

"What's happened to the Spic? Ain't she on kitchen detail?" A black girl, her hair covered by a blue bandana, might ask as she wiped and stacked the tin trays. "She relaxin' in a sauna bath somewhere?"

"I couldn't tell you," Martha would say, and the potato peelings curled away from under the grinning gadget in her hand. "I guess she's working somewhere else."

And when the black girls would be out of sight, using up what remained of the pats of butter on pilfered slices of bread, Isabelita, her fingernails scratching at imaginary drippings in remote corners of the stove, would say:

"What's happened to the colored girls? Ain't they supposed to be working here?"

"Maybe they called them over to the laundry or the sewing room," Martha would say as the carrot shavings fell away, bright orange and as clear as light, onto the dishtowel on her lap.

"I couldn't tell you," she'd answer to the questions they put to her about one another, but what she could talk about was the other lieutenant, the one who wasn't there any more. "Not the one you'll see stepping down the hall like in a fashion show," she said to Athena. "Not Miss America." The other lieutenant had been there for nearly fifteen years, and she'd known her for eight. "I swear to God, in all that time, when I was coming in and out, I saw her only twice in uniform, and that was when she knew the county or state inspectors were coming in to nose around. She'd never clap any girl in the hole unless talking to her first wouldn't quiet her, and lock-up was empty half the time. She said I'd served too much time already. 'God knows you've served enough time for every crime in the book,' she'd say to me," Martha said, wasting nothing of the potato as she carved the skin away. Sunday and Wednesday nights, she used to read aloud to them in the library, this other lieutenant did, and when Athena asked what kind of things she read to them, Martha had nothing to say, because the books and the words were not what mattered. It was just that the lieutenant sat down in the library with them twice a week and opened a book, and read to them, not as if they were children, but as if they were her own blood relatives, her sisters maybe. "The way she was, we could have had the same family name, and gone to the same church since we were born," Martha said.

She pulled the white threads of the celery, like harp strings, from the greenish stalk, and she said the name "rehabilitation" meant something then.

"I swear to God," she said, and then some self-evident truth that had slipped her mind for a moment stopped her short, and she worked in silence for a little while. "I didn't happen to get rehabilitated, and that's for sure," she said at last, "but if ever I get out of here with what's left of my sanity, I swear you can take a knife and cut my throat if I ever touch another drop. My husband, he could get a good lawyer to get me out, and that's a fact, but he has no understanding of life. Some nights at home, I'll want a little drink after supper, and what do I have to do but climb out the bedroom window, and go down the porch roof to get to the street, because he won't let me out the door. A glass or two of wine with your supper, that's well and good with him, but on the nights he'd lock me upstairs in the room, I'd start thinking about the lieutenant out here, the other lieutenant. She was around sixty years old, and I'd think to myself that maybe if I could talk to her I'd be able to understand a lot of things better, and I'd climb out the window and run 'swifter than arrow from the Tartar's bow,' as the saying goes, the two blocks to the corner bar. I give you my word, it was more getting back to see her that I wanted than getting a nip those nights."

"And then the barman or someone would call the cops right away?" Athena asked, watching Martha's deft hands, she herself trying to scrape and peel the vegetables into shape with a like precision, a like economy.

"Ah, no," said Martha, "it was different. It wasn't like that. An off-duty officer, or maybe an officer finishing his beat, on his way home but wearing his uniform still, one or the other might drop in, and by that time I'd have had two or three, and I'd have a couple more with whoever was there, so that's the way it would turn out." She was silent for another moment, her hands, like two well-trained servitors, working quickly, indefatigably. "I swear to you, if my husband had ever walked down the street with me just one night in the week, and we'd had a couple of drinks sitting in a booth together, with a little lamp lit on the table, and some nice tune playing, there'd be a different story to tell. I wouldn't be cooking year in, year out, for a regiment of women I have nothing in common with. I'd be home keeping house for my husband and my sons, God bless the two of them, instead of them fending for themselves. This time," she said, pulling off between flexible thumb and forefinger the onions' dry, papery skins, "this time you can cut my throat from ear to ear if ever I touch another drop, once they let me out of here."

The rear door of the kitchen opened onto a courtyard and as she worked, Athena had seen the two white women whose principal area of activity it seemed to be. They carried long, slender poles which, from the distance of the kitchen, might have been taken for billiard cues, but which were pronged on one end. The duties of these two women were to spike all stray debris with their poles, and to pack it firmly down into the dozen or so monster garbage tins, as well as to keep the length of grass on the garden side free of cigarette stubs and drifting wisps of paper, and this they did with leisurely dignity. It was clear they were in a category of their own: one with darkly henna-ed hair, and an inch or two of white showing at the roots of it, and the other with iron-gray hair cropped short, as men's hair was once trimmed. Somewhere they had got themselves rubber gloves for this unworthy work, which they wore as if they were imports from France, cut from the finest pastel kid. And what these women were serving time for, Athena was never to learn, for unless such information was proffered one did not ask any more than one asked in the outside world about another's moon and planets, or whether he was a Christian or a Jew. The look in the prisoners' eyes, and the words they spoke, or did not speak, were their history and their credentials, stating the case as gossip could not, or prison records, or the hazards of astrology. They might have been mistaken for Gertrude Stein and Alice B. Toklas, these two inseparable companions, Athena thought, watching them move with their poles in their green-gloved hands across the garbage-saturated cobbles, retrieving the visible and offensive evidence of lesser women's negligence.

In the middle of the morning the trucks could be heard arriving beyond the courtyard wall, and at once, in a wild flurry of discipline, Corporal Anxiety spun like a dervish into the kitchen, driving before her the two ladies with their poles, and herding them all, Martha, Isabelita, the black girls, and Athena, into the lieutenant's private dining room. Then she took up her post, with arms folded high across her chest, inside the partially closed door.

"The men are bringing in the week's supply of meat," Martha said in a low voice to Athena, wiping her hands on the dishcloth she carried with her, the beads of her eyes fixed in resignation on the total irrationality of men and women and their lives.

They could hear the sound of the men's boots on the kitchen floor, and the slamming shut of the freezers. They could even hear the men's contraband voices in a brief exchange of words, and one of them went so far as to whistle a small, light-hearted tune as he carried his load in. At this, Corporal Anxiety, her arms still folded, with the toe of one neatly shod foot pushed the door a little further closed.

"They've a thing about love at first sight," said the parody of Gertrude Stein, and she winked her eye at Athena. She smoothed one hand over her clipped gray hair, drawing her open palm down to the nape of her neck and letting it linger caressingly there. "When the garbage trucks come at two o'clock, they get out the shackles just in case Cupid lets fly with an arrow," she said, her heavy shoulders quivering with laughter that made no sound.

"Up theirs!" cried out the phony Alice B. Toklas. She stared fiercely out of the white-edged, dark auburn frame of what was scarcely the texture of hair any longer, after the years of bleaching and tinting. Her gaze stabbed with its dual blades through Corporal Anxiety's back, who stood guard on her fleshless, lath-like, giraffe-wooden legs. "One of these days I'm going to make it out of here in a garbage can," the woman who wasn't Alice B. Toklas said. She had placed her pole in a corner of the private dining room, but the elegant green plastic gloves still clung, skin-tight, to her gesticulating hands. "With the lid on tight, and spinach hanging around my ears, nobody will be the wiser," she said. "The men out there would heft me up and carry me straight out to the truck, and it would be fol-de-rol and tiddley-doo from me to all of you girls here in the finishing school."

The African queen, tall as a cypress, snapped her limber fingers softly, steadily, as they waited, and moved her high behind first up, then down. She bopped over to the window and looked out on the garden, studying the maple tree that leaned back in weariness against the wall, studying the wall itself, topped by its row of rusted iron sabers, around which the labyrinth of barbed wire had been strung.

"Once you made it to the top of that tree, there wouldn't be nothing could stop you," she said, her voice high, wondering, artless, the music and words of it scored for Corporal Anxiety alone. Her fingers were snapping softly, softly, against the firm bluish cushions of her thumbs, and her feet in the prison sneakers kept time to the unheard blaring of freedom, freedom, freedom, and the bonging of savage, silent drums. "They could blow their whistles until they popped, and them red eyes on top their cars would be spinnin' round and round, but they couldn't lay a finger on you, 'cause you'd be gone, gone, gone," she said, and her rump moved up and down with the scraping and bowing of her feet.

"You get your ass in a sling, you try anything like that," said another black girl. "They got bob wire strung all along in an outta them branches. I tried it once. I know."

"The day you make your getaway, Alice," said the travesty of Gertrude Stein, and as she addressed her lifelong companion her shoulders still quivered with the laughter no one could hear, "we'll all be thinking of you standing up there at the Hilton bar with your gin and tonic, and then sitting down to dinner with a bottle of red wine." She looked at Athena again, and winked her shrewd eye. "Just be sure you get the coffee grounds out of your hair, Alice, before you walk into Trader Vic's," she said.

"A glass of red wine never did nobody no harm," said Isabelita, scratching her feathers.

"They say it's good for varicose veins," said Martha piously.

Then Isabelita stepped closer to Athena, and she began speaking in a low, hurried voice, her thin fingers picking at her dress, her eyes panicked now beyond endurance, like the eyes of a fox in the open fields with the hounds behind it in full cry.

"You got a education, so maybe you know," she said, speaking furtively, with a glance this way and that as if for a way to change her course now that the hounds were yapping at her heels. "You ever hear of a baby committing suicide—you know, making up its mind it didn't want to live no more?"

The question was asked in such a hushed, hurried voice that Athena could not be certain it was this she heard, but there was no time now for anything else to be said. The men were leaving in their trucks, and Corporal Anxiety began herding the women back to their duties again. As they filed through the door, the caricature of Alice B. Toklas mentioned her own death.

"One thing I've always asked my buddies is that when they see my name on the obits page they're not to send flowers," she said. "I'd prefer a fried pork chop and cauliflower with cream sauce instead."

At eleven o'clock the line formed outside the dining hall for lunch, and at half-past four for supper. After breakfast and lunch, the prisoners returned to their dormitories for bed count, and then went to the sewing and ironing rooms, or the laundry, or the kitchen. At six-thirty on weekday evenings, two deputies brought to the dormitories the string-tied bundles of already sorted and censored mail. As the names were read out from the envelopes or postcards, the lucky ones rose from their cots and walked separately to the two women in uniform, and received the letters from their hands. It was the second night when the deputy called out Athena's name, and she was as startled as if a hand had struck her. She got up from her cot and walked, dazed, down the aisle to where the deputies stood. There were two letters and a telegram, and her heart was shaking as she took them in her hand, but she could not put a name to her fear. For a while she could not bring herself to look at these messages, which the prison authorities had already opened, for they came from a world whose dimensions had altered for her, and whose sights and sounds had faded as in a dream. She sat down on the edge of her cot again, her mind wiped blank, her will in abeyance, and then she took the telegram out of its yellow envelope and read the words typed on it. It came from Paris, and it brought love from Sybil and John, who somehow knew. The air-mail letter was from Paula in New York, and it said that she and Leo had just read in the *Times* of the arrests. (She remembered Paula's fear of thunderstorms, and Paula flying to her like a delicate madonna from a cathedral portal to seize the metal bracelets from her, Athena's, wrists, and the typewriter from under her fingers before the fatal lightning could strike.) "Please, Mama, send us your lawyer's name, or ask him to telephone us. Or could you wire us so that we'll know you're not having too terrible a time? We didn't know you were planning to do this." (*I didn't know it either*, Athena answered in silence. *I wasn't absolutely sure. You read* "this government, which continues to violate the consciences of its own citizens, no longer deserves the obedience of its citizens," *and you know this is true. You read that* "to obey such a government violates our responsibility to the Vietnamese people and to the American people." *And so you go at six o'clock one morning to an Induction Center, not quite certain what is going to take place, and you sit down with people you have never seen before in one of the doorways, and when the paddy wagons come, a proclamation is read aloud, and you are offered a choice, you are free to get up from the doorway of this public building and go*

*or else you will be placed under arrest, and you do not get up
and go.*)

The second letter was from San Francisco, from the black
man who had an upholstery shop at the corner of Athena's
street. He wrote in green ink on the letterhead of his store, The
Metropolitan Upholstery Establishment, in an easy, flowing
hand. "Dear Mrs. Gregory," the letter went; "I heard the news
on the radio and the banks were already closed. I went to a
couple of friends and raised the two-hundred-fifty-dollar bail
money without going to a bondsman, so that saved the 10%.
I drove over to the Oakland City jail, where they said you were
incarcerated, but you turned it down. Maybe the message didn't
get through to you. I felt bad about this. Maybe you can drop
me a line. Yours, Luchies McDoniel."

There was no way to tell them that you could not write, that
it took a week to get commissary privileges. There would be no
contact with the outside world until the lawyers came again.
Melanie. She said the name in silence, sitting on the side of the
cot, holding the letters and the cable in her hands. *Melanie.*
Melanie. But Melanie did not answer from her distant place.

Instead, it was Calliope's voice, muted and low, that spoke
from the next cot.

"Athena, I have to let all the hems of our Dior models down
again. Tonight, this minute. Orders from the executive branch,"
she said. "But they don't know yet about 'peace' and 'love' in
the men's shorts."

In another moment she would start laughing softly and fool-
ishly, taking the needles and thread and the blunt scissors out
of the night table drawer; and Callisto lying on the cot beyond
would laugh, and then voices throughout the dormitory would
call out: "Why are you laughing? What's there to laugh about?"
And then nobody could stop laughing, not even Athena as she
helped Calliope let out the hems.

VIII

"SHE'S BEEN OVER TWO YEARS in a commune, my youngest daughter, Melanie," Athena had wanted to say for a long time to Calliope, for there were things about women and their daughters that she wanted to talk about with her, but it was not easy to find the words that would make the questions as objective as history and free them of any murmur of complaint.

Every day after work, Athena and Calliope would walk twelve times the quarter-mile length they had staked out in the prison garden, and twenty times on the Saturday and Sunday they were there, walking from the north end of the fence (black, softly rotting boards reinforced on the other side with sheets of corrugated tin, topped with a row of scimitars entangled with spiked wire), past the rusting daggers of the iris plants to the maple, complacent in its chastity belt, and then back again to the molding boards of the fence. And this time she must have said it aloud, for Calliope was asking in a low voice as they walked:

"But still you saw her during that time—you saw her and the children?"

"Yes, oh, yes!" Athena said. (But where to begin, Calliope, where to begin? Not with the portrait of Charles Manson hanging in the children's playroom, because that isn't the beginning. It was later, much later that they hung it up there, a framed picture with prison bars drawn in, etched in, across the seated figure of the man, and behind him an outline of a fallen cross, and the keyhole drawn so large in the iron lock of the cell that it would seem a child could have fitted a key into it with no trouble at all. The lines under the picture read: "Pluto in the fourth house, the house of Cancer, the home, the seed of the Soul, conjunct the part of fortune is the black force of his soul being released within the nucleus of his self-created family. They were his instruments of destruction, the very same instruments that eventually betrayed him from within." But that came later, as did my question about the cross in the picture being in the corner of his cell, and one of the commune girls was to say in answer that Manson had carried his cross to Calvary, but once he was in the actual process of being crucified, he had set the cross aside. And the sound of Melanie's voice crying out in defense of Manson, that also had come later. "His planets are rooted in Pluto!" she had almost shrieked. "That left him no choice! Can't you see that he had to act at that moment as he did?" Melanie was halted there forever in her long paisley dress, leaning over to fasten the snow boots of a commune child, her face flushed in impatience with every concept that excluded the authority of the stars. "All the lies and hypocrisy about love and the progress of civilization and democracy and working for peace, how can you take part in it? Manson showed this society up for what it is! He was effectual, he acted, he accepted his destiny!" But all this was later, a good deal later, like the playing of the tape of the LSD trip, and my throwing the iron skillet that could have killed anyone in the kitchen that night if murder had been intended. Perhaps begin with the Sunday afternoon that Lucky and I went to the church together.) "Perhaps everything I'm trying to say will be clearer if I begin with the day that Lucky the Disciple and I went to the church," Athena said as she and Calliope followed the quarter mile from fence to wall, from wall to fence again. "That was at the very beginning, before everything turned bitter as wormwood or gall, whichever is the bitterest. It was in April or May, over two years now, and

I'd read about a Buddhist priest who was sitting in a chapel of a church in the same city where the commune was, sitting there in the ninth week of a fast to the death against the war in his country, Vietnam. Lucky was new to the commune, and he was looking right and left and upstairs and down for acts of faith to be made, because he himself couldn't act. He was looking for someone who could speak for him, either Pete the Redeemer, or Charles Manson, or the Vietnamese priest, for he himself had never found a way to speak . . ."

"Perhaps most of us haven't," Calliope said as they passed the strong, long, serpentlike roots of the maple that reached out from the soil.

They were certainly not on death row. It was nothing like that. They were just two women (and sometimes more than two) walking steadily past the beds of dying iris, walking as far as the molding fence, and then turning in their tracks to walk to the maple again; but the moments in which they walked were as crucial as if the last meal had just been eaten, the small glass of brandy almost drained. The stretch of ground they had marked out had become the confessional, and once in the times that shy, young Ann walked with them she told them that she was afraid of becoming a woman because she feared she would become, not *like* her mother, but exactly the same woman her mother was.

"Sometimes I think," she said in clear-eyed perplexity, "that all girls are afraid of that, and so they run away from home, and commit crimes, and cry all night and day in their search for other mothers."

Once St. Theresa walked a little way with them, not far, and not for long, just the time to speak of how she had come to set aside her nun's habit for the first time in eight years. She kept her head lowered as she walked beside them, and it was difficult to hear the rapidly spoken words of her confession. She said that religious dress, like any distinctive dress, could be like a foreign language, one that alienated people because they could not find an interpreter or dictionary for such an archaic tongue. She repeated to them the words of a sister-nun who had said: "Clothing can express rejection of the community. Examples of this are rebels and hermits, who speak their repudiation of the rest of us through their eccentric clothes." And not being a rebel or a hermit, St. Theresa said she had for a long time felt uneasy in her religious dress, her coif, knowing that these articles of clothing were closing off ways of communication with others. That day it was one of the college girls who asked her as they walked if she, St. Theresa, was authorized by the Church to be here among them, and she shook her head.

"There is an American sister at the Vatican Council, only one," St. Theresa said, "and she says that nuns have a place in the front lines of any movement that works for the benefit of humanity. But I don't know if my superiors share this belief. I came without permission," she said, and at that moment her small tense face seemed to Athena like a fist clenched to beat forever, if forever was required, against the panels of a long closed door; "but I know I have the sanction of Pope John, who told us that the Church must go where the people are, not where it wishes them to be."

Calliope's confidences were more complex, for it was her wish never to have mysteries of any nature explained.

"You've certainly seen the rainbow that arches over the window in the cockpit of a plane," she said to Athena one day as they began their second mile. "I mean, when the sun strikes the glass at a certain angle, and you're standing on the ground looking up. I simply don't want to know how it happens to be there. And I don't want to know what ecclesiastical brimstone will be poured on St. Theresa's perishable flesh when she's released from one prison and goes back to the other. I want it all to end with Pope John defending the worker-priests simply by *knowing* they were there, and with Father Groppi—was it Father Groppi?—calling the runaway children of our time 'the children with windy feet.' That's all I want to know about the Church, except for those other priests, who poured blood on the draft board files. So please go on with the story."

"Well, a very young minister opened the basement door of his church that day and let me and Lucky the Disciple in," Athena went on saying. "A ladies' luncheon had just taken place, and the basement was like a cocktail party, all bubbling conversation, and people laughing, and ladies in little flowered hats, and husbands in good gray suits, and the remains of potato salad and luncheon meat and jello being cleared away, and a cake sale about to begin. The minister was a little distraught when I told him why we were there. He was the one who had given sanctuary to the Buddhist priest, and he said he hadn't been able to change the church calendar and cancel the luncheon and the cake sale, or switch them to some other time. And the time would have been difficult to gauge, he explained, because there was no way of knowing how long a hunger strike to the death might last."

"Oh, God," Calliope said.

"He led Lucky and me to the stairway beyond the cloakroom, saying nervously that probably not many members of the congregation remembered that the Buddhist priest was still fasting to the death over their heads."

They mounted in silence the little flight of stairs, Athena went on saying, and Lucky had not spoken at all, but then Lucky never spoke. At the top was a heavy swinging door padded with russet leather and studded with brass nails, and when Lucky pulled it open, she said, they were met for a moment with almost total darkness, and then, at a little distance, the flickering pool of candlelight took over, and they could see the wisp of a man sitting on the chapel floor. He was sitting with his legs crossed under him, his shoulders incredibly narrow and frail, his knees incredibly pointed, the tongues of light from the double row of tapers that stood, fan-shaped, on either side hollowing and polishing his face and brow into an ivory skull.

"He wore the black cotton gown of the Indonesian priest or scholar, a very shabby looking gown, and a black cap like a rabbi's," Athena said as they walked, "and his scrolls and brushes with bamboo stems, and a little jar of India ink, were arranged on a low pallet in front of him. You had to squat down or kneel in order to speak with him," she said, "and when Lucky and I did this, we saw his eyes were closed. He was like a dead leaf, the weight of a dead leaf, and I was almost afraid to breathe, but I knew I must tell him why we had come, and so I spoke to him in French. He must have been waiting for the sound of that language, for even if it was the tongue of his colonizers it was also that of his learning, and his eyes opened at once in incredulous joy." The sunlit October air was growing cool in the prison garden now, and there was not much time left before bed count would be called. "He told us that in his country, in Vietnam," Athena said, "fasting was an act of personal purification, that in fasting you emptied yourself of all extraneous matter and became a cleansed vessel to bear the tender spirit of Buddha to all those who waited. He said that when he was purified of food he could pray more devoutly for the awakening of the conscience of humanity. And Lucky—this is the whole reason for the story—Lucky knelt there in a kind of trance of reverence while I translated for him the things the Buddhist priest was saying. And Lucky heard the Vietnamese priest say in all humility that he was ashamed of being so helpless in the mission he had set himself, and finally Lucky, who never could find the words to speak, said he had a question he wanted put into French. He wanted to ask the priest if anything except the war coming to an end in Vietnam would make him give up his fast, and the little priest said yes, there was one other thing. He said he would end his fast if he was enabled to go to North Vietnam with a group of other religious men, American, French, Canadian, English, any and all religious men; and then he and the others, perhaps having no language in common except the language of peace, would set out on foot from Hanoi, and they would walk through the intervening jungles to Saigon to prove— no, that's not the right word—perhaps just to *say* that men could still walk, without arms and without fear, through destruction, and under and beyond the instruments of violent death. The priest unrolled one of the scrolls, and it was a map done in pastel colors, and he showed Lucky and me with the point of a brush the route they would take. He knew the country well, and which bridges were still left standing across the gorges and rivers, and his hands, one holding the map up in the candlelight, and the other holding the brush, were no larger than a child's hands . . ." Athena stopped speaking for a moment, as if silenced by his actual presence there in the prison enclosure as they walked, and then she went on: "He said such a walk could be like a metaphor for life, because that is all life is, walking in the company of people you believe in from one destination to another, and there is always a jungle lying in between."

"And is that what he did, or did he die?" Calliope asked.

"No," said Athena. "I mean, I don't know. After three months, he was taken to a hospital. I read that in the newspaper, and then I didn't hear any more. But Lucky—you see, this is why I'm telling you the story—Lucky was almost overcome by that tiny man, and he knelt there before him, and wept, because he was so new to the commune then that he had not yet given his will and his conscience into a bondage that eliminates, at least for the duration of the bondage, the courage of individual choice. That was the year before," she began saying, but she did not finish the sentence. She did not say: *before the tape about the girl and the Hell's Angel.* "Lucky talked that afternoon," she said; "the first time and the last time I ever heard him speak."

On the way back in the subway, Lucky had said that sometimes he felt himself crowded in the commune, and sometimes when he came home at night and found someone he didn't know sleeping in his bed, HIS bed, he was really hassled, because he hadn't got yet to where the Buddhist priest was. He didn't seem to be able to stop talking, saying that listening to the Vietnamese, and looking at his face that was like a carving, so different from a white man's face, he wondered why so far they hadn't got any black or Third World people into the commune, and he wondered if groups living in political isolation could make any real changes in the world. There were days when his head was so fucked up that he couldn't function, he said, and the Buddhist priest had made him feel there might be maybe a kind of simplicity to life, if only you had the strength and the faith to accept it, if you could see the world like a territory stretching out wide and simple, just that, just a territory to be walked across, whatever lay in the way.

And then about communes, he said, he who had never had any use for words, barely able to say it fast enough and loud enough now above the rushing of the subway train, saying he thought it might be better if decisions inside communes were made by consensus instead of at a higher level, that sending out a xeroxed sheet of directions to all the commune houses every morning was like being back in school again or in the army, and that's what they were getting away from, that's why they'd left home and college and whatever, to escape that kind of authority. The Buddhist priest, Lucky said, was free of any kind of authority, even that of the temple; he was fasting and meditating and writing his scrolls without directions being given to him, and in the end he would probably walk through the jungles quite alone.

"That little Vietnamese scholar had so impassioned Lucky," Athena said, "that Buddhist priest, whom you could have held in the hollow of your hand, had cast such a light on the darkest area of Lucky's perplexities that in the church he had not so much as noticed the terrible odor of death or putrefaction that comes from the mouths of people who have fasted a long time."

"Oh, God, I didn't know that!" Calliope cried out.

Lucky had been a free man talking then, because it was perhaps before the final initiation rites, and certainly before the making of the tape, and he had said he wondered if commune policy shouldn't be interpreted differently for different commune members, like some people still had some of the old hang-ups and guilt feelings about ripping off things, ripping off food from the supermarkets, and tools that you needed from Sears, and books that you wanted out of bookstores; and then there was the matter of dissent, dissent inside the commune, the pressure being so strong on you against dissenting that you felt threatened, even physically threatened, and you ended up not knowing what the shit you thought, he said. And yet everyone's supposed to go out recruiting, recruiting new members, and if you start thinking in terms of recruiting, he said, you might as well join ROTC.

"For that one afternoon," Athena said to Calliope, "he was a questioning, eager kind of person, and Melanie was once that, too." There would be only a few minutes longer, for the sun was nearly gone. "Perhaps all of them in the commune were once reasoning, questioning, willful people at the beginning, and that's why they were there," she said; "and because of their reasoning and their questioning, Pete the Redeemer forbade them to doubt and he made their wills his own."

"But how does anyone make the wills of others his own?" Calliope asked, and she added quickly: "Don't tell me. I couldn't bear to know."

"But I don't know how it is done!" Athena cried out. "I don't know, Calliope! That's why I threw the frying pan one night, a big iron skillet. I threw it across Melanie's kitchen, and it went sliding and bouncing along the floor, and finally broke a dish."

"My non-violent sister in penal servitude," Calliope murmured.

"The kitchen sink was piled with dishes," Athena said. "About a dozen commune people had just finished eating, and I'd been out teaching all day, and I was trying to cook supper for the children, and I suddenly lost my mind. Some of the commune girls were in the next room sitting around the fire, and one of them said, 'Granny's cleaning up and baby-sitting the kids tonight, so it doesn't matter if we get stoned,' and another said, 'Granny's loaded. She could easily pay the telephone bill.' And I threw the frying pan at the redeemer, wherever he was, and at the evil magic of his power. And I threw it at myself for being so weak as to allow their voices to take over. There are times when I'm feeling self-righteous that I think I threw it as well for all the musicians he stripped of their music, and the painters of their painting, and the writers of the words they needed in order to write."

"And after you did that—?" Calliope asked.

"That was over a year ago, and since then nothing," Athena said. "For a while I went on writing to her, or trying to write, that is, but my letters came back, the envelopes marked in that enormous, crazy, schoolgirl hand 'Return to Sender.' And Paula tried telephoning, month after month she tried, but Melanie was finished with both of us . . ."

"Athena," Calliope said quickly, softly, at the door as they went in, "this isn't the end. There are things that we can do."

At the distribution of mail that evening, Athena indulged herself with the fancy of a letter arriving now, this very moment, addressed in the tall schoolgirl hand, with the dots over the *i*'s not dots but perfect little zeros. And although it did not come, something unexpected did take place. On top of Callisto's letters lay a sheet of folded copybook paper, and as the Grecian deputy handed Callisto the pile of mail, she said quite simply to her:

"It's a beautiful letter, but I have to return it. Mail between inmates cannot be delivered."

Callisto walked back to her cot and put her handful of letters on the night table, and then it could be seen that across the folded page torn from a copybook was printed the name Eric Simon, and the address Men's Quarters. But neither was this to be accepted as an ending, for now Callisto, sitting on her cot, her thin shoulders a little bowed, began to sing, and her separate act of love and defiance was transformed by her voice into a declaration of mutiny that involved them all. She sang:

> *The waters of Jordan, Oh yeah,*
> *Are muddy and cold, Oh yeah,*
> *They chill the body, Oh yeah,*
> *But not the soul, Oh yeah.*

As she sang, the black and the Chicano prisoners and the demonstrators clapped their hands in rhythm with this singing that made the dormitory another place. The hands clapped, and Callisto sang:

> *Na, na na na na, na na na na,*
> *na na na, na na na,*
> *want my freedom now!*

There might have been no uniformed deputies in the room as the prisoners sang with Callisto, for those who were the substance of the prison, its subjugated flesh and its outraged blood, had ceased for the moment to look on the demonstrators as uninvited visitors, and the words of triumph and insurrection they shouted stamped into oblivion the deputies standing there. They sang:

> *Paul and Silas, Oh yeah,*
> *Were bound in ja-il, Oh yeah.*
> *Didn't have nobody, Oh yeah,*
> *For to go their ba-il, Oh yeah.*

"Want my freedom now!" they sang with Callisto, until not only the dormitories, but the women's lock-up rooms and the black depths of solitary, and then the men's quarters, and next the countryside around them, must have sounded with the rhythmic beating of their hands and the power of their voices, and finally the entire world.

IX

ONE OF THE FIRST SOUNDS in the early morning was that of Lydia slapping the circulation back into her legs, the rat-tat-tat of it chattering like machine-gun fire in the dormitory. After that came the havoc the college girls made of the ritual of bed count. One day three or four voices would answer simultaneously in different keys when Corporal Anxiety, the clipboard in her hand, called out a prisoner's name; and another day they would argue hotly among themselves as to which name belonged to whom, confusing the deputy so that her voice trembled when she spoke. One morning they stood erect and silent at the foot of their cots with their pillowcases drawn over their heads; and another time, when three of them were summoned before dawn to kitchen detail, they had quickly braided one another's hair into multitudes of little plaits, skinny as rats' tails, which stood out as if wired from their skulls. As they ladled oatmeal into the waiting bowls, the Grecian deputy stopped them short with a snap of her broad white fingers.

"You'll have to go back to the dormitories. We don't like inmates making clowns of themselves," she said in a low voice of reprimand.

"We did it out of respect for the pure food laws," one of the college girls said in mock indignation, looking for approbation at the tittering women in the breakfast line. "Hair in the scrambled eggs or in the oatmeal, ugh!"

"So you're telling us it's a crime to laugh in this place?" another of the reprimanded cried out, and she flung her ladle down.

"If you do laugh here, then for the sake of the regular prisoners, it would be better not to laugh too loud," the Grecian deputy said. "Take your aprons off and fold them and leave them on that chair."

"So we don't get any breakfast?" one of them asked in a high, wounded voice as the deputy walked with them to the kitchen door.

"I would say that's relatively light as punishment," the deputy said.

Athena was seeking almost in desperation to believe that she had come to the end of quotations from other people's books, and other people's speech, and even to the end of mythology. These things had given her the courage to come this far, but now she wanted to function out of her own experience, her own history, and to speak with a vocabulary that was her own. That morning in the kitchen, she saw in helplessness that this could not be done so quickly, that it might take her the rest of her life to free herself of all she had borrowed; for now the Grecian deputy was suddenly transformed into Dryope, that woman of myth whose prison sentence was to become a tree. Athena laid the strips of bacon on the hot grill, remembering that Dryope's feet had taken root in the ground one day as she idly picked lotus blossoms for her young son, not knowing that the lotus bush was actually a fleeing nymph who had taken on this guise. And as the nymph's blood dripped from the broken lotus branches, bark began to creep upward over Dryope, covering first her lovely, naked legs, then her soft, vulnerable thighs, and then her torso. Just before her arms were encased forever, an interval of grace was allowed by the gods, and she was able to give her little son into the keeping of her husband and her father, and to beseech them to bring him to play in her shade when she would be entirely a tree. They promised this, and they knelt down and, as the cruel bark covered her arms and breasts, her throat, and finally her head, they watered her roots with their tears.

Athena watched the deputy returning, walking across the crowded dining hall as if coming directly to her, making her way past the long tables where the women sat eating. But she did not come around the zinc-topped counter into the kitchen area, but went instead into the private dining room beyond. And Athena, lifting the last strips of bacon from the grill, said to her in silence: *Escape the hardening of the bark while you still can.*

But the activities were so numerous that the deputies and their stylish uniforms came to play less and less a part in the demonstrators' lives. Lydia had been grieving over the state of the iris beds, and in the last hour before sunset each day she showed the women what was to be done, recruiting them after the sewing and ironing and washing of clothes in the annex was over with, and when kitchen duty was in abeyance for a little while. She told them that every two years iris plants must be taken out of the soil, and their sabers clipped short, and the long, prawnlike bulbs divided, so that one plant became two. Four trowels and four of the round-nosed pairs of scissors from the sewing room had been allowed her, but these were not enough to equip the dozen or more demonstrators who came, so they knelt and dug the bulbs out with their fingers from the neglected beds. Exactly like giant prawns they were, these earth-clotted bulbs, cocking their sweet-potato eyes at the women who wrested them from the earth; exactly like prawns' spidery legs, their white roots that dangled in the autumn air.

"My husband and I used to fish for them in Brittany," Athena said, kneeling on the parched grass.

"For iris?" one of the housewives asked, and Athena said, no, for shrimp, and she laughed because the other woman laughed, and with the cushions of both hands pressing hard, she split another bulb in two.

"They're said to be very loquacious," one of the college girls said. "I read in a natural science magazine that when underwater microphones are lowered to the ocean floor, shrimps will push eels and crabs and lobsters and every other curious onlooker aside and actually scream into the mike."

"But what could they possibly have to talk about?" Ann asked, her eyes wide in wonder. She sat on the grass of the prison's one strip of dying lawn, forgetting to dig.

"Well, shrimp power, among other things," said a librarian, and the powerless in their gray dresses kept on laughing at whatever was said. Only St. Theresa, her face tight and pale like an ailing child's, the scattered freckles on her cheekbones and nose turned topaz in the autumn light, did not seem to hear.

All about them lay the detruncated army of irises, banners lowered, a bivouacking legion that doubled and tripled in strength as the women split them apart. The professor's wife with the blue-gray curls was there, working diligently with the others, but no regular prisoners had joined them, the thought never having come into their heads, it may have been, to sit down in the garden with these ladies who were no more than vacationing here. Calliope murmured to Athena that Callisto had been commanded by the lady lieutenant, by Miss America herself, to come to her private quarters and talk with her about where she would be singing in the winter season ahead.

"Fawncy that!" Calliope said, and she laughed her quick, nervous laughter. "Callisto will probably tell her that she'll be singing right here, where the fun is," Calliope said, struggling with the blunt-bladed scissors to clip the beards of the iris plants close to their chins.

It was at night that other things were spoken of, beginning at mail distribution time, and not stopping until the night was nearly done. Once a slender, young black woman, wearing the trim blue and white uniform of the long-termers, stood up before them in the dormitory and asked them to consider the situation concerning visitors. She addressed them with the coolness of a top executive's private secretary, her mouth not about to smile, her eyes masked from them by granny glasses in mauve plastic frames.

"One to four every Sunday afternoon. You realize that's a very short time," she said. Her hair was fitted like a soft, black cap to her poised head, and her ears, carved and ornamental, lay close to her neat skull. "You seem to be educated, intelligent women," she said with apparent civility, but still it was an accusation she made, a rebuke to all their lives had been. If the demonstrators filled in the official slips with the names of family and friends they would like to see, she told them, standing neat as a bookkeeper before them, reliable to the eye as a loan consultant in a white man's bank, facing them without mercy, then the time in the visiting cage would be cut for the regular prisoners to less than three or four minutes per inmate, per week. "So I think you will have to agree that it would be a self-indulgent gesture on your parts to deprive of their visiting time those who are serving long terms here. And I'm scarcely speaking for myself, you know, for I shall be leaving, but there are women here who have six months, nine months, still to go."

And now Ann, like a schoolgirl in the classroom, timidly raised her hand.

"How long have you been here?" she asked, speaking scarcely aloud.

For a moment it seemed there would be no answer, and then the young black woman appeared to stand even more erect before them, and her clipped words came with even greater efficiency.

"Eleven months tomorrow afternoon," she said, and she adjusted her granny glasses with one slender, coffee-colored hand.

Perhaps half the demonstrators wrote "No Visitors" on the slips they had been given at mail time that evening. But before the young woman had got back to her cot again, one of the housewives suddenly cried out that she would do no such thing.

"Take it however you wish!" she cried to the young woman's

back moving down the aisle. "I'm writing down my mother's, and my husband's, and my brother's names! You don't accept us as equals, as individuals, but only as members of another race, different from you!" She, too, was young, and her hair was like corn silk, and her cheekbones high in a strong, icelandic face; but for all her daring, in another minute she might begin to cry. "You don't see us as women, but simply as *white*. I swear I don't see you as black. I'm not going to give you any special consideration. I want our privileges and our punishment to be the same, so I'm going to have my visitors too!"

The black woman turned and looked at her for a long moment, her face expressionless, her eyes blank within the mauve-colored spectacle frames. In total silence she surveyed the brain, the heart, the white exempted face of the fair woman whose underlip trembled.

"Would it occur to you that I *wish* to be black, that I *choose* as an adult to be black?" she said at last. "There's a chasm between you and me and between our races. Sex can cross that chasm. Nothing else can," she said. "I wouldn't try."

And at night, after bed count was done with and the dormitory darkened, the underground woman within Athena would write a number of letters in her mind. She wrote to her three daughters, and to her dead mother, and then she took on her academic responsibilities and wrote the recommendations that graduate students had asked her for and which she had not yet had the time to write. Such letters were addressed to "To Whom It May Concern." They followed a similar pattern, perhaps beginning: "During the autumn semester of 1969, Marvel Banewort [or Harris Egocent or Jane Atvariance] was a student in two courses of mine. Mr. Banewort was so profoundly committed to relevance that he dismissed the golden bridle episode between Pegasus and Bellerophon as out of date because horses are now anachronisms, which is a typical example of his wit. Hercules as a Mafia-type murderer of his wife and children was the highly original theme of one of his term papers, which were

frequently handed in six months late." If sleep did not inter-
vene and put an end to this, another letter might begin: "It is
a tribute to Mr. Egocent's tenacity of purpose that he was never
for a moment touched by the plight of Prometheus, nor was he
thrown off balance when Io, the girl who looked like a heifer,
and who wandered the earth in search of understanding, cried
out: 'I am a girl who speaks to you, but horns are on my head!'"

The faces, if not the names, of a long procession of students
drifted into obscurity as sleep approached, and then the clang
of words would startle Athena awake again. "Albert Camus had
a good idea, but he was never able to put it across," either Mr.
Banewort or Mr. Egocent began a term paper, and the two of
them looked at her through horn-rimmed lenses, certain beyond
any doubt that the critical mind would prevail. Or Ms. Atvariance might come into the dormitory with her twenty-page
paper on "Contemporary Playwrights," which included a comparison of her own work with that of Samuel Beckett. "While I
am concerned with embellishing and broadening the relationship
of my personae," she had written, "Samuel Beckett strips his
characters of every shred of human glory. This leaves his audience in a state of deep depression, and everyday living is surely
hard enough without that. However, Beckett and I do share a
similar approach in our writing, and that is in our conception
of Fate: we agree that Fate is there, whether you like it or not.
In my one-act play *Animal Crackers*, and his two-act play
Waiting for Godot, we both personify Fate as a character who
never makes an appearance on the stage. Eventually I came to
feel that Beckett and I were avoiding an important confrontation by deliberately keeping Fate off the boards and in the wings,
as it were, and I felt this was a betrayal of audience participation.
So I brought Fate right out on the stage in *Lovers at Last*. Mr.
Beckett has so far failed to do this." The eulogies written by
the underground woman usually concluded: "I recommend the
subject of this letter [whether Mr. Banewort or Mr. Egocent
or Ms. Atvariance] to a world I do not function in with ease."

But there were others, other students, who came to life in the night hours in the dormitory. There was Eduardo Guerrero, a black student with a well-shaped helmet of hair, wearing a pea jacket that had survived his three years in the Navy, whose thoughts ran quicker than mercury in his elegant skull. As he faced the Tactical Squad on campus, he had shouted out to the plastic visors: "Be men, man! Let's see your eyes!" He knew what Melville had in mind about race relations when he wrote *Benito Cereno*, and once he had reminded Athena about Dylan Thomas saying: "I agree with Schopenhauer (who, in his philosophic dust, would turn with pleasure at my agreement) that life has no pattern and no purpose, but that a twisted vein of evil, like the poison in a drinking glass, coils up from the pit to the top of the hemlocked world." And there was Shawn Wong, who told the story of his forebears, writing: "The night train, the old night train filled with Chinamen, my grandfathers, fathers, all without lovers, without women, struggling against black iron with hands splintered from the coarse cross-ties, this night train stopped at the edge of the ocean, the engine steaming into the waves that lapped against the iron wheels. The ocean was humbled before the great, steaming engine; its noise was iron; the moonlight on the ocean gave the sea its place, made the water look like waves of rippling steel. The Chinamen worked all day on the railroad, but at night they built the great iron engine that brought them to the edge of the sea, pointed them toward home, the way west . . ." He took lines from his great-grandfather's letters, and wrote: "Spring begins in the Sierras with the first thaw in late January or early February. These are months of apprehension for us. Those who are not laying track forward through the mountain passes move back along the track we laid in the hard winter, going from camp to camp, finding the frozen bodies of our lost friends, lost to the winter nights, men who couldn't keep warm, or were caught in their sleep by the softly falling snow, thick snow that left them invisible by morning. . . . Spring was a season of mourning for us. We'd look for spots on the ground where the sun had melted the snow away and begun to thaw the earth. The ground was softer there, soft enough for a shallow grave. . . . The creeks of ice-water began flowing then. The land in flux brought back the sounds of birds, leaves, waters, the land began to breathe and melt, and the train began to rust. When the railroad is finished, I will ride back home in the springtime, pay homage to graves, camps, the whole flux and rising of the earth in this new season."

On one such sleepless night, Athena found herself sitting on the side of Calliope's cot in the dark, asking her a question.

"Listen," she whispered. "This is important. I suddenly realized an astounding thing. No black, no American Indian, no Chicano, no oriental student, has ever asked me to write a good academic word for him or her. How can you explain it?"

Calliope's voice was muffled as she answered, as if she was yawning or trying not to yawn.

"Maybe because that kind of recommendation isn't needed for the revolution. I think that's pretty right on."

Athena went back to her own cot, and before she fell asleep she composed a letter to the tobacco and pipe shop on East Forty-second Street in New York City, asking them to stop sending Rory their catalogue of all the handsome, manly things (like cigarettes and monogrammed silver cases and teak-wood humidors) they had for sale. "Dear Sirs," this letter went; "I appreciate your kindness in sending Mr. Gregory your very colorful and attractive booklets of suggestions for 'The Man Who Has Everything,' everything, even cancer of the lung, including death," she wrote.

On another night, a girl was brought into the Rehabilitation Center very late, which had certainly happened on other nights, but this time her screaming awakened them. One of the college girls slipped from her cot and crept down the half-lit corridor toward the office, keeping close to the wall so that she would not be seen. When she came back, she gave the whispered word that the office door had been partially open, and that she had been able to see the shrieking, cursing girl trying to break the grip of the handcuffs, fighting to wrench herself free of the deputies who held her, biting and clawing like a cat. The story flew from cot to cot, from regular prisoner to demonstrator, and back to regular prisoner, the girl and her history pieced together in a barely audible exchange. Within five minutes they all knew that she was small as a ten-year-old, that she was black and wore her hair in an enormous Afro, that she had feathery artificial eyelashes, and that her eyelids and fingernails were done in frosty white. She was wearing one of those tweedlike, ankle-length, sheath skirts, and white, high-heeled, crinkle-leather boots, the college girl reported, but whether or not there had been the time to note all this in the split second she had seen the girl, nobody asked.

"Could be Marcie," one of the black girls whispered. "She ain't been gone but two weeks, maybe three."

The big-bosomed, motherly deputy could be heard shouting that they were going to get the lieutenant out of bed to deal with her if she didn't stop her noise.

"Could be Myrtle," another prisoner said. "'Member her always talkin' 'bout gettin' herself white boots with heels?"

But the girl's name must have been Bea, for that was what she screamed out half a dozen times as she fought the deputies, crying through her clenched teeth that they weren't going to get Bea down on her knees, not yet, not ever, shrieking with the fury of a cat cornered in an alley by its battle-scarred oppressors, striking out in terror against their flattened ears, their lashing tails.

"Seems like Bea got a lot more cool than that," another hushed voice said.

"Sound like she lost it all this time, whoever she be, whatever she done," Tallulah said in the darkness. "If that Bea, she know better than to carry on like she outta her right mind."

"Bea was shootin' up three-four times a day, costin' a hundred dollars flat. Tha's what she said," another whispered. "If that

Bea cuttin' up out there, I know for shu she not twenty yet, an'
she got a kid she leave with her momma, 'cause she been in and
out too many years to count."

"Could be she gone so far off her head this time, she don'
know her way back," Tallulah said.

"You don't get Bea's clothes! You don't take away her
clothes!" the words came tearing, ripping, down the hall and
into the dormitory where the women lay.

And now the struggle became fiercer as the deputies stripped
her of all she owned. Her furious outcry changed its direction
when they carried her to the hole, and slammed the heavy
door on her, and her cries climbed higher and higher as she
beat the handcuffs against the stone of the floor. The women
in the dormitory no longer spoke, but they had begun to hum
in chorus, to moan a muted accompaniment to her piercing
anguish, their dark, steady voices weaving a hammock of sound
in which to rock their sister in her pain. Slowly, slowly, their
lament gathered power, flowed through the wide doorway,
past the toilets and sinks and showers, flooding into the other
dormitory beyond, until it seemed that the two long rooms
would overflow with the moaning, humming tide of the prisoners' voices, and the women would have to rise from their
cots to save themselves from the deep, lapping tide. In the
end, when it could no longer be borne, the women would
fling aside the worn sheets, the patched army blankets, and
leap up, trembling like aspens, and gyrate in increasing frenzy
until, like horses stampeding, they would collide with one
another, neighing in panic, their voices slashing the darkness
in inarticulate answer to their sister's voice crying out from
the cavern of the hole.

There were no words left for anyone to say in any language,
the only communication being the thin, frenzied screaming of
one girl and the requiem of the prisoners' response. And yet
the lieutenant was speaking, or trying to speak, through the
barred aperture of the hole, smartly uniformed, it might be,

her dark hair elegantly coiffed, flanked by a bodyguard of deputies. The sustained pitch of Bea's fury did not waver or break, and the humming, the keening, of her sisters rose ever more tender, ever more enveloping, no single voice ascending above the others, but the voices becoming one voice that swept away in its melodious grief whatever words of threat and warning the lieutenant might be forcing through the bars.

"Oh, sing out loud, please sing out loud!" Ann whispered fiercely to Callisto. "Please sing the Vietnamese song you always sing to us! Sing 'How many children must we kill before we make the wave stand still?'! Just that, oh, please, very loud so everyone can hear!"

But Callisto gave no sign that she had heard what Ann asked, and she did not sing that song or any other, but hummed the tender hymn of desolation as the others hummed. For they were learning that night that they were not, and had never been, a hundred women lying on their cots in the dark, isolated, and thus lost, in their own identities, women now who were neither black nor white nor Chicano, but all with interchangeable skins. The attack upon one girl in the darkness of her cell was an attack on their flesh, and the handcuffs on her wrists were on their wrists as well, and when at last the sheriff was called from the men's side, the picture came suddenly into focus, as if caught in a telescope's clear, uncanny eye. Outside in the wide, starlit night could be seen the lookout towers set high above the fields, above the fences topped with barbed wire; inside the fences sprawled the low, barracks-like prison buildings, with barred windows and barricaded doors; and within the buildings were gathered the lieutenant's deputies and the sheriff's officers, their waists cinched with leather, the men with the revolvers in holsters at their belts and handcuffs dangling on their hips; all this, the fixed barriers, the uniformed women and men, the leather, the steel, the loaded weapons, mobilized to silence one naked black girl in her solitary cell.

The sheriff unlocked the door of the hole and lobbed the tear gas in, and their sister's screams ceased, but louder and louder the women's voices hummed and moaned and keened as one voice. They could picture her coming out on her knees, crawling out gasping, choking, nothing left to her of all she had chosen to define and fortify the role she had selected to play, nothing except the artificial eyelashes and the moonlight varnished nails.

"There is to be quiet in the dormitories," Corporal Anxiety said from the threshold. She had switched on the lights to verify that the prisoners were all in their designated beds. "You are to be silent!" she said, the lantern of her jaw swinging on its invisible wire; and the sound of the women's voices came to an end.

X

THE LATE AFTERNOON was flooded with the purest golden light. It touched with radiance the thorns of the barbed wire above their heads, and lent to the demonstrators' faces a singular lambency. The lady psychiatrist and the accountant had somehow managed to tie back against the rotting boards of the fence the lean, straggling arms of the rose bushes, using doubled and tripled strands of thread they had filched from the sewing room. Lydia and a half dozen others were working on their knees by the iris beds when Calliope smiled at Athena over the intervening shoulders and said:

"What about a spot of walking?" And once they had got up and begun walking their accustomed stint, she went on saying that she would be going East with her husband at the end of October. "Arion will be conducting two concerts, one in Boston, the other in New York. So I could make a quick visit to the commune, if you thought it a good idea." She spoke with a deceptive brightness, as if disclaiming that there was any kind of emotion connected with the plan. "But perhaps I should know a little more about it. I'd like to hear more about the commune, of course, but also"—and here her voice hesitated for a moment, but still with no hint of sentiment altering its bright sound— "perhaps I should know," she said as they walked together, "what it is that you hope, that you wish, for Melanie."

Athena could not bring herself to answer that it was perhaps nothing more than the sound of Melanie's voice that she wanted, or the words written out in Melanie's elaborate hand that the ties between them had not been slashed like a cut jugular vein. She thought of saying to Calliope that the commune was not for an instant a revolutionary place, but rather one man's adaptation of Christianity and the plainest bourgeois values to a setting of his own defining. Pete the Redeemer is Christ, she wanted to say, and the redemption he offers is fame and fortune, these words of promise given his followers like a Bank of America card or a Master Charge plate. But she said instead:

"The children—there were about twenty of them then—they're all obedient, and well combed, and well washed, because Melanie is the mother in the commune. In the morning they sit at table and chant to their porridge, 'Pete is God, Pete is God,' and in the evening they chant the same thing to their soup."

And behind their chanting, the two words "fame" and "fortune" could always be heard as steadily as the beating of a drum. All the pretty, long-haired girls, and all the handsome, lost young women with dark, brooding eyes, and the overweight runaways, the truants not only from school and the parents but from life itself, all clung like the drowning to these words. The footloose young men, hard-working, ambitious, vain as they were, set aside their pride and became taxi drivers, ceased wondering and became masons, carpenters, house painters, plumbers, and brought their earnings back to Pete, the humiliation of their days and nights endured not for Pete alone, but as passing tribulations on the journey to fame and fortune that was to be their lasting reward.

The women became models in art school studios, stripping themselves naked before strangers for love of him, or became typists, or salesgirls, or cocktail waitresses, in the disdained society of the outside world; or they performed the household duties for the men, and for the community children they bore, sustained by the pledge that one day fame and fortune would be theirs. Before this year or the next was out, they believed that

Pete the Redeemer would be acknowledged the greatest folk singer since Woody Guthrie, and his albums would outsell even Dylan's. *He doesn't tell stories about real people in his songs,* Athena had once said to Melanie. *And what about your men and women of ancient Greece?* Melanie had cried out. *How real are they?* They had sat in the children's playroom, listening to the tape of Pete's voice and his harmonica playing, and Athena had thought the harmonica had a nice lilt to it, but the thin, flat voice and the words of the song were something else again. *For a folk singer, he doesn't seem to have heard about the rich and the poor, or peace and war, or even about love,* she said, and Melanie had cried out in fury: *Why should he be like everyone else? Why should he when he's God?*

They knew with reverence, the commune people, that the book Pete was writing about his life and his revelations, his prophecies, his acid trips, his prison regeneration, his turning of water into wine, would one day be translated into twenty-eight languages and become the acknowledged Bible of the young. It was simply a matter of serving him without question, of working with ever greater devotion, and then the triumph would embrace them all. As for those whose belief had faltered and who sought to leave the commune, they were tracked down by the strong-armed Iron Squad and beaten into subjugation again.

"However you consider it, whichever way you turn it to the light," Athena said to Calliope as they walked, "at the commune the imponderables of the spirit have gone out to lunch, and only renown and riches remain."

Athena could see Melanie sucking her thumb still when she was hungry or when her heart was broken, no matter how old she had grown. At any time of the day or night, there was the pliant schoolgirl thumb popped into her mouth, and the records played over and over when times with Pete the Redeemer were bad. "Cryin' time has come again, you're goin' to leave me," came one record's complaint, the sound of it heard clearly now in the dying afternoon. And "Heartaches by the dozen, troubles by the score," tap-danced another record, and Athena could see Melanie with a baby in her lap, always with a baby, looking out of the commune window at the end of the world. And then came the song that would bring tears to even a Greek statue's cold, marble eye. "Put your head on my shoulder, say the things you used to say," it pled, "and make the world go away." It was these words that Melanie was crying out in the far place where she was, but nobody could hear her, for had not the adult members of the commune taken as their own the anguished supplication of the song, the voice of each serving only to drown out all the others? "Make the world go away!" even the Iron Squad was asking as it beat up the defectors and threw them into the makeshift cells. This was the desperate message that Pete the Redeemer had garbled so successfully, cutting the wires of communication short as he slipped in and out of jug bands with the harmonica at his lips, in and out of young women's lives, in and out of time served for possession, demanding godhead in exchange for the fame and fortune that he promised them all, giving no quarter to any language, any tongue, that did not pronounce his name.

Maybe seeking to salvage it all from abject tragedy, Athena began telling Calliope then about another tape that Melanie had once played for her. That was in the old time, in the perilous time of uncertainty, Athena said, when it was still believed that she would come to acknowledge Pete as the redeemer in the end.

"In moments of crisis," she said as they walked in the prison garden, "the young women of the commune turned for guidance to the prophecies of the Ouija. Perhaps they didn't want to know that the name the inventor had given it in warning is 'yes' in two foreign languages. The tape of the séance Melanie played for me seemed somehow to suggest," Athena said, "that the commune Ouija board was better attuned to man, for whenever a male member of the family asked the questions, the answers became obsequious. 'Pete,' it gently counseled the redeemer, 'the world has hurt you, but don't be sad. Your spirit is destined to rule the universe.'" "How soon?" was the question Pete the Redeemer had put to it then, sick and tired as he was of waiting around. But when the Ouija prophet spelled out, "Maybe a month, maybe a year," Pete lost his temper. "Why can't you be more explicit?" he asked impatiently, and the little three-legged contraption, with the fingers of the young women balanced lightly on its back, had replied: "Not until you have been carried to Venus will you rule."

"Why Venus?" Calliope asked as they passed the iris beds again. "Why not Orion or Betelgeuse?"

"Perhaps because Pete the Redeemer would accept only a feminine planet as his territory," Athena said, "or perhaps because Venus is the brightest of all the planets in the solar system."

"No hand-me-downs for him," Calliope said in a strangely altered voice, and Athena glanced quickly at her face and saw that Calliope's eyes were wet with tears that did not fall.

I shouldn't go on with it, the underground woman rebuked herself. She has seen the entire hideous tragedy is in this tape. But still Athena went on with Pete the Redeemer asking the Ouija prophet how the hell he was going to get to Venus from where he was. The answer could not have been more simple: a spaceship made of an alloy of silver would take him and the commune members to the planet Venus, where Charlemagne and Abraham Lincoln and FDR were waiting for them to arrive. "How come the spaceship just don't pick me up right now and land me on the football field in the middle of national television?" Pete had asked then, and the answer spelled out was that the moment for world recognition of him had not yet come. For an instant, Pete the Redeemer appeared to have lost sight of the spaceship made of silver alloy and manned by Venutians which would bear him off to triumph, for like a wanderer staggering in the desert, with the vision of the oasis ahead turned to shimmering air, he had suddenly cried out: "I hate the world, and I'll hate it until it's completely destroyed! What am I going to do, either here or on Venus, with all my hatred and contempt? Answer me that!" The young women's hands so delicately arched above the three-legged Ouija, their fingertips resting lightly, lightly, on the varnished wood, may have trembled in apprehension a moment as Pete gave his own answer. "All those who have betrayed us have got to pay!" he shouted. "Whenever I think of those bastards who fear and hate me, I want to kill!" His voice sank to a whisper as he spoke the final, querulous words, asking the little wooden turtle that moved on the magic board: "If I'm so much greater than him, why can't I raise people from the dead and walk on water the way he did?" And then the tape was done.

"If you felt you could go, if you had the time," Athena said to Calliope, "just for a moment, just to see how she is . . ."

That was Friday, and they were told that in the evening a lady minister would hold services in the chapel, and a sense of excitement came alive in them all. It might have been opening night at the opera that was offered them, and after supper they lined up before the deep kitchen sinks to wash in a hurry the outsized pots and pans and cutlery; and it was then that St. Theresa said to Athena that she too intended to go.

"It's not right for me to do it, but still I shall," she said. Whatever penalty she would have to pay for the sin of demonstrating against the war, and the sin of attending a service outside the Catholic faith, she would pay without cavil; but now there were even graver things on her conscience. "I've become strong here in prison, and for the first time I'm not afraid to face the truth." Her small hands were under the slimy water, scrubbing at the blackened bottom of a frying pan. "I knew that for centuries bishops and priests and abbots and popes were so afraid of the energy of women that they closed them all away. But I never wanted to say to myself, 'yes, this is true,' and now I can." Her lips were so tightly set that the color had gone from them, and the words barely escaped them as her hands scrubbed furiously in the opaque water in the sink.

"Don't let Martha hear you speaking against the men of the Church," Athena said, scouring the layer of grease from first one plate and then the next, trying to make the commonplace words sound funny, for she had never seen St. Theresa laugh. But St. Theresa did not seem to hear.

"I wonder if you know that way back in the sixteenth century," she went on saying, her profile small, white, intense, "St. Angela Merici sent the Ursuline Sisters out of the cloisters to serve the people? Did you know that?" she asked as if life itself depended on the answer Athena would give.

"No," said Athena, and on the other side of her at the sinks Callisto asked if she could borrow the copper-haired sponge, asking this in the uncertain way in which she always approached Athena, undecided, it might be, as to what roles they played in relation to each other: daughter and mother, or singer and writer of myths, but roles which somehow served to make them ill at ease together. They smiled almost shyly at each other as Athena gave her the metallic sponge, and then both looked quickly away. "No," Athena said to St. Theresa, "I didn't know."

"For almost a century," St. Theresa went on with it, and she plunged a monstrous pot into the water in the sink. "And when their work was spoken of everywhere, all over the world, Athena, the bishops and priests and abbots and popes decided they would have to bring it to an end. So the women were taken away from life and cloistered in silence again. They set us apart from the destitute and the imprisoned because they were afraid that we might bring Christianity back on earth. After Pope John died, what did they do but take the worker-priests out of the factories and send them back into the churches, away from the people, back into prison. Once Pope John stood up in the olive fields and said to all the dignitaries who kneeled down for his blessing that Jesus was not crucified in a cathedral between two golden candelabra, but on a cross between two thieves." The slime of grease that floated on the water gathered in rainbow circles around her wrists for a moment as she turned her head to look up at Athena's face. "Can you tell your students when you go back that books have failed?" she asked in the same low urgent voice. "Can you tell them that there is a library here in prison and that more than half the prisoners don't know how to read?"

"Yes, I can tell them that, and I can tell them other things," Athena said quietly.

When they were done, they dried their hands in their aprons and hung them on the row of hooks outside the larder, which Martha had bolted and padlocked for the night, and then they hurried up the hall. Past the library they went, where the lonely books waited on the shelves, and where they could see the closed-circuit TV screen jerking and flashing with animated cartoons, past the processing offices and the lock-up wards, and into the snow-white chapel, just around the corner from the isolation cells. There were perhaps a dozen demonstrators and twice as many regular prisoners, and when they crossed the threshold the whiteness of the walls, and of the pulpit and pews, struck their eyes like sudden light. A blanched tide of virtue had seemingly flooded into this bare, simple room, and there it remained, land-locked and stagnant, yet antiseptically pure. The four narrow windows in the western wall were arched like church windows, the leaded glass of them stained with the color of sunset. The prison bars fixed to the outer sills could be seen like the slender stems of trees against the evening sky. Dead white were the covers of the hymnals in the dead white racks that ran along the backs of the pews, and chalk white the seats of the pews into which the inmates moved silently.

There before them on the platform stood the lady minister, a tall, spare, wooden-boned woman resplendent in green silk and brassy ornaments, her hair henna-ed stiff and bright, with rouge in abrasions on her cheekbones and in the wrinkled, sunken caverns of her cheeks. The prisoners were demeaned even be-fore they entered this place of worship by their gray dresses and their ill-fitting tennis shoes, while the lady preacher and her organist beside her had the proper outfits in which to sing the praises of the Lord.

"Oh, God, it's the sideshow at the circus!" Calliope murmured, for the organist standing there above them on the platform was scarcely larger than a dwarf, with legs grotesquely bowed beneath a pink wool skirt, and pastel sequins trembling on her rosy blouse. "Oh, God, I'm cruel!" Calliope whispered, her head held high, the gentian eyes seeming ever bluer between the short, thick charcoal lashes.

The organist wore high-heeled, white, patent-leather pumps, with satin rosebuds serving as buckles, and rosebuds were scattered in the brittle nest of her hair. She told them, the little girl voice fluting out of the middle-aged, care-seamed mouth, that she had found salvation as recently as five years before. It was not too late for any of them there in the chapel, she said, it was never too late for anyone to be saved, not the drunkard lying in the gutter, not the drug addict, not the blasphemer, not the woman who had strayed. The lady preacher, standing tall and bony in the merciless light of sanctity, her gaunt face manlike under her helmet of orange hair, put the seal of approval on all the organist said by pronouncing at intervals the cabalistic, ancient word "amen."

Twenty-two years she had been coming to the Rehabilitation Center, the minister snapped at them once the organist's testimony was done; twenty-two years of bringing the word of God to those who had left the path of righteousness. She had stepped into the pulpit now, and her bracelets rang aloud as she set her hymnal and conductor's baton on the lectern before her; twenty-two years of self-sacrifice for the sake of the unfit and the unworthy, and she fixed one prisoner after another with a wild and bolting eye.

"I was called upon to sacrifice my husband, my married life," she told the congregation, "for I could not serve two masters. I was called upon by the Lord to leave my husband and divorce him. The Lord had put His finger on me, and I bowed to His will."

"How do you feel about women's liberation?" one of the college girls asked, but the minister gave no sign.

"Once I had cast off my marital bonds," she went on saying, "I was free to listen for the Lord's directions. My ears heard anew and my limbs were strengthened. I could follow in His footsteps without faltering. The temple of my body was purified, and no sinful flesh stood between me and my Savior."

"Oh, yes, yes, Lawd!" Tallulah moaned aloud from the back pew. "Praise the Lawd, amen!"

"One day I shall stand on the right hand of the Lord in everlasting glory," the lady preacher said, "but you will not be there, none of you will stand with me and my sister by His side unless you repent and mend your ways."

"I've been mendin' them, Lawd! They almos' mended now!" Tallulah cried out from the mountainous weight of flesh that rested on her knees. "Praise the Lawd, oh, praise the Lawd!"

"What kind of an outfit will you wear up there in heaven, ma'am?" another of the college girls called out. "Don't you think if you and the organist wore gray dresses like Tallulah and the rest of us do, you would be more acceptable to God?"

"No one is authorized to speak during the service!" the minister cried, her voice not yet beginning to shake. She gave a sign to the seated organist, and the dwarf's hands pounced on the keys. The preacher raised her baton and opened the brightly painted trap door of her mouth to lead the singing, the fillings in her back teeth as golden as the collar at her haggard throat. "Hymn forty-one!" she commanded them, and the prisoners took the hymnals from the racks before them.

The organ quavered and throbbed, sighed deeply as the women got to their feet, their voices thin and tentative as they began to sing. "Jesus is our Savior," they murmured in hesitation, feeling their way until Callisto's clear voice soared above the others, drawing the voices of the reluctant from their throats.

"Jesus is our Savior!" they declared in triumph, and now a tide of joy rose higher and higher in the chapel, and the surging of the prisoners' voices lifted Tallulah from her knees, and she held to the back of the pew, singing and swaying, but whether the tears that ran down her face were from crying or laughing could not be said. And without apparent effort or intent, the words began to change then, and as the organ played the voices sang: "Black and white together, black and white together!" The lady preacher snapped her mouth shut and struck her baton sharply on the wood of the lectern. At once, the organ gasped into silence, and slowly, separately, the prisoners' voices died.

"Some of us," said the lady in the pulpit when all was still, "some of us are singing. Others are just having a good time."

"Excuse me," Callisto said, her narrow, gypsy-dark hand raised, "but isn't being joyful a reverent thing?"

Athena stood just below the pulpit, and she could see the cords in the lady preacher's neck lashing and writhing, no longer veins or arteries, but snakes imprisoned in her flesh. Their doom was to turn and twist forever in their hideous convulsions, strangling her and themselves, unable to escape and slither away.

"Those of us who will continue singing respectfully may remain in the chapel," the minister said as the snakes writhed in purple wrath. "Those who are here for a good time will leave—will leave at once, AT ONCE!" she shouted; and then the serpents abruptly ceased in their contortions, and the woman spoke in awful quiet, her shaking fingers holding to the lectern, her mouth reaching for air. "The voice of the Lord is gentle . . . His voice is gentle," she said, each word a separate shudder in her throat. "He has written me a love letter . . . He has written a letter that only the pure and the respectful are privileged to read. *Your* eyes, they cannot behold it," she gasped. "The Lord has written His love letter to me in the chapters and books of the Bible. He has not raised His voice against me as sinners have done. He does not, does not, raise His voice," she whispered, her trembling hands still clinging to the lectern. "Now go," she said, barely aloud, "now go."

In a rustle of movement, the prisoners placed the hymnals in the racks again and, demonstrators and regulars alike, they filed through the doorway, humble as cenobites in their ill-fitting dresses, and the lady minister and the organist were left alone. As they moved down the hall to the dormitories, past the lock-up wards and the offices, past the library, where the TV screen still flickered with its travesties of life, they could hear the far, tremulous cry of the organ calling after them, the sound growing fainter, ever fainter, until it was finally lost entirely as Callisto began to sing to them, part in humor, part in grief, that she was a poor pilgrim of sorrow, traveling this wide world alone.

XI

CALLISTO TOOK THE CADENCES of the women's snores at night
and improvised on them. There were the basses and the altos,
the soprano whistlers, the basso profundos and the falsettos,
and Callisto did contrapuntal phrasings of them and gave their
discord a musical form. These concerts took place in the first
total death of those who slept, before the reprieve of dreaming
began, and the regular prisoners forgot the misery that circumscribed their lives and laughed like zanies in their beds, laughing
in stifled hysteria as Callisto's voice told them that ordinary
things could be taken so far away in fantasy that they need
never return to where they had always been before. (Once she
had made the steady dropping of water from a kitchen faucet
into a flute solo.) The demonstrators on their cots, who saw
themselves at odd moments as part of the conscience of their
time, in that half hour of demisemiquaver forgot the gravity of
their mission and shrieked their muffled glee. Even the awakened snorers themselves laughed, certain that it was someone
else, just over there, in the cot beyond, who had bugled aloud,
or scraped and sawed the catgut strings in the discordant sym-
phony.

And then, three nights before their time was up, something
took place for which no explanation was ever offered: Athena
was awakened in the darkness by the voice of the dreadnought

deputy blasting through the fog of sleep. She said that Athena was to dress and go at once to the processing offices.

"But what's happened?" Athena whispered, her heart gone cold with fear. "Did a telegram come? Is it something about my children?"

But there was no reply, for the single eye of the deputy's flashlight was already at the other end of the dormitory. Athena slipped quickly out of bed and flung off the flannel nightgown, and pulled on the prison-issue underpants and the gray dress. The sneakers had taken off in directions of their own, and she dropped to her hands and knees to feel for them under the night table, under the cot, her lips mumbling the names like the beads of a rosary: Paula, Sybil, Melanie; Melanie, Paula, Sybil, Melanie. She ran in panic down the dark, silent hall, carrying the sneakers in one hand, her heart crying, Sybil, Paula, Melanie, and once in the brightly lit office she saw that the clock above the two desks said half-past four. The only black deputy in the place was seated before the second desk, leisurely chewing gum, and she reached down for the pillowcase, tied at the top with string, that held Athena's clothing, her shoes, her handbag, her identity.

"Check out the items as I call them off," the deputy said, and she waited, holding the typed list, chewing her gum, until Athena had undone the string. "One wool skirt, one wool jacket," she began, but Athena's hands were shaking so that she could not find these things.

"But where am I going? Could you let me know where I'm going?" she asked, and she looked at this woman who wore the uniform casually, the collar of her shirt unbuttoned on her strong, dark throat, and the necktie loosened and jerked to one side. "Could you tell me—?"

"One pair white earrings, one gold wristwatch," the deputy began again, but she stopped when she saw that Athena was doing nothing at all.

"You're going to court," she said then. "Your trial's coming up. A lotta girls here would be glad to be going instead of waiting around out here."

"But I've been sentenced," Athena said. This deputy was nicknamed Miss Karate by the regular prisoners, for she was stronger than any two other deputies put together, they said. It was she who was called if no tear gas was handy, and her time was usually the night shift. Miss Karate appeared ready and willing for action at any moment, prepared to toss any number of lesser men or women over her head and onto the strip of red carpet and sawdust of a circus arena; standing before her, Athena wanted to laugh out loud in relief, for Melanie and Paula and Sybil were not a part of what was taking place. "Why aren't the others coming with me?" she asked, not trembling any more.

"They'll be others going with you. Don't worry about that," the deputy said, and she went on saying: "One girdle, one bra, one pair nylons." She looked at Athena over the desk, the gum moving faster in her jaws. "Start checking them out," she said.

"Yes, I am—one girdle, one bra, one pair nylons. I have them here," Athena said. "But why am I going to court again?"

"Ask the judge that," the deputy said. "Athena, you check your things and sign this release. You can't keep everybody waiting." In another instant, the tried patience in her deep voice might break. "One blouse, one slip, one pair underpants, one make-up kit . . ."

Then it was done, and Athena put her name to the list, and Miss Karate stood up from the desk. She chose a key from the ring of them attached by a chain to her leather belt, and pushed Athena ahead of her to the varnished panels of a closed door.

"Get ready quick," she said, putting the key in the lock, and Athena walked into the small, crowded room. "The car leaves in ten minutes," Miss Karate said, and the door closed behind her, and was locked again.

There were eight women struggling to get their clothes on in the dimly lit room, some stooping to tighten the straps or laces of their shoes, some smoothing the lint from their wool coats and skirts. Others stood arranging their hair and their make-up before the two small mirrors on the wall, shouldering one another aside, and drinking black coffee from paper cups—eight prisoners who were strangers to Athena, and a ninth who was Tallulah, standing enormously naked and weeping, a girdle dragged halfway up her monumental thighs and halted there by the quivering blockades of flesh.

"I cain' get 'em on, my clo's," she said to Athena. "I put on fo'ty, fo'ty-fi' poun's since I come in here." And because of the sorrow in her voice, the women forgot their own reflections in the mirrors, forgot the lint on their dresses, the wrinkles in their skirts that they had been seeking to press out with their open palms. They set down their paper cups and their combs and their lipsticks and gathered around her, and they tugged and pulled, with their underlips caught in their teeth, but the girdle would not go any higher. So they dragged it down over her tremendous dimpled knees, her great smooth sable calves, and when her giant feet had stepped free of it, they threw it onto the table among the drained paper cups, for time was getting short. "I cain' go if I cain' hole my nylons up," she said, speaking almost in hope now. "Yo' tell her that. Yo' tell her I cain' go if I cain' get my clo's on." The tears were sliding down her face, but she did not seem to know this. "They gets all the work outta yo' they can, an' they throws yo' out when they ain' got no more use for yo'," she said, weeping not for the clothes she had grown out of, but because they were sending her away. And then one of the black women cried out:

"String! We'll tie your nylons up with string!"

They knotted together the bits and pieces of string from the pillowcases emptied of all they owned, and they got Tallulah seated, and knelt down before her, struggling to get the nylons over her broad toes and up her legs. Athena wore the gray dress still, and her hair was not combed, but what mattered now was not that she was going, or that she was the only demonstrator going but the wild drama of getting Tallulah dressed in time. She and another white prisoner worked feverishly, forcing the straps of Tallulah's brassiere over the bowed yoke of her shoulders, seeking to knead the wallowing breasts into the mesh of the soiled bra. And now the bra was discarded like the girdle, and two of the black prisoners rapped on the locked door until Miss Karate brought them a needle and thread so that they could change the hooks and eyes of Tallulah's brown skirt.

"I can't leave the scissors with you," the deputy said, the gum in her mouth speaking a tough language of its own.

"Then hold them there for us until we're done," said the smallest black girl, sewing fast. "That'll give you some re-laxation from your duties for a while."

Miss Karate stayed as they ripped open one side of Tallulah's yellowing slip and pulled it over the multitudinous little braids lying close to her skull, and the infinite byways and alleys of scalp that ran between. Athena stretched the neck of the pink sweater as far as it would go, and dragged it over Tallulah's head, and now the fiercest struggle of all began. They got her arms into it, but however fiercely they pulled, it would come no lower than just short of her nipples, the pink wool having seized her armpits in a throttling grip.

"Well, her coat, her coat will cover it all!" somebody cried out. But the old brown coat gave a hearty laugh and split its seams, and its sleazy lining hung down to her heels behind.

"It's good enough," the other white prisoner said, tugging and hauling to close the front, but the buttons and buttonholes had taken the bit into their teeth and refused to meet.

"I ain' goin'," Tallulah said, and her underlip trembled. "I ain' goin' to go like this. W'at my chillen goin' to say?"

"You can't stay here. You been here a year," the smallest black girl said, buckling Tallulah's sandals, this bright, quick girl, efficient enough to handle them all. "You know that. You know the law. They gotta get you outta here." She stood at the glass now, her mouth made into an upright oval as she painted the lipstick on; then she went to Tallulah and carefully painted her mouth as well. Miss Karate had unlocked the door, and she and the dreadnought deputy stood on either side of it. "You look good, Tallulah," the smallest black prisoner said. "Stop crying, sweetheart. You going to be free."

The official station wagon was black, and as long as a hearse, and it held ten people and the driver with ease, three prisoners on each of the wide rear seats, and Talullah spread over two seats in the front beside the sheriff's deputy who drove. A filigree of chicken wire was patterned in all the window panes, and the car doors were locked electronically. Two holsters buckled to his belt held the deputy's revolvers, and a grinning pair of handcuffs dangled at his hip. The other white prisoner was seated beside Athena, and she began talking in the most ladylike of voices about the possibilities of what might lie ahead. She was a comely woman, probably just over forty, who could have been mistaken at first glance for a suburban housewife, but in her bold blue eyes and the set of her rosy chin there was a recklessness that was at odds with the look of her decorous flesh. She carried the role off very well, sitting there with small brass hoops piercing her ears, dressed in a gold-and-lavender brocaded sheath and platform-soled, gilt sandals that she must have been wearing at a cocktail party on the far summer evening of her arrest.

"I'm really looking forward to going to Corona," she said pleasantly, "prinicipally because of the opportunities there to become a trained cosmetologist." She might have been chatting about where she would spend the winter season that was almost upon them, whether in the Bahamas or the Virgin Islands, or on the Italian Riviera. "I'm not completely certain yet," she said, smiling her forthright, attractive smile, "but I'm really hoping. Such broadening experiences are offered, career-wise, at Corona, if you have the sense to take advantage of them. It's gratifying to know your time's being well spent—your hours," she corrected it, the word "time" having slipped out inadvertently. "For instance, brushing up on your shorthand and typing, if you like that sort of thing. I started out as a private secretary," she said with a little laugh. "That was the first rung of the ladder," and the brooding black prisoner sitting on her other side picked up courage and spoke.

"They says they has coffee machines all over the place at Corona," she said.

"Why, of course they do, in the reception rooms and the lounge. That's quite natural, isn't it?" the white woman said in her well-modulated voice; and another girl leaned over from the seat behind and asked if it was true you could wear your own clothes there, and have visitors twice a week for an hour at a time, and go out to the movies on Saturday night. "Why, of course," the white woman answered, as if truly amazed. "Why, naturally, if you're properly chaperoned." She spoke as if this had been the custom as well in the vacation spot they had just left behind. "I feel pretty conspicuous in this outfit," she went on saying to Athena, laughing again as she smoothed the gold brocade drawn tight across her knees. "I just didn't think in time to bring a coat along. If I'm going South, it won't be any problem, but I hope I'll have the time to pick up a dress or two before I go."

Corona, Corona was a magical name in all their ears, the mere syllables of it transfixing them with its dimensions and its promises. Another place the white women spoke of as they rode was Eureka, but it did not evoke the same glamor in their minds.

"I heard Corona wasn't integrated yet," the smallest black prisoner startled them all by saying from the rear seat, speaking brightly and quickly, with no hint of malice; and yet they knew the attack had begun.

"Well, some of the girls might lack the education or the background needed to get in," the white woman said. With one lady-like hand she adjusted the brass hoop in her ear. "At Eureka," she went on saying to Athena, "I'm told the accommodations are not as comfortable, and the library isn't as well equipped for the courses you may want to take."

And then from the seat just behind, a prisoner put the outlawed question to her.

"Was you workin' in one of them night-clubs?" were the words she asked.

The white woman looked at Athena and made a little moue of horror at the ignorance of those with whom they rode.

"Good heavens, no. I've always held executive positions," she said, not turning her head.

"Was you a cashier?" another prisoner asked, and the white woman cried out in a genteel disdain:

"A cashier? My heavens, no."

"An' could be yo' was caught wit' yo' hand in the till," another voice said.

"Or maybe caught shopliftin'," said a voice from far behind in the car; and then the prisoners began to laugh, laughing and laughing as if there was no grief in the world, and no reason ever to stop.

It was half-past six, but it might have been any hour of the day or night when they reached the underground garage of the city jail. They were led into breakfast, then to a holding cell smaller than the one into which the forty-odd demonstrators had crowded the week before. But these cells were otherwise as alike as one Howard Johnson restaurant is to the other, each with identical benches along the two walls in which there were no doors, identical toilets behind identical partitions, identical drinking fountains, and an identically cold television eye watching from above. The door they came through opened in from the long corridor, and opposite this now closed and bolted door, another led into the courtroom. The life of the ten women locked in the cell, their actual being, seemed extinguished by weariness, and they no longer spoke. They were neither wholly asleep, nor entirely awake, immune to the meaning of their own pasts now, as to their futures, women in limbo, waiting for nothing except the sound of their own names to summon them back among the living again. The heavy burden of Tallulah's flesh no longer mattered, and the word "Corona" was not even an echo in the silent room. At intervals, as the hours passed, the door into the courtroom was unlocked, and an officer called out a single name, and one by one, without a gesture of farewell, without looking back, the women left. Once they had entered the courtroom, they did not return.

By half-past eleven, there were three of them left, and when the courtroom door opened again and a name was called, and a prisoner rose and left, only the smallest black prisoner and Athena remained. They lay, half asleep, on separate benches, and Athena thought of dreams, and that cats are said to pass three quarters of their lives in sleep because of dreams more alluring than reality.

"Dogs sleep much less than cats," she said to the girl lying with closed eyes on the other bench. "They say it's because of the difference in their dreams."

"How could anyone tell that?" the girl asked. She had come suddenly awake, and she lifted her bright, alert head.

"Some kind of electronic equipment records their dreaming time," Athena said. "Not what they dream, but how much they dream." Perhaps visions offered of luxury and leisure without end, she thought; halcyon dreams, without feathers or the teeth of mice. "Dogs seem to have only one dream—you know, chasing a rabbit, with their paws going like mad. And so they get bored with sleep. Cats can hardly wait to go back to sleep again."

"Cats know a lot that dogs don't know," the black girl said. She stretched, lying on her back, then drew her knees up and clasped her hands under her head. "They know something dogs never heard about. They got something to fall back on," she said, so bright and sure.

"Something different from chasing squirrels," Athena murmured, thinking: *In a minute or two I'll be asleep.*

"Yeah, like dreams," the little black prisoner said; and then almost at once the door to the courtroom opened again, and a name was called, and the girl swung off the bench. Before she went through the open door, where the officer stood, she turned her head quickly and winked one eye at Athena, "Have a nice day, lady," she said, and in that last instant Athena saw that her face wore a small, tight mask of fear.

Now she was alone in the holding cell, alone with her black wool skirt and jacket, and her soiled white blouse, and her wristwatch and white earrings, and the old, haunting dream took over, the dream of the lung which the first surgeon had said could be likened, not to a grape, but to a bunch of grapes, the pale fruit inside each grape pellucid until the blight set in. The blight had fingers blackened by tar which squeezed the substance from the grape skins, the surgeon said, and there they hung, shriveled and empty, unable to serve any longer as wineskins of air. The chest, he said, speaking outside the door of Rory's hospital room, is a finely finished box, lined with red satin or silk, like the instrument case of a musician, and it holds an accordion which breathes rhythmically out and in. The actual music it imparts for the purposes of respiration is, of course, supplied by the nervous system, he explained, but there is no agreement among medical men as to the role the brain plays here. The lung, he said in the kindest way possible, is tinted pink by blood that flows into it from the right side of the heart, a flow which is computed at twenty to thirty liters per minute when the subject is active, and three to seven liters per minute during rest; "as your husband is resting now," he said, and he paused a moment. "Only his lung is not pink any longer, since the requisite quantities of air per minute cannot ventilate the respiratory system; his lung is stained yellow, like the two first fingers of the hand of a nicotine addict." And therefore he will die, he did not say aloud.

The second or third surgeon in the next hospital said that the lung is like a honeycomb, with the air pockets in it not pearl-colored as in the comb, but exquisitely pink, like the petals of a rose. When you break a rose from the bush, he said, you can sense the pouring of life from the main stalk of the plant into the heart of the flower, and this is an ideal analogy to demonstrate the total vulnerability of the lung. Its purity can be maintained, he continued briskly, until—and abruptly his energy subsided. "Until what?" Athena asked now in the dream. "Until the carcinomata come," he answered in a low voice, his eyes not meeting hers. "Intervention for the removal of carcinomata of the lung is rarely possible, due to the late stage at which patients come under observation"; and he went to the trouble to describe the army of yellow-bodied spiders, spinning their webs in smoke and nicotine, eroding the substance of the hive. And the fourth or fifth surgeon said quietly: "There is a center in a man which can be said to resemble a telephone exchange, from which rhythmical messages pass down the nerves and connect the message with the respiration. At each breath, a message is sent back up the vagus nerve," he said, "but the precise nature of the message is not known to us"; and he added in sincere regret: "When the messages cease to come, the breathing ceases as well."

In the middle of the dream, the door from the long hall was opened, and a new group of prisoners came in. Athena sat up on the bench and smoothed back her hair as they crowded in, as frisky as colts, their young legs slender, their skirts short on their thighs. Their dark breasts could be seen in the deep cut of their necklines, and cigarettes were on their lips or carried in their fingers. They were black, except for one Chicano girl, who stood apart from the others, beside the water closet partition, quite alone. The voices of the black girls rippled with laughter, the airy, innocent smoke blew from their mouths, and their subtly painted nails held the cigarettes like fresh, clean chalk with which they wrote their signatures on the air.

"Filter tips don' do yo' no harm," one of these new prisoners said, for cigarettes were their communication and their currency. "In fac', they's advertise lak bein' good for yo', lak trippin' out to the country." And another said: "I was swearin' off on account the expense, but what you do, you go roun' ruinin' everybody's evenin', just sittin' there not smokin', like you was criticizin'." And a third one said: "My Auntie, she's goin' on eighty-six an' she ain' dead yet, been smokin' sence she was ten, so I gotta while to go!"

Their laughter filled the holding cell, and Athena saw within their dark, young breasts, and did not wish to see, the blood flowing from the right side of the heart (twenty to thirty liters per minute when the body is in motion, the first surgeon had said) into the clusters of firm, clear-fruited grapes that he had likened to the still unblighted lung. Lively and talkative, they drew the smoke into the constantly playing accordions of their sweet, heedless chests, while the Chicano girl stood apart in her pale green coat, her fingers nervously pulling at the buttons of it, blind and deaf to everyone there. The watch on Athena's wrist said one o'clock, but neither the woman deputy who opened the hall door nor the officer who summoned prisoners into the courtroom, had made any mention of food.

"What happens about lunch?" Athena asked the black girls in the holding cell, and they whirled like a flock of starlings to where she sat on the bench.

"Lunch?" one of them repeated, her voice mocking and high. "They done give us lunch before they processed us, and yum, yum, was it fine! We had crab salad, an' T-bone ste'k, an' more French fries than you could eat!"

"An' aspar'gus an' mix ice cream," another girl said. "They sure musta forgot 'bou' you"; and this was enough to start them laughing again, all but the Chicano girl, and to send them waltzing from place to place in the cell, laughing and blowing the cigarette smoke in delicate, bluish spirals on the air. "The cou't clos' down twelve to two, everybody eatin' 'cep' you, lady. You better up an' tell tha' ol' TV up there you ain' been treated righ'."

And now the Chicano girl walked on her out-of-fashion, high, white heels across the holding cell, walked with eyes fixed like a sleepwalker's, to where Athena sat. She halted before her, a strong, young peasant woman who might have been standing in the dust of a Spanish square on a Sunday morning, dressed awkwardly for mass, as much a part of the earth she stood on as a tree rooted for centuries in the same soil. Her eyes, with a singular cast in them, were bovine, docile, and the wiry, dark brown hair that grew low on her broad forehead was parted in the middle, with small, gold earrings showing below the strands of it that were drawn low on her ears and back into a chignon behind. Athena saw her suddenly as the wandering Io, whom Zeus had loved, and for whose sake he had wrapped the earth in a thick, black thundercloud so that his jealous wife would not discover them; and when she did, he quickly transformed the maiden into a heifer white as the moon. (Sometimes she was white, said the records, and sometimes black, and sometimes the color of the violet.) Under the pale green coat, Athena saw that her belly was swollen with pregnancy, and the child would thus be Epaphos (*My God, my brother!* Athena thought).

"You gotta kid?" the Chicano girl asked her, but the answer was of no interest at all to her. Athena moved to make room for her on the bench, but the girl stood motionless before her, saying: "I hadda kid, real pretty. She wasn't one year old. She die last week. Lemme tell you, lady, she already dead when I walka in. I leava her witha the sitter and go to the Welfare, and when the sitter go home, she high school kid, I taka the bottle out of the fridga, I don't know nothin', nothin', I think the kid is lika sleepin'. I pick her up, and she feel cold. I lighta the oven, and I holda the kid in fronta the oven, but she don't get warm, and I try with the bottle, but she ain't breathin'. She wasn't not one year old. But she gotta black curly hair like he got, my husband—"

Without any warning, one of the black girls said: "You ain' got no husban'." They were gathering around her now, smoking their cigarettes, not laughing any more. "Whatcha talkin' 'bou' a husban'?"

"I gotta husband," said the Chicano girl, looking straight at Athena still, the heifer-girl, the moon-cow who had clambered up the cliffs to where Prometheus sat bound to his rock, and spoke to him about once being a princess and a happy girl, now changed into "a beast, a starving beast, that frenzied runs with clumsy leaps and bounds." "My husband, he didn' lika hear her cryin', wakin' him up night cryin'. So he says, you keepa the kid from cryin' or I getta out tomorrow, I getta out and don't come back, so I says she a good kid. I gotta get to the Welfare, so I leava her witha the sitter, she a high school kid, and maybe she drop her on the kitchen floor, maybe she hit her too hard."

"You got a ce-ment floor in that kitchen?" one of the black girls asked her. They were moving back and forth, back and forth behind her, stalking their prey. "Spic, you lyin'," another said, and they moved in closer, closer, their cigarettes in their slender fingers.

"I holda the kid in fronta the oven, and thena I run down the stairs with her," the Chicano girl said. "I run alla the way to the 'mergency, and I tella them there, I tella them I leava her witha the sitter and go to the Welfare, and the sitter go home, and I take the bottle outta the fridga, not knowin' nothin', and I think the kid is lika sleepin'—"

"What 'bou' that ce-ment floor?" one of the black girls asked.

"Yeah, the floora cement," the Chicano girl said, the word without meaning to her. "So I lighta the oven, and I holda the kid in fronta the oven—"

"Spic, yo' lyin' in yo' teeth," a black girl said. Now they were moving in between her and Athena. "They got yo' under arrest, yo' better tell it like it was."

"Lemme tella, she already dead when I walka in," said the Chicano girl. "She already gettin' cold, so I lighta the oven—"

Her fingers twisted the buttons of her coat, and her moon-struck eyes were fixed on Athena. "I trya with the bottle—"

"Lissen, Spic," another of the black girls said. "Lissen. We got kids, all of us got kids, an' we don' leave 'em with no baby-sitter. When we goes to the Welfare offices, we leave 'em with our mommas, with our aunties, yo' hear? We out on the streets 'cause we want to do the best for our kids." Closer and closer they came, butting their soft, small hips against her peasant hips, blowing the cigarette smoke in her moon-cow face, closer and closer, until there seemed no more air left to breathe in the cell. "You got a ce-ment floor in tha' kitchen, o.k.? So what yo' do, yo' drop tha' baby head down on the floor, tha's what you do. You so 'fraid of losin' tha' man who ain' yo' husban', you think this a good way to stop tha' baby from keepin' him awake, ain' tha' right?"

"We don' kill our kids, uh-uh, Spic," another of them said, her lips drawn savagely back from her white teeth. "We don' have to put up with havin' no men roun'. Tha's not our prob-lem, gettin' a man or keepin' a man, but it sure seem to be yo's. We wan' our kids, whether they cryin' all night or not cryin'. We don' bash they brains out. They our warriors, an' our mommas an' our aunties they lives a long time, they lives till they ninety, 'cause we needs 'em, an' our kids, our warriors, they needs 'em, an' tha's to do with love, tha's to do with paradise, not fuckin' some curly-head dude, you Spic."

"I lighta the oven, and I holda the kid in fronta the oven," the Chicano girl said, looking straight at Athena. "I come back from the Welfare, and the sitter, she go home, she high school kid, and I taka the bottle outta the fridga—"

"You is lower than the worm in the mud, you is lower than the rat in the cellar," one of the hovering black girls said. And an-other cried out: "Leave the high school girl outta it!" They had begun to pull at the velveteen collar of her coat, to flick their snapping fingers at the gold stars in her ears. "Spic, you the one beat out the brains of yo' own chile, yo' own flesh and yo' own blood," another of them said fiercely, while the eye of the television camera above them looked carefully away from what was just about to take place. "Take off yo' coat," another said. "Take it off so's we can see what kinda shape you in," and the burning end of her cigarette rested for a moment, as if by accident, on the back of the Chicano girl's hand. Then they dragged the pale green coat from her shoulders, jerked her arms out of the sleeves, and threw the coat onto the floor, kicked it like a dead thing across the cell. She stood before them now in a white lace dress, a pregnant, cataleptic bride with a cross on a slender chain around her neck. "You is as low as the ole Tom cat that eats his own chillen," a black girl said, bringing her face close to the Chicano girl's. "You is low like the sly, ole man-eatin' shark."

Athena got up from the bench, and she put her arm through the girl's bare arm, and now the shifting, shoving circle of women closed around them, cigarettes in their fingers still, their varnished nails sharp enough to rip the white lace wedding dress from neck to hem, to slash wide open the peasant throat, eyes and voices savage enough to carve the heart out of her breast.

"Let her sit down. She's tired," Athena said.

"Tired?" one of the black girls mimicked in high derision. "Tired from beatin' her kid's head on them pavin' stones? How you fixin' to get ridda the nex' one, Spic, the one you got inside you now?"

And then the door from the courtroom was unlocked, and the officer standing in the opening called out the separate names from the list he held. One by one, the black prisoners answered the summons, one by one moved toward him and waited at the threshold where he stood.

"Put your cigarettes out before entering the courtroom," he said wearily to them. "You been here enough times to know."

After the flurry of movement, the prisoners, the flock of starlings, were gone, and Athena picked the Chicano girl's coat up from the floor, and shook it out, and she put the girl's arms into the sleeves of it, and buttoned it over. She managed to draw her down on the bench, and they sat in what seemed a long while of silence together, Athena's right hand holding the girl's left hand. And if I were Calliope, thought Athena, I would take her in my arms and hold her close, but I cannot do this, and why I cannot I do not know. "Why cannot I be either the black girls or Calliope?" she asked herself. "Calliope, who demands nothing, no past, no future, no moral obligations, or the black girls, whose demands are more inexorable than those that will be made on Judgment Day? Why am I condemned by no one but myself to fall between the two?"

When the courtroom door opened again, the officer called out a single name, and Io, the sleepwalker, with her patiently parted hair, her untroubled brow, released her hand from Athena's hand, and rose from the bench, and followed blindly where the court officer led.

"Lemme tella—" her voice said before the door closed, and then there was absolute silence in the holding cell.

It was half-past three by Athena's wristwatch, and she knew that the court would soon cease operations for the day. She had accepted now that she would sit here alone, forgotten, perhaps sit all night, for there was no sense in her having been brought here, and no reason why she should ever be taken away. But in another hour, as she lay half dreaming on the bench, the door from the hall opened, and a woman deputy looked in, keys dangling at her waist, and asked Athena her name.

"Your name isn't on any list," the deputy said when Athena had answered, and she turned the pages on the clipboard that she held. "You shouldn't be here. There's enough going on without us having to deal with complications like this. You should be in the Rehabilitation Center where you came from," she said in something like accusation to Athena as she led her down the hall.

XII

THEN ATHENA WAS BACK, and processed into the Center again, and after the paperwork and the fingerprinting, and the shampoo and showering were done, supper was long past. Again she wore a clean but ill-fitting, gray prison dress, identical to the other, and a pair of sneakers other women had worn, and over her arm she carried a towel and washrag, a pillowcase and two folded sheets, a ruffled nightgown, and a cake of soap in one hand. Down the hall she walked, exactly as before, a little lightheaded with hunger, quickly passing the library, where the television screen spoke loudly out, and where she glimpsed for a moment the intimately known faces of Calliope, Callisto, St. Theresa, Ann; and in the hall, just beyond the door, the Grecian deputy was halted. In the deliverance and gratitude of her return, Athena saw the deputy as someone as dear to her as were the others, despite the uniform, despite the title, a smooth-skinned, straight-nosed emblem of clarity incongruously present in this place.

"I found a book you had written on the library shelves today," the deputy said almost shyly, "a book you wrote about the ancient Greeks, about their mythology." Athena wanted to ask her urgently then if she had ready the story of Dryope, but instead she stood silently before her. "The Center is given books that the public libraries clear out," the Grecian deputy said.

"The ones that aren't in demand any more," Athena murmured, but before the deputy could speak again, Calliope was suddenly there with them, her face submissive and demure under the soft crown of graying braids.

"You're back, you're safely back," she said in a gentle voice, and then she addressed the deputy, holding her wit and her levity in check. "Athena invented the flute, you know," she said.

"She gave up playing the flute almost immediately after inventing it," Athena said, looking from the deputy's face under its soft helmet of red-gold hair to the muted beauty of Calliope, whose eyes burned marvelously dark and blue in her gypsy-wanton skull.

"She probably wanted to give more time to the bridle she was working on," Calliope said.

"Your account of her says she also developed legal ideas," the deputy said gravely and shyly, and now the bark appeared to drop from her lower legs, and from her thighs, falling away before it could reach the vital organs contained in her flesh.

"That's exactly what she was doing in the city courthouse all day today," said Calliope, and she ventured a low, nervous laugh.

"It seems out of character," Athena said, "but I'm obviously wrong. Every authority seems to agree that she gave up the flute because she didn't like the sight of herself with her cheeks puffed out."

"I hope nothing like that interfered with her plowing," Calliope said, and then she spoke of the book she held in her hand. "I found a life of Mozart in there," she said.

Athena had a burning need to know now about the lives of these two women, about Calliope's childhood and girlhood, and about the deputy's, a furious longing to see their mothers' and their fathers' faces, and to know whether father or mother had made them the gifts of heart and spirit that they bore. Because of the opposed choices they had made, there was a chasm between the two women that the voice or the hand of neither could reach across; but at what moment the choices had been made, and what had caused them to be made, she could not know until she had glimpsed the others who stood forever like sentinels behind them. Another time I'll ask them if it was the books they read or that were read to them, and what music was playing in their ears when each decided what she would do. Another time, another time, she thought, so giddy with hunger now that she could scarcely hear the words the two women were exchanging as she moved away.

The dormitories were abandoned at this time of the evening, and once Athena had found a cot whose vacancy was signified by a folded blanket at the foot, she sat down on the edge of it and mindlessly put the nightgown and towel and washrag in their designated places. In a minute, she would open out the sheets and stuff the stained pillow into its pillowcase, she thought, but now she lay down on the sagging mattress and closed her eyes. If she could dream at once, it would not matter about eating, but however desperately she willed it, she could not summon the familiar vision of the woman in biblical dress who carried a stray lamb through the blue of dusk. Instead, the hands of her three daughters drifted onto the screen, and an almost unbearable loneliness engulfed her. Paula's hands were the quick, eager, limber hands of a young boy, the backs of them tanned, the fingers expert on the strings of a cello, practical enough to clean the carburetor of a car and to thread a worm onto a hook without concern. Melanie had square-tipped fingers, like Rory's, and her knuckles protruded now, and heavy veins ran from knuckle to wrist, hands in sharp variance with the untouched beauty of her face; for these hands had scrubbed incalculable numbers of diapers; year in year out forced the coarsest materials under a sewing machine's bright, leaping needle; winter after winter clutched a shovel and flung the deep snow away from the commune doors. Sybil's hands did not belong in the same family as the others, or so it seemed, yet Athena had always known they were her own mother's hands returned to life, small and blue-veined, with absurdly childlike fingers, hands that were ill at ease with tennis rackets, brooms, and saucepan handles. These seemingly incompetent fingers could hold an artist's brush, or a palette knife, or a pen to write out the lines of poetry. There was Sybil's whale poem beginning:

> *The big cradle on the rippled waters*
> *Bowed to some silver coins: the jelly-fish,*

the words drifting, drifting out of Sybil's girlhood, like the current of the Gulf Stream flowing through Athena's memory:

> *The Empress whale flowed on.*
> *She laughed in a ladylike fashion*
> *And adjusted her waterfall crown,*

the words drifting, flowing, the tide moving in and out, the waves rising and falling, saying:

> *The whitest, richest cannibal had left a snail's*
> *Widest trail which none could follow without a coffin . . .*

But the dreamer could not accept that word as the last, not that as the ending, and Sybil's girlhood poetry flowed out of the sea, and across the beach and into the green fields filled with light, saying:

> *For Mama: I cannot add*
> *Nor even subtract*
> *Nor multiply*
> *Neither divide*
> *The number so simple*
> *The only figure*
> *I can understand*
> *But one, the only one*
> *One and all,*

and Athena dreamed that if she could touch their hands now, nothing, nothing else would matter, nothing else would ever matter in life, and then a hand was laid on her own, and she looked up, startled, into the black beads of Martha's eyes.

"I brought something for you to eat," Martha said in a low voice, and she took it out from under her apron, fixed neatly on a paper plate. There was a slice of buttered bread, with thin rounds of hard-boiled egg laid neatly on it, and on each round a curlicue of mayonnaise with a small fern of parsley planted in the center. "It was the best I could do," Martha said in the dimness of the dormitory, and she sat down on the edge of the next cot to watch Athena eat. "They drag you from pillar to post, and never so much as a thought given about where your next mouthful to eat will be coming from." She spoke in a hushed, surreptitious voice, barely louder than breathing, as if in fear of the bugging contraptions that might be placed under the mattresses, or in the drawer of the night table between them, or in the unlit bulbs in the low ceiling over their heads. "Year after year, I've been through it, and I'll tell you this much: sometimes I think it's the reason I started drinking in the first place. They drive you to it, with their lack of human consideration. They think nothing at all of keeping you in a holding cell from dawn to dark, cheek by jowl with women you wouldn't pass the time of day with if you were to meet up with them anywhere else. I'm not judging the prisoners themselves, poor souls, may the saints be my witness to that. There're enough others around to pass judgment on them and send them without rhyme or reason into 'the hell of dungeons and the scowl of night,' as the saying goes. It's the officers and the deputies, eating like royalty themselves and begrudging half a meal to anyone without brass buttons and braid plastered all over them. Isabelita, starving herself like a martyr for her mother and children, you can see she's been putting on weight since she's been in here." And then she stopped speaking for a moment, for the argument had turned itself the wrong way round, and she sat quiet, watching Athena eat. Her hair, free of the canvas kitchen cap now, was striped like a zebra's hide, jet black and pearly gray, and her penguin arms were tied delicately in at the wristbones, her thumbs leaning over backwards in their pliability. "Another thing that's on my mind," she began saying then, "is why didn't they teach Tallulah how to read and write in the solid year she's been locked up in this place? The answer to that is, they wanted to separate her from her children. Oh, they have their ways of destroying your life, the lot of them! I've been writing to my youngest son," she went on, and her eyes looked quickly at something else, perhaps at something she carried inside her like a nightingale in a cage. "It'll be his birthday in three days, and I've been setting down a lot of good advice for him about how to lead his life. He'll be nineteen, and he wants to be a singer," she said, her voice still cautious and low, as if even this might be used against them in some future time and place. She took out of her pocket a wedge of cheese and a half apple wrapped in a paper napkin for Athena's dessert. "Last year I got him an album of John McCormack singing, but this year I can't go in for anything like that. You should hear him singing 'Sure, a little bit of heaven dropped from out the sky one day,' every bit as good as McCormack, if not better, and there's one McCormack himself didn't have enough poetry in his soul to think of singing, and my son sings it to me on Sunday evenings when I'm home. Verse after verse the song has, and one of the best of them goes, 'I could scale the blue air, I could plow the high hills, Oh, I could kneel all night in prayer to heal your many ills!' It's a song about Ireland, about the country itself, and there's an Irish saying that every man with a good tenor singing voice goes to the devil, but I can't always be looking on the dark side of life. One day I'll take a trip with him over there, the youngest of the two. The other one's more like his father. I've never set foot on Irish soil," she said, her voice increasingly hushed, "but that's where we'll go, for God knows they don't pass the same kind of judgment on you over there. If I could live my life over again, I'd grow up in Ireland, first as a child, and then as a young girl, and there I'd meet a young man, maybe the age my own son is now, my youngest son, and he'd be a good dancer, for I loved to dance when I was young. And I'd have a drink with this young man of my heart, and no harm to it, and 'Spanish ale shall give you hope, Shall glad your heart, shall give you hope, Shall give you health, and help, and hope—' That's another of the verses of the same song," Martha said, her longing for Ireland possessing and consuming her now. She would shed America, this country that belonged to the past and the present, but not to the future; she would cast it aside, every moment and every memory of America wiped out as dreams are forever wiping out reality. "Oh, I've taken great decisions this time, I can tell you!" she said, her voice still wary. "I've made up my mind about what I'm going to be doing from now on, and no fooling about it! Never another drop, so help me God!"

"I'll tell you a few lines of a poem now, too," Athena said, getting up from the cot and picking up a still folded sheet. "It's a poem written by an Argentinian poet, a man named Borges, to an Irish writer named James Joyce."

"It was Joyce wrote *From Here to Eternity*, wasn't it?" Martha said. "They had the book in the library here a long time back, until one of the deputies had a look at it one day, and then they took it off the shelf." Martha had taken the other end of the sheet that Athena opened out, and she said: "Lay down on the other cot, Athena, and get some rest while I make up your bed for you."

"We'll do it together," Athena said. "Listen. The poem goes, 'In a man's single day are all the days of time. . . . Between dawn and dark lies the history of the world.' I think he's saying you don't have to go back in time to begin again, but that every day is a new chapter in history." They spread the worn sheet over the mattress and tucked the frayed ends of it in over the broken coils of the springs. "And it goes on," said Athena, "'From the vault of night I see at my feet the wanderings of the Jew, Carthage put to the sword, Heaven and Hell.'" Athena slid the stained pillow, flat as a doormat it was and not much cleaner, into the ragged case.

"As a matter of fact, and this is God's truth," Martha said, folding the top of the second sheet evenly down over the khaki blanket, and then smoothing it across with her quick, sure hands, "I wanted to ask you tonight for a line or two of poetry to put into the birthday letter I've been writing for him, for my youngest son. I brought along a bit of pencil and some paper." She took them out of her apron pocket and handed them to Athena across the cot. "There's nothing we can do about the sagging in the middle," she said. "These poor beds have to bear the terrible weight of all of us who have sinned."

"Shall I write, 'In a single day are all the days of time,' and, 'Between dawn and dark lies the history of the world'?" Athena asked.

"Maybe just a few words not quite so final as that," Martha said. "They don't give you much hope for the future, do they, all that about the vault of night, and the dawn and the dark, and the wandering Jew? It would be better to send him something to hold onto until I'm out again."

Now the prisoners were beginning to return, coming singly or in twos or threes, drifting back to the dormitory from the library shelves and the television screen. Athena sat on the side of her cot and put the paper on the night table, and after a moment she began to write.

"This is from the poem of an English poet named Blake," she said, and Martha stood with her hands folded under her apron, watching the few simple words being written down. "If the sun and moon should doubt," Athena wrote, "they'd immediately go out." She gave the paper and pencil to Martha, saying: "If this isn't what you'd like for him, I'll try to think of something else."

"I think that'll do," Martha said after a little silence, and she folded the paper over. "We'll see what comes of it," she said.

It was before final bed count, just before the lights were lowered, that Lydia told them she planned to work in the garden the long stretch of their final day. She wanted to get the last of the iris bulbs split apart and replanted so that they would be able to breathe in comfort for another year or two. And their minds must somehow have solidified in their skulls, Athena thought afterwards, for none of them recognized then that she was asking for accomplices, for accessories to the crime she was preparing to commit. Quite logical and right it seemed, when she spoke of it that evening, and none of them said either yea or nay as she swung her ear trumpet in one direction and then another, her white eyebrows cocked in question for the answers that did not come. Two nights and one day lay between them and liberty, and so far they had survived; surely nothing sensational could happen to them now. Indeed, the daylight hours had taken on an almost bearable progression, and it was only when night closed in on them that the presence of the women in the deeper regions of the Center pushed cement and stone and wood aside and assaulted the virtuous order of the dormitory dwellers' lives. The ceaseless pounding of fists and open palms against the closed and bolted doors, against the damp, crumbling walls, against the iron teeth of the bars, began with the coming of the night. Imprecations were shouted out from the solitary cells, strangled cries of rage, and from the lock-up wards came sobbing so broken, so despairing that it stopped the heart with its pain.

These women they could not see, but whose grief and outrage engulfed them in the dark, were like creatures on another, swiftly revolving planet crying out for succor as they spun past. They were not women who slept in prison-issue nightgowns between sheets, but disembodied souls, the wild spirits of the still undefeated, who had fought their way out of the castigated flesh to howl like beasts, to moan as if in excruciating labor, to shriek their protest against the unendurable anonymity of what had been offered them as life. They were the articulation of Martha's compliance; they screamed out Isabelita's repudiation of her unending acquiescence to man; they were the lunatic outcry of the silenced black girls, and the rage of the garbage ladies with their hands in pastel rubber gloves. They were the total wrath and virulence of all the disarmed and persecuted and subdued, shouting and cursing as they reeled from wall to bolted door and back to wall again, stampeding (save in those intervals when the deputies went to quiet them) from barred window to window that opened on nothing but a long hall of unending despair.

"Oh, Momma, Momma!" a voice cried out that night, accompanied by the screams of others, at times sharper than the ears could bear, at times attenuated, distant, as the planet on which the tortured were held captive went hurtling past in the dark. "Oh, Momma, Momma, my Momma, I never done nothin' to nobody! Oh, Momma, come take me back home! Momma, Momma, I don' need no whup, I don' need no chain!"

Athena sat upright in her cot and cried in a strident, unfamiliar voice:

"We have to stop this! We have to help them! This can't go on!"

And from the far end of the darkened dormitory, a black girl spoke lazily, as if roused from sleep and yawning between the words.

"Forget it, lady. They ain' doin' nothin' to her they ain' done to all of us. Tha' sister's fifty years ol' if she's a day. She never had no momma. She's fantasizin'. Don' go interferin' with her trippin'," she said, while the women on the other planet pounded their frantic messages out against the doors, the walls, the doors, the walls again, and on the tables where they laid their heads to weep.

XIII

AT SIX O'CLOCK in the morning, just before breakfast, Lydia touched the arm of Corporal Anxiety, who stood on duty at the kitchen door. Neither her old fingers nor her old voice trembled as she said she would not be able to work in the annex that day. She waited, half smiling, for an answer to be given, the ear trumpet raised in the direction of the deputy; but Corporal Anxiety simply turned her angular head away and looked past the breakfast line of women, looked up the long corridor, past the dim dormitory beyond, looking farther and farther into total vacancy. Because there was no answer, Lydia went on saying that it would be immoral for her to spend time sewing or ironing, or sorting clothes or blankets, when the irises were choking to death. She would leave the Center with a sense of accomplishment, she said, if she could see them all standing free of one another, not crowded and throttled, but upright, with the clipped fans of their sabers all curving the same way.

"Toward the sun, dear guardian, toward the sun," she repeated, saying it over and over like the deep tolling of an angelus. And, driven to it by Corporal Anxiety's silence, Lydia said at last: "I intend to work in the garden on our last day here, dear guardian of the peace, or I shall not work at all."

When she had come to this decision, the other demonstrators did not know, for she had not openly asked them for support, but merely smiled at them with her wise, knowing smile, strong as a giant, refreshed as long as Gandhi and Tolstoy were her accomplices in history. Yet even though no signal appeared to have been given, before Lydia could take her place in the breakfast line, the motherly dreadnought, breathing audibly, steamed down the hall and through the kitchen door, and she and Corporal Anxiety led Lydia away. They removed the black silk cord from around her neck, with the trumpet swinging at the end of it, perhaps classifying it as a deadly weapon, or perhaps in the belief that Lydia might use the cord as a noose to hang herself in whatever place of confinement they had in mind for her. It was certain that she did not for a moment suspect what the destination was to be, knowing nothing until the iron door, with its barred peephole grinning at the lock-up ward across the hall, closed her into the damp dark of the hole. But Callisto, coming down the corridor, had seen it taking place, and now she stood before them at the entrance to the kitchen and dining hall, facing prisoners and deputies alike, needing no one now, not even Calliope, as she gathered into her narrow hands, into her own direct circuit between impulse and act, the uncertainties and bewilderment of them all.

"Lydia has been taken away to be rehabilitated," she said, neither tragedy nor comedy in her ringing voice. "So I think all of us, all the demonstrators, should go on strike. I think we should refuse to work today, either in the kitchen, or in the annex, or in the garden, until Lydia has been restored to us. We will not eat until she is free," she said, and the demonstrators already seated at the long tables laid down their forks in guilt and set their coffee cups aside. "Even if it means we will not be released tomorrow, I think we have no other choice," she said.

The two deputies on duty made no move as the demonstrators at the tables, and those waiting in line just short of the stacked breakfast trays, followed Callisto out the door and up the hall. Athena put down the spatula she had been turning the pancakes with, and untied the strings of the denim apron, and laid it with the canvas cap on the larder counter. She could see

Callisto walking as if alone, moving a little ahead of the others, delicate-boned as a Vietnamese woman, her black hair hanging nearly to her waist, muted and modest, without anger and without fear, and all of them following where she led. But their final destination could only be the dormitories, and there they halted, while Callisto went on alone to the processing offices to ask for an interview with the lieutenant; Vietnam asking to speak with Miss U.S.A., Athena thought bitterly. And alone Callisto returned to the dormitory, where the women sat on the sides of their cots, waiting in silence for justice to be done. Although it was not yet seven o'clock, the deputy on duty had said the lieutenant was gone for the day.

"I wonder if Jesus knows what's happening on earth these days," Callisto said in a low voice the first time she came back. "Don't bother coming around, Jesus," she said without looking at anyone. "You have no boots on, and you have no helmet or gun. Better stay away." All that day, the ear trumpet, no longer conduit for speech or laughter or the sound of weeping, lay on the night stand by Lydia's cot. Once someone spoke of Lydia's arthritis, and another murmured that Lydia's heart was not strong, and that she was eighty-four years old; and through the long hours they saw her as their own deferred courage, as the act and the vocabulary of all they had not quite dared to do or say. The second time Callisto came back, she said to the demonstrators: "An Indian philosopher named Krishnamurti says that the only real creativity takes place when the mind is still. But how do we turn a shallow, noisy, racing little brook into a quiet lake, deep and reflecting and still, so still that the falling of a leaf on it can make it tremble with excitement? He says that if you have a strong enough desire for stillness, then you will find a way to it. I cannot be of much help to you, for what may be my most successful techniques for quieting the noise in my mind might not work for you at all. Sometimes I think it is enough to say that if we don't sit down and shut up once in a while, then we'll lose our minds even earlier than we had expected." The third time she came back, she did not speak, but even in her silence they knew she had not met with the lieutenant. The fourth time she spoke to them of Gandhi, saying: "I'm sure you're all feeling terribly hungry by now, so perhaps we should remember the greatest hunger-striker of all time, who fasted without mourning. He asked those who were arrested with him to enter prison joyfully, as the bridegroom enters the bridal chamber."

And without any warning, and from wherever she was far outside the prison, Athena thought she heard Lou, the harbor pilot's daughter, crying out with a snort of laughter:

"He must have said that before he got a good look at the bride!"

It was growing dark when the ornithology professor's wife, whom the pigeon named Daughter had lived with for three years, sat up on her cot and began to speak. Day by day, since they had been locked away from the world, her gray curls had turned into the wisps of a witch's hair, and her once rollicking laughter had come to have a cackling, hollow sound. But now that Lydia and the black girl called Bea had taken leave of them as finally as if in death, it may have been that she offered in homage the story of a hummingbird the professor had named Vervaine.

"It's the next to smallest bird in the world," she told them in the twilight of the dormitory, not crying it out hilariously, as was her wont, but still with a touch of waggery in it. "The only smaller bird is the Cuban Bee hummingbird, *Calypte helene*, and my husband has never been able to get his hands on one of those!" Ha, ha, she laughed, or tried to, but the new and terrible uneasiness that had stricken her now gave it a grimmer sound. "Vervaine is about three inches long and weighs less than an ounce," she went on saying, "and once a year my husband and his students have to clip her nails, all eight of them. That's because her claws curve out, and there's the risk of them getting caught in the branches of the miniature forest they've

set up for her. Her legs aren't any thicker than a thread of sewing silk, and if she struggled to get them free, she could snap
them in two." The story, with all its minutiae, took a long time
to tell, and in the growing dark they came to see the dazzling
green and gold of Vervaine's coloring. "It takes two to hold her
when they trim her nails," the professor's wife said, and she
added that *Mellisuga minima* was the Latin name of this verbena
hummingbird. Ha, ha, oh, God, ha, ha, ha, she laughed again at
the thought of two grown men holding a bird not quite three
inches long. And as if she had not already made it clear enough,
she spoke of the furious courage of all hummingbirds, saying
that even the Cuban Bee, the smallest bird alive, will fight any
bird that approaches its nest, no matter what its size. There were
experts in the field, she said, who maintained that hummingbirds
have the courage of a lion, and that they would attack beast, or
snake, or even man himself, if there was a threat to the tiny,
jeweled honey-suckers of its kind. "My husband saw Vervaine
attack a heron once," she said, and now she was undone by the
anguish of her laughter; "and not once, but over and over, until
the heron panicked, and picked up its long legs, and went flap-
ping off. Well, courage, not all of us have it," she began saying,
but she did not finish it, and whether or not Bea and Lydia were
in her mind there was no way to know.

And then Ann, sitting tense and upright on her cot, said in a
low voice:

"But they're not really non-violent then, are they? I mean, as
hummingbirds."

It seemed to Athena then that she must have fallen asleep as
she lay on her cot, for the professor's wife had ceased to speak
and now she could see Lou quite plainly, Lou on her crutches,
with her leg hanging down in its plaster cast and the two peace
signs inked on it, swinging across the dormitory, as palpable as
life itself, although by some slip-up in time she couldn't be there
until Christmas came around.

"Shit on your hummingbirds!" Lou shouted out with all the

old anger and contempt. "Lime-white, bird shit! Look, lady, we're in jail! What's the matter with that for reality? Can't we talk about where we are and about what we've seen happening in this place? Can't we talk about that instead of this crap about hummingbirds?"

But whether asleep or awake, Athena knew now that there was someone lying underneath the sagging mattress of her cot, under the broken springs. There had been no movement, no sound, and until she opened her eyes Athena thought it could be no one but Ann, frightened and lost in the presence of still another situation for which she had not been prepared. But then she saw Ann still sitting erect on the side of her own cot, murmuring about violence and non-violence in feathered bodies weighing less than an ounce, and at that moment quite another voice spoke in a whisper to her from the floor.

"O.K.," the voice said, "it's Isabelita come to say good-by, maybe to ask you about something you could do. Five o'clock tomorrow morning, you go, all of you getting out." Athena turned on her side and reached down with one hand, but Isabelita did not seem to see it there. For now she had begun the endlessly whispered story, claws and beak scratching frantically for sustenance in the barnyard as she talked, the story about children, and how they know very well, oh, very well, she said almost craftily, what's going to happen to them, talking so fast that some of the words were lost in the whispered bubbling of her fatal wound. "Kids keep on watching, and you and me, we don't know what the hell they're watching," she said, "maybe watching just to see how things are going to turn out"; and she said that was what her baby, did, the kid that died, because after kids have watched long enough, they make up their own minds whether to die or live.

"He kept watching my other kids, looking out of his crib like he was in prison," she went on with it. "He was always seeing my mother taking the other kids out, like when she went shopping, and leaving him behind. She didn't have no cart to take him along, no stroller-like. Maybe that was the first thing he was watching," she said, the words rushing softly, softly. "Or maybe the first thing was about eating. He was ten months old, so he didn't get to eat the same like the other kids, and he was maybe thinking he wouldn't never be able to catch up and get big like they was, maybe that. Who the hell's to know if he was thinking that if he wasn't big he wouldn't be able to get as much food as the others was getting? Maybe something like that." Swiftly, swiftly, the steady, muted hammering of her voice came from under the cot where she lay. "Or maybe it was something else," she said, the words coming faster and faster. "Maybe he'd be watching for me through the bars, like he was in prison, waiting for me to come home on Mondays when business wasn't no good, and when you're ten months old how you going to tell Monday from Tuesday, or tell Monday from any other day of the week? And so you gets tired of waiting, you ain't waited a long time, like everybody else in life, so you just stop breathing, and that's what he done. He died on a Sunday, like he'd been waiting all week for Monday to come around. He just stopped. The doctor said he just didn't go on breathing no more."

"I could go see your mother," Athena said. "San Mateo isn't far." For an instant she thought she would ask the mother and children to come live with her until Isabelita was free again. In her mind, she moved a bed from one room to another; perhaps bunk beds would be needed, or at least two youth beds, she thought. "I'll tell her you're working in the kitchen here, and eating well."

"I'll give you the telephone number," Isabelita whispered sharply. "You tell her I'm putting on weight. Maybe tell her to try treat all the kids the same way, no one treated no different to the others. Tell her I got a public defender working on my case. We don't know nothing sure, but maybe I got six months to go. They ain't going to let you take no paper out," she went on saying, "so I'll write it on your ankle. I seen girls doing that one time. I got a ball-pen with me," she said, and Athena sat up on the edge of her cot, and put her bare feet on the floor, and in the half dark Isabelita wrote the seven digits on her left anklebone. "There's a coupla colored girls hiding under your friend's bed over there," was the last thing she said, "under Mrs. Calliope's bed. They been talking like crazy to her over there. They oughta be ashamed of themselves, sneaking in when nobody's looking. I oughta tell the deputy and get them kicked out," and then she wasn't there any more.

XIV

JUST AS THEIR CLOTHES, their handbags, their bracelets and earrings, their identities, had been taken from them when they entered prison, so their protest was now subverted. They had been given no receipt for it, it was honored by no acknowledgment, and therefore it had never taken place. At five in the morning of the tenth day, they were all set free.

"I had a very satisfactory night's sleep," Lydia told them as they crowded in relays into the dressing room, carrying with them the pillowcases which held the apparel of their separate lives. Lydia's coarse white lashes hung heavily over her almost opaque, brass-colored eyes, and they kissed her withered cheeks and shouted their homage to her through the ear trumpet that they passed with reckless gaiety from mouth to mouth. They were about to go free, free as the wind, and nothing else mattered now. "When you're old, sleep is always not far away, ready to accustom you to what lies ahead," Lydia murmured, trying in the confusion to distinguish her own sneakers from the prison pair that she must leave behind.

It was half-past five when they walked out into the chill of dawn toward those who waited at the gate, toward the known faces, the familiar cars, moving numbly back into their own lives again. "We couldn't sleep last night because . . ." one of them might begin saying to husband or brother or friend, and then was unable to finish it; or another might say: "We've been on hunger strike for twenty-four hours . . . ," and not be able to go on; but the invisible thread that had bound the women together had already begun to stretch thinner and thinner, finer and finer, until it seemed about to break, but it would not break. Those who had come to take them home had not worked in the sewing and ironing room, or in the kitchen or the laundry, or in the garbage courtyard, and had not heard the names Martha and Isabelita and Tallulah, or looked on the anonymous others to whom the demonstrators were committed forever in uneasiness and guilt.

Calliope, in her emerald velvet suit, was fast in the embrace of a lively, stubborn-fleshed man with dark, Spanish eyes, who moved as if dancing on the balls of his feet. He wore a jacket of soft, heather-colored tweed, and a white shirt open on his handsome throat, and energy zigzagged visibly from his solid shoulders, like the rendering of vibrations around a figure in a comic strip. He was not tall, but this energy that snapped and crackled in an aura around him gave him a look of height and of authority. This would be Arion, Athena knew; and whether it was envy of their commitment to each other, or the grief of jealousy that constricted her heart, she did not know; but she had to turn her head from the sight of this flamenco dancer of a man holding Calliope close in his arms in the clear light of the still unsullied day. Siddhartha, in his woven yellow cloak of the ascetic, was not met by poonghies in religious robes, but by an abashed, middle-aged couple, overcome, it seemed, by their own unworthiness to be the parents of this dedicated, shaven-pated man. And was not the father, Athena thought with a start of recognition, a man who worked behind a wicket at the main post office, who had said to her in weariness one day: "Twenty-five years of window work, mostly money orders"; and once, when an irate man in a business suit had elbowed others aside to shout through the wicket that he was not going to tolerate having his office mail delivered by a long-haired, barefooted post-man, had not this man who now placed his arm around Siddhartha replied: "All I can tell you, sir, is that he had shoes on when he left here."

Lydia was led away by a half dozen of her communards, who packed her into a Volkswagen bus; the librarians and school-teachers were met by other librarians and schoolteachers, and were borne off, taking St. Theresa with them. The college girls were met by other college girls, wearing ankle-length skirts and bulky sweaters; the young minister with downy cheeks was re-trieved by other grave young ministers; and for a moment Athena saw the poet in his bowler hat, his silver-headed cane under his arm, standing melancholy as a heron on the cement walk, and then three young women with flowing hair and swirl-ing paisley skirts ran to him on sandaled feet and swept him into their car.

Athena and Ann, who had no relatives to meet them, were to ride back to the city with the bearded professor who had traveled in the paddy wagon with them ten days before. His wife was picking him up, he said as his eyes searched the bleak landscape for her, and when he saw her at the wheel of their car, with its bumper sticker reading "Another Family for Peace," the gray of his face and the gray of his beard seemed to kindle with light. She slid over on the seat so that he could drive, and then she turned to look with tired, violet eyes at Athena and Ann seated behind. The lawyers had told them the demonstrators would be freed around six, she said, but she couldn't wait, and had come at four, and watched the morning star fade from the sky.

"Probably Venus," said the professor, clearly an authority on any subject that might arise. Athena could not remember which department he was in (psychology, political science, interna-tional relations?). "Unless, of course, the planets took it into their heads to change their habits while we were behind bars." He spoke with a great show of joviality as he turned the key in the ignition, and in the instant before they left, Athena's eyes were drawn to the car window, summoned there as if a voice outside had called her name. Beyond the waiting cars and the freed prisoners and the strangers who had come for them, beyond the sheriff's deputies with their holsters at their hips, Calliope stood quite alone, separate from the others, separate from Callisto and the tall, haggard, praying mantis of a man who must be Eric, apart from Arion even, looking at Athena, giving her this sign and signal concerning all that lay ahead. "Did you have the oil changed?" the professor asked his wife, and then the car moved off between the barbed wire barricades.

"We've heard the classes at college went off well," said the professor's wife. Her arm in the navy and white checked silk of her sleeve lay along the back of her husband's seat, and she spoke across her shoulder to Athena. "All the teaching assistants did nobly," she said, "and your students' papers are waiting on your desk. I saw them when I looked in at your office on the way to pick up Lionel's mail."

"Oh, we had a great time! We held seminars as usual every day!" the professor said, and his ears moved back a little as he grinned.

"You didn't have daily jobs to do?" Athena asked, but because her heart was at peace now, she spoke absently. There was a covenant between her and Calliope, and the voices of these others could scarcely be heard.

"They couldn't make up their minds what to do with us," the professor said, laughing outright as he drove. "They couldn't very well ask us to dig potatoes or work in the carpentry shop the way the regulars did."

"But we did the same work as the other women," Athena said.

"Probably *jure divino* in our case!" the professor said, driving fast. "We had an excellent seminar in Eastern religions from a young man who had studied in India, and another in international relations, and a very fine one in ornithology. I gave a class of a kind in Latin," he said in a modest aside. "Our professor of ornithology was quite a remarkable old boy, seventy-three years old and due to retire this year. I learned from him, for instance, that the nomenclature 'falcon' is a generic term applying to any bird of prey that is trained to hunt small game for man. So in this sense, although most falcons are hawks, owls and eagles can also bear that name if they have been trained for falconry. We learned a lot about hummingbirds, too," he said.

"How fascinating!" his wife cried out.

"I'm driving fast," the professor continued, the tone of his voice not changing, "because I want to get home in time to have breakfast with my kids, and then drive them to school, which is what I usually do. Where is it you people would like to go?"

"Where do you want to be taken, Ann?" Athena said to the side of the girl's cheek, and to the lengths of vermilion wool that had been woven again in and out of the glossy braids. "Where do you live, little Ann?" she asked.

"I can't go home, I can't go there," Ann said softly, her face still turned to the window and the wind-swept hills.

"But what else can you do?" Athena asked her, her voice low so that the others would not hear. "Perhaps this is a good time for you to go back, after ten days of nothing being said."

"I want to stay with you," Ann said, still not turning her head.

Athena gave the professor her address, and she took Ann's hand in hers, and as they came to the city the professor drove faster and faster, risking the crossing of intersections on yellow lights, swinging around cars that had halted at stop signs, impatiently blaring his horn. Athena felt Ann's fear pass through her flesh, and she looked down at the long tapering, utterly helpless, feminine fingers, knowing that to be without defenses is in itself a ruthless defense.

"Your hands are not like my daughters' hands," she said. "My daughter Sybil has my mother's hands."

"My mother . . ." Ann began saying, her profile set in child-like perplexity against the window on the other side. The professor drove faster, faster, he and his wife hastening home to their children and to the seclusion of their life together, barely able to wait to get the two strangers who rode with them out of the car.

In another five minutes, Athena and Ann stood on the sidewalk before the three-story, white Victorian house, its ground floor veined with ivy, a flight of granite steps leading up to the front door. Athena took out her key and looked at the shrublike tree that grew in its square of soil beside the steps, not a dark cypress, which might have been more in character here, but a handsome enough little tree, its golden and light green tassels giving it a blithe, springtime air. She saw in relief that its branches had not been freshly broken, although through the years its crest had been whipped off a dozen times by passing children, or passing drunks who left their empty half pints at its roots. The sign she had thumbtacked to its trunk a month ago was there still, the words printed on cardboard with a heavy black marker: "This tree wants to live as much as you do. Please help it to survive." But under this message, someone had written now in blue crayon: "Bless you, my dear," and another hand had slashed across it in red: "Fuck both of you!"

Above was the dark green door and the curved bay windows framed in the same deep green as the polished leaves of the vine. And there was the gold leaf scroll set like a signature at the end of the last century between the first and second floors. Athena and Ann mounted the flight of steps to the portal, the vestibule, the propylaeum, the nook or cranny, whatever name it should be given, Athena could never decide, where four smooth white columns bore the flower-heads of their Corinthian capitals on high. Behind the beveled glass pane in the door hung a delicately tinted poster that illuminated the portico like an actual light. In the foreground of it were green rice paddies, and bent figures in wide straw-colored hats working in them. In the background, flames of destruction blazed into the sky, and above the tranquil countryside of Vietnam, the eagle of the American Air Force, black as thunder, was poised in hooknosed wrath.

"I love this house," Ann said in wonder as Athena unlocked the door.

"I'll get the hose out right away and wash the sidewalk down," Athena said, and then she saw that the ivy, reaching so eagerly around the basement windows below had recently been watered, for drops clung still to the dark, polished, open-palmed leaves. "Probably Luchies McDoniel," she said. "He's the man who has the upholstery shop at the corner. It's only eight o'clock, if you can believe it!"

Behind the house, the garden waited in the first light of the sun, waiting without complaint for bird calls to return in another season. Although it was October, roses bloomed still, some tea-colored with ivory hearts, some with full-blown petals as thick as cream, nor had the dripping hearts of fuchsia altered in color. The oblong slope of lawn had prepared the way for winter with an outlay of lush, daisy-studded grass. Only the Japanese plum and the tremulous young eucalyptus had begun to shed their leaves.

"It was a dump five years ago," Athena said as she took Ann down the back steps onto the grass. "My daughters made it into what it is now." A Monterey pine stood fuller and taller than any other tree in the garden, and Athena touched its silky tines. "Our first Christmas here, Paula got it from a nursery across the bay. It was so small that she carried it in its swaddling clothes— you know, the sacking they put around uprooted trees to keep them damp." She led Ann across the grass that softly and deeply embraced their feet. "And here is the eucalyptus," she said, and she heard her own voice go strangely grim. It had never learned to stand alone, and now, although lashed to a strong bamboo pole, it leaned, half fainting, against the house. "Senseless mauve leaves," she said, not calling them tears, "always clogging up the rain gutters and the drain. Melanie, my youngest daughter, planted it. It was about a foot high that year," she said, and for a moment she did not say any more. Sybil's tree was the single redwood, the sequoia, in the corner by the high driftwood fence.

It was barely as tall as a man, and its fernlike branches seemed never to cease in movement, its needles shimmering, shimmering in the subtlest of timeless mysteries as its great roots reached down through the covering of dark earth to sand, and through sand to the iron rock of a long dead age. "When we bought the house, it was a dead stump," Athena said. "I wanted to have it hacked out and hauled away. But Sybil sees the possibility of life in everything, not dramatically, but really quite sensibly, as though things—people even—were blank pages or empty canvases that she can do something with. And she transformed it—"

Ann had not spoken, but now the look in her eyes interrupted Athena, and she was startled by what she saw. *Oh, God, not pity!* she kept herself from crying out. *This I will not, cannot have! I am the one who reaches out a hand to those who are engulfed in the wave! This is what the Greeks demanded of man, simply by the way they lived and died. Tragedy, gallantry, and fortitude they asked of man, but not his pity! Have I presented myself as one bereaved?*

"If I could stay with you, I could help with the garden and everything in the house," Ann said, speaking in almost craven humility.

And *No!* thought Athena, and she moved toward the wooden steps leading to the kitchen, on the railing of which lemon-and-orange-trumpeted nasturtiums twisted and turned and intertwined their zany way. *Never, never!* But another part of her mind was strangely tempted. She put the kettle on for tea, and took the pound cake from the refrigerator.

"Perhaps you could get the cups and saucers out of the cupboard, Ann, and the spoons out of the drawer," she said, thinking: *Ann could have the little bedroom on the garden. I could move my papers and typewriter, and even the files, down to the dining room.* She put the pound cake in its foil trough on a straw mat on the table, and set a knife beside it. *She could just walk out on her family and stay here,* Athena's mind went on with it, *because she is going to do that anyway, and this would*

be a stopping place for her on her way to living her own life.
Aloud she said: "After we've had some tea and cake, you must
try to sleep. The sofa in the living room is wide as a bed. I'll
bring a blanket down. And then I have to drive quickly, quickly
up to college and get my papers straightened out. At nine tomorrow morning, I have a class."

"I won't be able to sleep," Ann said, her eyes a little wounded.
So fragile she was, sitting there eating a slice of cake and drinking the tea. Her skin was like tinted porcelain, her eyebrows
fine as the sable-tipped paintbrushes in Sybil's watercolor box.
"I could work in the house while you're gone, or do some shopping for you," she said.

"I'll be back some time in the afternoon. I'll do the marketing
on the way home," Athena said, "and then we'll have lunch or
supper, or whatever the meal will be. But now you should sleep.
Sleep brings all kinds of answers."

"But I already know the answer," Ann said.

Alone in her bedroom, Athena stood for a time before the tall,
oval mirror, brushing out her hair. There, to the right, on the
chest of drawers was Rory looking at her with such sorrow and
wisdom, his head and shoulders imprisoned in a silver frame.
There he was, and there was her own reflection, and she spoke
harsh words to it, saying: *Now that you have learned to do without anyone, you have put yourself into solitary confinement, and
you will allow no one the authority to set you free.* She wanted
the underground woman who had set the barriers to have the
power of speech and hearing and action wrested from her. She
wanted Calliope, with her quick, extenuating humor (which
was courage), and Callisto, with her bell-like singing (which
was courage), to drive the other woman out. She saw her hollow
cheeks, and the high arch of her nose, and the almost stern set
of her mouth in the glass as she brushed her hair, and she remembered the poet Gabriela Mistral saying: "Let me be more
maternal than a mother; able to love and defend with all of a
mother's fervor the child that is not flesh of my flesh. . . . Grant

that I may be successful in molding one of my pupils into a perfect poem . . ."

And then she willed herself to accomplish the old miracle of self-effacement, as she had often done as a child, and as a girl, and as a woman: standing motionless, she stared at her own face in the glass, seeing through it and beyond it, until it was there no longer, until first the face and then the body below it were entirely wiped away. Once Rory had swung her around from the mirror and said: "Suppose you wiped yourself out permanently, suppose you never came back on the screen! How in the name of God would I ever find you again?" And now the glass before her was completely blank, and Athena said to it: *Now I can start over again.*

After she had changed her earrings and put fresh lipstick on her mouth, she went down the softly carpeted stairs, skirted the living room, where Ann slept on the sofa, and quietly closed the front door behind her. The garage was two houses down in this block of totally disparate houses, some painted pink, some gray, some olive green, and as she passed the tasseled tree in its enclosure the final words on the cardboard sign tacked to its trunk shouted out after her and the underground woman, "Fuck both of you," and she began to laugh.

XV

IT WAS SIX O'CLOCK in the evening when Athena came back to the house, carrying in her arms two heavy paper bags packed with the food and drink that would make the blood course faster in their veins. In one was a bottle of red Dubonnet and a Paul Masson burgundy, and she sat it on the kitchen table with care. In the larger bag were three filet steaks, and she thought of them with pleasure, each the size of the palm of a hand; beneath them was a round container of whipped butter, a head of soft-leafed garden lettuce, a loaf of sour French bread, a riddled square of Swiss cheese, a ripe avocado, and strawberries in a little green basket of woven plastic. Ann stood by the table watching her take one thing after another from the bags, watching Athena with brown, light-flecked eyes that seemed to bear a reproach, a rebuke, in them. Her braids had been re-done and they lay as smooth as satin across her shoulders, and, as she watched, her small hands reached forward to help, then fell useless by her sides again. She said she hadn't known whether or not to water the garden, and that a tall black man had rung the doorbell in the afternoon, a big man with a pointed beard, asking to see Athena.

"It was certainly Luchies McDoniel," Athena said. She opened the refrigerator door and took out a tray of ice cubes, and put ice into two squat blue glasses that had been waiting for ten days now, upside down on the drying rack. Then she cut two twists from a parched half lemon left in the refrigerator's vegetable drawer. "I'll call him after we've had something to eat," she said, and she poured the ruby-red Dubonnet in over the ice.

"If you left directions with me every time you went out," Ann said, standing there hesitant, defenseless, her eyes holding some kind of nameless blame, "like, vacuum the dining room, or mop the kitchen—well, then I would know, and I could be of help to you—"

"There's an artificial lemon somewhere for the salad," Athena murmured absently. "I forgot fresh ones. It will have to do." She seemed not to have heard Ann speak, but within her the words "every time" that Ann had spoken were tolling in the room like a tocsin, like a death knell. *So now*, she thought, *I shall have to commit the murder. Now I shall have to say things that will stab over and over into her heart.*

"Did you meet with students today?" Ann asked.

Athena was taking the lettuce and strawberries from the upright bag, and although Ann's voice was casual enough, in it Athena discerned the unmistakable sound of—(*what?* she asked herself; *was it actual concern over the presence of others in her life, the trembling, inexpressible fear of loss of the entirety of love?*). But Ann was suddenly released to action now, and she carried the basket of strawberries and the silky-leafed head of lettuce to the drainboard, and then she reached into the cupboard over her head with uncertain authority and took the salad bowl from the shelf. To Athena it seemed that every gesture Ann made was affirmation that this place was her own habitual setting, and whatever she touched, table or chair, bowl or fork or spoon, and even the moments of Athena's daily life, had become familiar possessions that she would not, could not, share.

"I talked with a dozen or so students," Athena said; "talks the college likes to call 'conferences.' I'll tell you about at least one who makes the walls of that place crumble away." It was always the first swallows of Dubonnet in her veins, when she had not eaten and needed sleep, that started her talking fast and recklessly. She lit the oven and put a half of the loaf of French bread in, and then set the table quickly, while Ann washed the lettuce at the sink. "He is my dark-eyed Orion, the leaping hunter, who may or may not be Indian. He's been a student of mine for more than a year, he and his two handsome Samoyed dogs, who follow him everywhere. He's twenty years old, or twenty-one, with straight black hair down to his shoulders, and strong white teeth such as no Native American is legally permitted to have. Orion Sweetwater, Son of the Moon, that's his name," she said, and as she poured more Dubonnet over the ice in her glass she had an unexpected vision of Martha's round forearm, the skin of it like white crepe paper, the little red knob of the elbow at the end, and the hand reaching out for the glass Athena held.

"But who *is* he?" Ann asked, laughing at his name. She stood at the sink in her thigh-short dress, her bare legs tapering and slim, her narrow feet on the brick-colored tiles.

"He's my student," Athena answered. "One of the few—he and the Filipino students—the few in any year who turn the metal files along the wall into accordions playing, and who make the cold steel desk and the swivel chair run after them like mercury down the hall." The raw steaks sizzled as she placed them on the broiler, and she took another swallow of Dubonnet and went on saying: "Orion may be a name he's chosen for himself, but that's all right. Think of the saints' names that Catholic children are given, the name of 'Jesus,' for instance, given to little Spanish boys so they'll know in which direction to go. He had to find a name for himself because he doesn't know who his mother and father were. He was adopted at six weeks, so he had no set of saints handed down to him—not verbally and not in writing—and so he's seeking the right to his own name. Oh, the avocado!" she said. She took it from the bottom of the grocery bag and handed it to Ann. When she had folded the bag and put it with the stack of them under the sink, she poured more Dubonnet into her glass, and drank, and said: "I'll make the dressing while you slice the avocado." She opened the broiler door and turned the steaks, and then took the half loaf from the oven in a folded napkin, and laid it in the flat basket on the table. "Because Orion was uprooted from his past," she said, "whatever that past was, because he was abandoned, adopted, he is seeking his way back in time, laughing a lot with those fine teeth, not blaming anyone, but seeking something way back at the beginning, something very different from those who abandoned him or those who adopted him were able to provide." She was mixing olive oil with celery salt and parsley flakes, and the second, or perhaps the third, Dubonnet was running like magic in her blood. "He follows the harvest, working hard at it," she said. "Pickets with Chavez, reads Paiute and Iroquois and Osage poetry," and she could see Orion laughing as he talked, and the Samoyed dogs at his feet yawning and looking up at him in hope that he was about to move on at last, and she could hear his voice saying: "I have to find my father and have it out with him. That's why I'm always in a hurry." Athena pulled out the broiler rack, turned off the gas, and searched for the artificial lemon on the refrigerator's lowest shelf, and found it, and returned quickly to Orion. "Whether he's Indian or not," she said, "he's almost certain of who he is when he reads aloud something from the prophet Smohalla, lines like, 'You ask me to cut grass and make hay and sell it, and be rich like white men! But how dare I cut my mother's hair?' And—wait a minute—" Athena took the steaks from the broiler, and placed them on a platter. "Put the salt and paper napkins out," she said to Ann. "Or lines like, 'You ask me to dig for stone! Shall I dig under my mother's skin for her bones? Then when I die I cannot enter her body to be born again!' The earth, Smohalla was writing about the earth," Athena said, hastening to rebate the name of mother before the small mask of personal distress could throw its shadow on Ann's face again.

"Did you too have to go on a search to find your father and

mother the way Orion does?" Ann asked, bringing the talk back
to where she wanted it to be.

She carried the salad bowl, filled to the brim now with lacy
green, to the kitchen table, and when she had set it down she
took the first taste of the drink that had stood untouched before
her place.

"I never found my father," Athena said. "I was too proud
to seek him out." She pulled the cork from the bottle of red
wine, and carefully filled the two small, stemmed glasses. "You
may not be able at this moment to accept the accusation we
have to face about our fathers," she went on saying, speaking
cruelly, callously, in preparation for the murder of this child's
mindless love. Ann had begun tentatively to eat, and Athena
broke off the heel of the French loaf and passed it to her.
"There's unsalted butter in that container," she said, and she
put the bowl of salad closer to Ann. She had drunk quickly down
the little glass of red wine as she talked, and now the sweet
butter spread on the ring of bread between her teeth was as fresh,
as pure, as if scraped two minutes before from the bedewed
hollow of a wooden churn. She remembered suddenly that the
last time she had eaten was the pound cake and tea at nine
this morning, and before that stretched the twenty-four-hour
hunger strike. As she began to eat, she was filled with inexpressible delight with the taste of the rare, tender steak, with the
browned crust of the bread, and with the delicate lettuce leaves.
If she had started to eat simply to keep the thoughts clear in her
head, she ate now because of the wonderful pleasure in it, knowing that all she had been trying to say must in the end be something more than ramblings poured out of a bottle of Dubonnet,
or that came, glass after glass, from a bottle of red wine. It was a
calculated report that she wanted to give Ann, a factual dis-
course on parents' loss of their children either in the finality of
death or the temporality of life. It was a canny appeal, without
a teardrop of pity in it, for those who had given their children
breath, and with whom they could no longer speak. "The silence

between fathers and children is like a tombstone set on the grave of the very meaning of life," she said, and because of the foolish sound of these words, she added quickly: "You must eat, Ann. You must eat a great deal! We haven't brought about peace yet. There is still a lot to do."

"There's more lettuce on the drainboard," Ann said, and she stood up from her chair.

"Yes!" Athena cried out. "You must eat everything!" She put the third steak on Ann's plate, and filled up her own glass with wine again. "Perhaps that is why the priest-confessor was brought into being in religion," she went on saying, "simply so that the child could speak to the father, and the father to the child, across that terrible barrier of fear."

"But I don't understand what you're trying to tell me," Ann said softly. She was sitting at the table again, her hands halted in the act of putting fresh lettuce leaves into the bowl. "I don't understand at all," she said, and the color seemed to have ebbed from her face.

"Once you told me you went to prison so that your father would be able to speak out again. Perhaps you said that because you sensed that if we can't speak to one another out of our own limited, circumscribed lives, then the wider reconciliations can't possibly take place," Athena said. "My father gave me my absurd name, but I never reproached him for the impossible burden it put on me. I felt it my duty to justify that name, and I went cringing and crawling back to the Greek myths, and because of the image of that other woman, I wasn't entitled to one false move. Every moment of the night and day was a separate demand to behave morally and responsibly. I was at the same time in the ridiculous position of being both the goddess of war and the goddess of peace, and I knew my father had condemned me to this duality. I blamed him," she went on, again filling her wine glass to the brim, "and the more I learned about the daughter of Zeus, the more fiercely was I split in two. I was a model daughter, trying to re-enact all that had taken place at least a thousand years before the coming of Christ. And while I became a part of that ancient unreality, I was also another woman—a girl like you, first of all—and I wanted to take part in contemporary acts of fortitude, and gallantry, and tragedy. I got married young, and had children, but for a long time I dared not reject my classical role. I was always two women, one visible and understandable to everyone, and the other one functioning underground, and both of them learned long after my father was dead that I should have gone to him one evening, on an evening exactly like this one, and made something else out of the silence between us simply by asking him to allow me a choice."

"But what choice?" Ann asked, speaking barely above a whisper. For the first time, she lifted the small, stemmed glass before her plate and took a swallow of wine, and her childish hand trembled helplessly as she set the glass down again. "I don't understand what choice you mean."

"I don't know the exact words," Athena said after a moment. "Perhaps the two words are freedom and submission. I've come to all my decisions late, and those are the two I've found it the simplest to use. It may be there isn't time in anyone's life for more complicated alternatives. But sometimes," she said almost uncertainly, "sometimes when you're young one word can get confused with the other, freedom with submission, submission with freedom, and then it's hard to work things out." She had never talked to Ann about Melanie, of the life she had submitted to in the name of freedom, and she had no wish to do so now. "Take the human weakness for community worship, the idolizing of one man, one seemingly unassailable power, that is truly submission, isn't it?" she asked. "Yet other, quite different names are given to it by those who have surrendered their wills. Do you remember Dostoevski saying, writing, that there are only three forces that can hold the weak and the unhappy captive, and these are miracle, mystery, and authority?"

"I haven't read Dostoevski," Ann murmured, "but I will, I will."

"A man may promise freedom to those who have come under his power," Athena said, and now the promise of fame and fortune, fame and fortune, that Pete the Redeemer had made them all was stampeding in her mind. "But he is actually binding and unbinding as he wishes the frail, trembling eucalyptus branches of each follower's bonded will. Freedom and submission are much simpler words than miracle, mystery, and authority. They may be the only words you will need when you start talking with your father."

Ann's hand was shaking still as she touched the stem of the wine glass again, but she did not lift the glass to drink.

"When I talk with my father?" she said barely aloud. "You mean that is what I should do?"

"Yes," Athena said; and now the murder had been committed, and she jumped up from the table, and carried their two dinner dishes to the sink, for the time to eat the strawberries had come. She set the dishes down on the drainboard, thinking: *Tomorrow. I can do them tomorrow. Tomorrow everything will be possible.* She held the plastic basket under the running water, tipping it one way and then another so that the cold, bright flow would not bruise the rosy flesh. Then she brought the strawberries and her mother's silver sugar bowl back to the table, where Ann sat stricken, the dagger quivering in her heart. "This is the way we used to eat them in France," Athena said.

She sat down opposite Ann, and she poured wine from Ann's glass into her own, and then she began plucking the stems from the strawberries, and one by one she dropped the soft, ripe fruit into the half-filled glasses of red wine. When the glasses could hold no more, she spooned sugar in, and she and Ann, as if mesmerized, watched the separate, glistening grains seep down through the wine and settle on the strawberries in drifts of rosy snow.

"You said that you should have gone to your father on an evening exactly like this one, so you mean I should not stay here with you. Is that what you mean, Athena?" Ann asked at last.

"Yes," Athena said again, and she stirred the strawberries slowly, slowly in her glass. "People of different generations should not try to live together. The demands can be terrible in their tragedies. You will make your own life, and you will not forget to come back and tell your father, and mother, and me, about it. But you will have to do it alone, for no god, no Buddha, no Mohammed, not even through the example of his own suffering, has ever been able to tell us how to live with other people, and so we have to find out alone. But first taste this special dessert I made for you!" Athena cried out with a show of gaiety. "Taste how good it is!"

Obediently, Ann spooned the strawberries out of her glass, and drank the sweetened wine. Before they left the table, she asked in a faint voice:

"Isn't the father always the outsider?" But Athena did not have any answer to give.

It was dark as midnight when they went out to the car, and into the chill of the Pacific coast. Athena drove leisurely, with a new sense of luxury, for it had been a long time since they had seen anything as beautiful as the shimmering lights of the city flung lavishly out below. The way to Ann's house was winding and steep, and as they drove higher and higher, far below the hills the variegated colors of the street and harbor lights took on a remarkable symmetry, a seemingly natural, predestined order, like that of the stars, a clear and steadfast design that delivered the night from its chaotic dark. Athena took deep, happy breaths in gratitude that there were no longer doors to close fast behind them and before them, no longer keys turning, and turning again, in iron locks. No longer was any limit set on the amount of air they were permitted to breathe, for now they were free in even the simplest of ways: free to move without explanation from one place to another, to look up at the sky without thickets of barbed wire tangled between them and the clouds by day, the planets by night. They were free to take decisions as simple as whether or not to buy a loaf of bread, or how to arrange the hours of the day to satisfy all that clamored for attention, free to be alone, in silence, if that was what one chose.

"Now we've really left everything behind, haven't we?" Ann said softly. In the seat beside Athena, she was leaning a little forward in order to see the ever widening, ever more intricate display of jeweled necklaces and tiaras that encircled the black satin of the water below, and the pendants and earrings of light that showered the black velvet of the land. "I don't feel any bars anywhere," Ann said, her voice singularly happy now that the decision had been taken. Once they had climbed as high as the land itself appeared to go, Ann said: "This is the house," speaking softly, and Athena parked the car at a tilt on the nearly perpendicular slope.

They paused for a moment, standing together on the sidewalk, and for a moment there was no distance between them because of the strong, the nearly irresistible pull of the night as it soared above them, the high, endless vault of the night arching without limit or interdiction above all that was imprisoned by gravity below. In the shallow wash of light from the streetlamp at the corner, a flight of rustic wooden steps could be seen mounting from the slabs of paving up, up the cascading slope of the garden, the streetlight falling like dust on the yucca swords and bleached hibiscus flowers, and on the pale, thick tongues of cactus, and the scrolls of giant fern. It was Ann who took Athena's hand to lead her up the steps, for now they had exchanged roles, and Ann became the guide and the protectress and Athena the child not certain of the way. Hand in hand, they followed the flagstones of the path through the hush of the densely planted garden, moving under the boughs of twisted, stunted olive trees toward the glow from the lanterns of fretted metal mounted high on each side of the front door. Fancy as lace, archaic as a phaeton, these lanterns were, Athena reflected; carriage-gate fixtures with no driveway leading to them, forever alien to the tropical, untamed growth of the garden on which they shed their light.

There was a long moment to wait for the bell to be answered, and then abruptly he stood framed in the narrow opening of the doorway, his heavy shoulders stooped, his whole being held in weary abeyance, this man who had been before no more than a faceless, fleshless symbol in their talks.

"Good God," he said, and when he opened the door wider to let them in, it could be seen that he held a pistol in his right hand. "Come in," he said, his voice tired, defeated, his glance sliding away. "The dogs are up in the country, getting some training," he said, not adding, "because with my capped teeth I can't whistle any more," and he went on saying: "My son's away at college, and my wife's out. You never know who may be marauding around the place." He dropped the pistol into the pocket of his tweed jacket. "Of course, we have a security guard on duty, covers the whole block. It's a good neighborhood, but far for friends to come. Friends!" he repeated, and he gave a short laugh as he closed the door behind them. Even though not in uniform, he was to Athena the likeness of every American colonel or major, or whatever the rank may have been, whom she had seen in the Post Exchanges and the Officers' Clubs, or passing by on the streets of foreign cities, except for the torment in his vein-lashed eyes. He turned to usher them past the mustard-colored, velvet portieres in the wide doorway to the left, and into the first of four large drawing rooms that opened one into the other; and, following him, Athena found herself studying the heavy, scarred back of his neck, the thick roll of flesh, from which Ann had said his hair had been uprooted to be transplanted to his crown. "I suppose you're from the prison?" he said, his faded blue eyes, his ruddy jowls, the small beak of his flushed nose, turned toward Athena. The three of them stood on the deep pile of the oriental rug, embraced by the light of an outsized floor lamp, but he did not look at his daughter. Communication was to be conducted between the two upholders of decency and order, this was his cunning plan, and Ann might not have been there at all. "We made inquiries and found out where she was," he said, his eyes so wretched, so bleak that it seemed they could never light with a spark of passion or tenderness again. He gestured wearily toward the group of overstuffed chairs that waited with richly brocaded arms and clenched wooden fists for whatever victims they could seize. "I suppose she's out on probation," he said. "I can assure you that her mother and I will keep a close watch on her. There won't be a second offense, if we can help it. I gather you were detailed to bring her home."

"But I'm not a deputy, I'm not a probation officer," Athena said, and she told him her name. "I was arrested with your daughter. We were released today."

She looked at Ann standing on her nail-studded sandals on the fine oriental rug, and Ann looked at Athena with her gold-flecked eyes, and the intensity suddenly relaxed in her tight, small face, and they both began to laugh.

"What a mess, what a mess," the father said, looking at the two women, who made no effort to stop their laughter. Surely even he saw this as something at long last stirring with life in this mausoleum of a house, something as unexpected as if parched flowers sealed in a tomb had begun to send out vinelike feelers toward the corpse who had perhaps not wholly died. As for him, nothing seemed to hold him together any longer, not the good tweed jacket, or the mauve and gray striped shirt, or the dark olive slacks. The gold band of the wristwatch on his gray-haired wrist was nothing at all, it had no meaning, nor did the cuff link shaped like the gleaming head of a red setter, with a ruby as its tiny eye. The khaki uniform had been taken from him, and with it his will and his intent. Up what street should he go now, and into which city, and what was the destination in the years ahead? War had been wrested from his grasp, and no longer did subordinates snap to salute when he passed by, no longer could he respond with the mere lifting and dropping of his hand, the casual, condescending gesture of the father, of Zeus, saying to them that he permitted them to stand at ease.

The Officers' Clubs of the civilized world could no longer be his haunts, for now they were alive with the talk and the vying and the humor of other, younger men. "My wife's at her modern dance class tonight. She'll be home shortly," he said. "Let's sit down and have a drink. As a matter of fact, I had just started to pour myself one in the kitchen when you arrived."

"I'll have a drink very quickly with you," Athena said, and the foolish laughter of the two women began again. "I'm a teacher. I have an early class tomorrow," she said, and even this sounded ridiculously funny. "In five minutes, I'll have to go."

"Don't go, don't go!" the father cried out. "I haven't heard people laughing in a long time! Just tell me what your brand is. It won't take a minute . . ." His bleak, grieving eyes were pressed on her, pleading for reprieve. "Sit down and talk for a little while. Sit down until my wife comes home. She'd like to hear the whole story from you. I know she would."

There was a spring in his step now as he hastened out the door, and Athena sat down on the edge of one of the wide chairs and spoke in a low voice to Ann, who would not sit, who could not bring herself to speak.

"It's half-past nine," Athena said, and now their laughter was entirely done. "The women are coming out of the library and walking back to the dormitories. In a minute, there will be bed count. You mustn't forget them. Whatever happens, you mustn't forget they're there."

"I'll never forget," Ann said. The father returned with an eager, springing step, carrying two glasses with small linen napkins folded around them; scotch and soda, and ice ringing against the glass. And Ann spoke again. "What story do you mean, Daddy?" she asked, her face gone tight and grim. "There isn't any *story*. There isn't any story in people sitting down in a doorway as a protest against drafting young men to fight the war. It's just a simple *act*, don't you see that, Daddy? It's people acting out a belief . . ."

"Ann," the father said quietly, grievously, still avoiding the sight of her, "if I had the courage, I'd take this arbiter of all arguments out of my pocket and put a bullet through your heart, if you still have one, or through your head, if any remnants of brains remain. I should settle it with you first, and then put a bullet through my own head."

"But why, but why?" Ann cried out in bewilderment.

"Because I have failed you as a father, as I never failed your brother," he said, his eyes still fixed on Athena's face. "In Frankfurt, Germany, I had my son placed under arrest." He straightened his shoulders as he spoke the words. "He was fifteen, going to school at the U. S. Army school there, and he got picked up one night in a Frankfurt tavern. He was getting drunk with a bunch of GI's and their Fräuleins. The MP's were making their rounds, and when they looked at his ID they telephoned me. Middle of the night, it was, and I thought he was upstairs in bed. They were going to bring him back home, no charges or anything like that, and I said, 'To hell with it! You keep him! I don't want him here! Let him face the consequences,' I said. 'Lock him up! Take him to the clink!' So he learned all right," the father said. "He learned once and for all that if you step out of line, you take the consequences. Consequences," he repeated to strengthen the argument, but as he picked up his glass to drink, his voice died slowly on the word.

At that instant, Ann moved quickly across the rug to where he sat, and she kneeled down before him, thrusting herself between him and his drink, putting her slender arms tightly, tightly, around his thickening waist.

"The consequences are that now you will *see* me, that you will speak to me!" she said in a fierce, low voice to him. "You haven't looked at me, you haven't spoken to me since I came home! Look at me, Daddy, listen to me!" she cried out softly, softly, as a docile daughter should, and she flung her head back so that she could look into his eyes. "Speak to me before Mama comes back!" she pled.

"You and your brother, both jailbirds!" the father said in a broken voice, and tears of pity for himself dampened his eyes. But still he reached down to where she was and put his arms around her, and for a brief moment he held her head pressed close against his heart. But not for long, for now he saw across Ann's shoulder that his glass was nearly empty, and he said: "I've had a hard time, a hellishly hard time. I'm going to get myself another drink."

When he had gone through the arch of the door, Athena stood up from the edge of the enormous chair, free of its ruthless possession.

"You'll be able to talk more easily after I've left," she said.

"Yes," Ann whispered in trembling uncertainty. "Yes. But then my mother—"

Carrying his glass with the greatest care, the father was back with them again.

"Oh, don't go, don't go!" he cried out to Athena. "Sit down for a minute! You aren't doing very well with your drink," he said in jocular rebuke. "I've just hit on a plan I'd like to discuss with you. Something really interesting. I'd like your reaction to it, Mrs. Gregson—"

"Gregory, Daddy," Ann corrected him in the softest of voices.

"I thought Ann and I might take a trip together," he said, settling himself by the coffee table again. "I'd like to go right around the world, having a look at the places where I had my tours of duty in the past twenty-odd years. Do it on my own money, not on my wife's inheritance. I've saved money through the years, and I have my pension. Not a fortune, but enough to finance a trip." He took a long swallow of his drink. "I'd take Ann with me. That would be the idea. Oh, sit down, sit down! There can't be that much of a rush! Sit down!" he cried out to them both, and Ann crossed the rug, and sat obediently and humbly on the broad arm of his chair.

"I'm afraid I haven't time to finish my drink," Athena said. "I really have to go."

"But, Mrs. Greggsby, Mrs. Greggsby, you'd be such a great

asset on the trip, if we could persuade you to come along!" the father said. "What about it? What about playing hooky from school and having a look at Tokyo and Athens and London and half a dozen towns in Germany? You're so damned easy to talk to!" he said, and if it hadn't been for the torment in his eyes, it might have been thought that he spoke in high elation. "You and Ann and I could have a ball!" he said.

It was after ten by the time Athena had put the car away, and cleared the kitchen table, and then she carried a paper bag of the remnants of food down the back steps to the garden, and around the wall to the paved area where the garbage cans stood. The outdoor bulb did not light up when she flicked the switch, and she thought: *Tomorrow. I'll put a new bulb in tomorrow.* She could see well enough by the square of light from the kitchen window, and when she had put the lid on the garbage can again, she could even see the two women. Alice B. Toklas and Gertrude Stein, with their pastel green gloves, and their divining rods, were moving in the shadows just beyond. Athena thought she would sit down on the cool stone by the garbage pails to discuss with them for a while the present state of American letters. She knew that inside the plate glass window of the front door the poster depicted still in delicate colors the Vietnamese peasants bowed in their rice paddies, and the black eagle of the air force that flew over their heads. But here in the paved courtyard there was no delicacy of painted pagodas or the rigid evil feathers of cruising death, but only the yellow square of the kitchen light fallen on stone. When Gertrude Stein and Alice B. Toklas saw her sitting there, they laid aside their forked poles, and took their gloves off, and sat down in silence beside her in the October dark.

XVI

IT WAS NOT UNTIL Athena had let the steaming water run into the bath, and taken off her clothes, that she remembered; for there on her anklebone were the seven numbers that Isabelita had printed out with care the night before. It was nearly eleven o'clock, and too late to call, for the children would be asleep, and perhaps even too late to reach Luchies, whose presence in life had also slipped her mind. She copied the inked digits onto the pad by the telephone, and then set the alarm for seven, telling herself that before she left for classes she would call them both. Then she slid into the tub, and as the water closed around her it became a cradle of anesthesia. She was drifting slowly toward sleep, saying to the warmth of the water and to the cake of soap she held like manna in her hand: "I cannot put others where they were." She knew without emotion, beyond any awareness of pain, that Rory and Melanie were never to be replaced. It was not as if replicas could be made of them in the way that the ancient, touching statues on the façade of a cathedral can be replaced by new ones set into the niches torn empty by catastrophe. "And is this not the true reason why I returned Ann to her home and to her monstrous life?" she asked herself, murmuring half aloud in the underwater stillness of the room; "not for her own good, however I may have argued it. And is this not why I cannot telephone Luchies tomorrow, or the day after that, or any day at all?"

At seven-thirty in the morning, sitting at the kitchen table with her coffee cup beside her, and a Brandenburg Concerto making its declaration of faith from the radio by the stove, she dialed the number that had been written on her anklebone. The distant ringing bored and bored into the tunnel of silence, and it might continue until the end of time, she thought, the low, persistent drilling, then the instant of remission, as if in that second the entire world ceased all sound and action to give ear. She tried to picture the room where Isabelita's four children might just be getting out of bed, the older two helping the younger ones to dress, but all she could see was Isabelita drinking orange juice behind the enormous refrigerator door in the prison kitchen, head thrown back, eyes, sharp and wary, skipping this way and that, the scrawny, plucked throat jerking like the throat of a drinking bird. Athena took a swallow of coffee and made the final promise to Isabelita: that she would move them, children and grandmother to this house. She tried again to see the room where the telephone bell was ringing, ringing, and then pausing, then ringing again, not being answered because the grandmother was perhaps out getting milk for the children, buying tortillas, maybe, so that there would be good things to fill them up before the older ones went off to school. She listened for a long while to the steady drilling, then to the half-expectant, half-despairing moments of silence, and then she put the telephone back into its cradle.

An hour later, Athena set her brief case down on the battleship gray of her office desk, and looked through the small pile of letters on her blotting pad, left there undealt with since the day before. There were communications from the American Federation of Teachers recommending new life insurance coverage that would increase the benefits to one's surviving spouse, and ads from textbook publishers who offered to simplify the art of teaching by the mere turning of a page. And there was a letter from Orion Sweetwater, Son of the Moon, which she had sorted out from the urgent messages and set aside in a gesture of self-discipline in order to write to Sybil and Paula and tell them she was free. His letter came from South Dakota, and it said that the sky was blue as a lake, and that the Samoyeds had scorched the cushions of their paws very badly, running through the wood ashes of a dying fire, and that he had bandaged their feet with Unguentine and was trying to keep them immobile in his covered truck.

There were also three communications from students, done on ruled paper and folded lengthwise, with Dr. Gregory and the course number on the outside. One was written in purple ink, one in green, and one in Spencerian red. The one in purple went straight to the heart of the matter, saying: "This semester has taught me one thing anyway: that burning the candle at both ends just doesn't work. I had to show my parents that I could support myself and get an education at the same time, so I've been working at the Greyhound Bus Station thirty hours a week, and as a result missed most of your classes. I think I've kept up with the reading though, Lord knows how, because I'm taking nine other units, but I won't be able to make it to class today for the discussion on Demeter. I'm sorry about this, as I had some pretty pertinent arguments to bring up. Next week I'll get a paper in on Zeus and if my grandfather (on my mother's side) doesn't take a turn for the worse and if I don't have to go home for the funeral, I'll definitely be in class next week. I feel I've accumulated quite a lot of data about the gods and goddesses and whatever, but next semester I'll work out my hours better as I feel there are certain areas I should cover more thoroughly." The signature at the bottom of the page was Harris Egocent.

The next one, written in green, said: "Matters of great emergency kept me from attending the last two sessions of your 'Greek Myths, 408.' I have also not been able to hand in any papers so far, but I am working on one that I think you will find very interesting. It suggests an approach to the Greek myths through the work of William Faulkner. I find that Faulkner explores the nature of ritual and myth in essentially modern terms (i.e., society pitted against the individual within it), in which comic and ironic juxtapositions of word and deed, conception and action, fantasy and reality, constantly occur and re-occur. I am convinced that you will find it a paper worth waiting for. I intend to stay home working on it all this week, so I won't be seeing you in class." It was signed: Jane Atvariance. The third, ball-penned in red, bore the signature of Marvel Banewort, and it began: "Although I have not as yet got around to handing in any papers to you for your 408, I would like to make an appointment to talk with you sometime about a long essay I am considering doing for a course I am taking in major authors. I think this essay could also apply to your class for my purpose is to show how the structure of *Moby Dick* and *The Sun Also Rises* is concerned with the investigation of the levels of consciousness apparent in the actions of the characters. The prime source of exploring the structural techniques will be each author's viewpoint as an operational means of involving the reader in the action of the story. I use the phrase 'operational means' because the two novels I have mentioned are concerned with a tone of progression which I think could be applied as well to the static struggling of the Greek immortals against the dynamic. Both novelists I have cited, as well as the Greek chroniclers, accept the historical use of a time sequence. All of them set up planes of abstraction which . . ."

Athena sat in the gray swivel chair, facing the gray metal of the filing cabinets, the floor gray under her feet, and the long gray hall outside like the prison hall. She folded the letters again, and set them aside, and picked up the telephone receiver, and dialed the seven digits. Almost at once, a child's voice could be heard softly calling:

"Manolita, Manolita!"

"Listen," said Athena. "I'm a friend of your mommy's. Can you hear me?" For a long moment the child's voice did not speak, and it seemed to Athena that the child itself was drifting away on an invisible current, drifting, drifting, like the head of a

flower on a slowly ebbing tide. "I'm a friend of your mommy's,"
she said again, and she saw her own hand reaching stupidly out
as if to take the child's hand.

"Manolita!" the voice repeated, and then a second child's
voice was there.

"You got shoes for school?" the voice asked.

"Listen," Athena said, speaking in haste before the undertow
of silence would suck them both away. "I saw your mommy.
Your mommy sends you her love. She says she kisses you."

And now the sound of tittering began, the sound of several
children laughing, insouciant as the thin, foolish cheeping of
birds swinging on a wire.

"You got *shoes*, kids' shoes?" the voice that may have been
Manolita's asked, and the far twittering of laughter flickered
across the wire and into the bleak office where Athena held fast
to the telephone.

"Tell me where you live," she said. "I can get you shoes if I
know where you live," but now even the laughter had ceased.
"Where's your granny?" she said, trying to woo them back to
speech. "Ask your granny to come and talk to me." She stared
hard at the black, perforated mouth of the lifeless contraption
she held, but only her own breathing answered. "Your grandma,"
she said, in a wheedling tone. "Could I speak to her, to your
abuela," she said, the word suddenly surfacing from memory;
but the children had laid their telephone down in the solitary
confinement of its crib.

In the classroom down the long, gray hall, twenty-eight faces
waited, sixteen white male faces, some with handsome beards
and wide mustaches, some with merely the mustaches, some
with dark glasses to shield themselves from detection, others
with bright blue northern eyes. There were three men with darker
skins, one round as a plum pudding, the two others slender as
gazelles, their cheekbones high, their eyes oriental; and nine
white girls with hair parted identically down the center of their
scalps, light hair or dark, hanging straight as scarves below their

shoulders. There was not a black or a Chicano face among the twenty-eight, and would not be for a long time to come, Athena knew, for this course dealt with a culture they could not recognize as theirs, to be dismissed as belonging to the world of the intellect, of pedagogic opportunity, to an exclusively Anglo-Saxon and oriental world. The floor of it was strewn with cigarette stubs and crumpled paper cups, and wrappers that had once clasped candy bars, and Athena wanted to sweep up the clutter of this world, but instead she lifted the lectern from the teacher's table, and set it down behind her on the floor. Out, out, she reflected as she dusted off her hands, at least with the crutches of authority.

"I don't understand why the name of Demeter's daughter was not to be spoken aloud," said a girl in the front row, dispensing with the raising of her hand. "I've been so brainwashed by that myth that I'm afraid myself to say the daughter's name!" And when other students laughed at this, the girl flung her long, straight raven locks around in their direction, and cried out: "It isn't funny! I felt a terrible mother-dominating thing in that myth! It really angered me."

Athena said quickly that it should not anger her, that it should rejoice her, for it meant she had understood the timeless pattern that myths define and re-define. For myths recount the childhood of mankind, Athena said, not adding that Thomas Mann had said this in far better words, for probably some of them sitting there before her had not heard of Mann; so she offered them his ideas as if they were her own.

"There is a deep well of time where Myth still lives, and will always live," she said, "because it is the primitive and mystical history of all men, and it draws us back over and over to the origins of religion and morals, of good and evil, as conceived from the beginning. In that beginning, Eve was once Pandora, and Pandora became Eve, and if you see in some contemporary situation a re-enacting of the story of Demeter and her daughter, then you have understood the meaning of the Greek word *mythologia.* It refers to 'stories,' of course, but also to their 'telling.' " Athena thought now of Padraic Colum's description of the hedgerow classrooms in Irish villages, where wandering teachers move from place to place, not tied to a desk or bound by schoolhouse walls, instructing the young in reading and writing through the echo-awakening of Irish myths, and Irish poems, and Irish history. For a moment she wanted to speak of the Irish poet, Colum, whose words sprang with a ringing life and music from the printed page; but who seated there in this room would know of Padraic Colum? Not wishing to make them ill at ease, she did not pronounce his name, but took the hedge-row classrooms as her own. "I think you're seeing now that myths are stories that deeply concern not only the narrator but the audience as well," she said, and she told them of the Irish teachers who went on foot from one village to the next.

"But why couldn't Demeter just have let her daughter go, without all that business of wandering around in disguise?" the girl in the front row cried out when Athena was done. "Didn't the daughter have a right to her own life? The way I read that myth, Demeter would have called anyone Hades, whether he was the devil or not, if he happened to seduce her daughter. She was overprotective. You'll have to admit that."

"Don't forget," said a young man in the back of the room, adjusting his dark glasses, "that it would have been difficult to identify Hades—the old man himself—because he is described as having his head turned back to front so that nobody could see his face. There's what seems to me an unnecessary element of mystery and secrecy to deal with in this myth."

Athena began to say again that the Greek myths had survived because they still spoke of the common experience of man, for did not the face of evil frequently wear a mask, or else was completely turned so that it could pass as virtue?

"The element of mystery, or secrecy, is part of the political stance," she said, "such as the presence of our country in Vietnam. The national countenance is turned back to front so that no one can see its features."

The orator of the class, the deep-voiced enunciator, silky-bearded, with grave eyes, withdrew from the banality of this and asked if he might read aloud the parts of the myth of Demeter which seemed to him as vivid as poetry, which was after all, he added with a forbearing smile, why this particular group of people was here.

"I can't agree with you about the contemporary relevance of the myths," he said, "for to me they are like a series of paintings, murals by Puvis de Chavannes or Maxfield Parrish, and obviously dated." The students, all twenty-seven of them, to whom these names meant nothing, looked uneasily away. And *hush, child,* murmured the underground woman. *I have been taught that mythology transcends the individual and contains the life stories of all women and men.* "'Demeter's daughter was gone,'" the orator began reading, his voice like that of a priest intoning mass, "'abducted while Demeter was sojourning on Sicily, and the year of her departure was a cruel one for mankind. Nothing grew in the vallies or on the hills; no seed sprang up; in vain the oxen drew the plowshares through the furrows. It seemed to all that the race of man, and the beasts that served them, would die of famine. Demeter had lost her daughter, and because of this the world was made barren. Not a single blade of grass struggled through the sterile soil, and the white barley, like all other grains, was no more than a cinder. Zeus saw at last that he must take the matter in hand, and he told Hermes to don his winged hat and shoes and go down to the Underworld and bid the King of the Multitudinous Dead to let his bride return to her mother, Demeter, the golden-haired Goddess of the Corn.'"

"Personally, I was relieved when the father stepped into the picture," said the girl in the front row. "Demeter was on such a trip, running around masquerading as an old woman, and putting other people's babies in the fire! It was about time Zeus appeared on the scene."

The orator paid no heed to the interruption, but continued reading in his fine, deep voice: " 'So Hermes went into the dark of the Underworld to persuade Hades to send Demeter's daughter out of the gloom and into the light. He found Hades at the bedside of his young wife, who was grieving and yearning for her mother. When Hermes pled with him, the eyebrows of Hades were raised in a smile, and he spoke to his wife, saying: "Go thou to thy mother, the goddess who now wears the dark raiment of mourning, and be no more so exceedingly sorrowful. Am I not brother to Zeus? I shall obey his will." But Hades secretly put into her mouth the honey-sweet seed of a pomegranate, so that she would be committed to return to him for a portion of each year. Then he harnessed the immortal steeds to his golden chariot, and Hermes took the reins and drove the black horses straight to the fragrant temple where Demeter dwelt. At sight of the chariot of the King of the Multitudinous Dead, Demeter leaped up like a bacchante, like a nimble-footed goat in the mountains, and her daughter sprang from the chariot into her arms and was held fast there.' " *All right*, Athena said to herself. *All right. That's enough.* But there was no stopping the handsome orator now. " 'They talked of what had happened to them both,' " he pressed dramatically on, " 'speaking the whole day enveloped in each other's love. Then Zeus sent another messenger, a great personage, none other than his revered mother, Rhea. She hastened down from the heights of Olympus to the barren, leafless earth and spoke to Demeter, asking her to restore to men the life which came only from her giving. "The Kingdom of Darkness shall hold your daughter for only four months of the year. Eight months shall she be with you, if you will in return permit the life-giving corn to grow again." Demeter was sorry for the desolation she had brought about through her grief, and she caused the heavy-clodded fields to sprout again with abundant fruit. She covered the earth with blade and blossom, and then she hastened to the Kings of Eleusis, and chose one to be her ambassador to men, to instruct them in the sowing of corn. She taught him the sacred rites, and divulged to him the secret of bringing the life-giving grain to flower in the fields. She initiated him in the mysteries which no one may utter aloud, for awe of the goddess was like unto a violin mute placed upon the tongue.'" As the student concluded, he combed the fingers of one hand through his silky beard.

A girl sitting near the windows raised her hand tentatively and said she thought it was a beautiful story; she could not understand why so much controversy was taking place about it in the class.

"It's not a story about a mother putting restrictions on her daughter," she said, speaking without fervor, as if from a dream. "It's about the changing of the seasons. The four months that Demeter's daughter must spend in the Underworld are the four months of winter, when nothing comes out of the soil. The third of the year that she must live without her mother are November, December, January, and February. It's a true and simple story about the seasons changing."

A young man in a light blue windbreaker suggested that it was frequently colder in February than in early November, and he would place the four months as running from the fifteenth of November to the fifteenth of March. No sooner were the words spoken than the girl in the front row again tossed back her hair and cried out:

"What about Australia? It would be summer in Australia in those months, so the whole idea of it being a story about the seasons is a mess!"

And what if the underground woman at this instant flung aside her disguise? Athena asked herself. *What if she should take my place at this table and say without any show of emotion: "There's really no use in any of us staying here."* The underground woman would be the only one with the courage to say this to the twenty-eight waiting faces, the fifty-six ears, the sound of her voice so cold that it would chill even Athena's blood. Standing upright at the table, a teacher facing her students, a textbook open in her hand, the underground woman would say: "We have to find some other way." But instead Athena said:

"Demeter and her daughter are perhaps closer to our own experience than are the lives of the other goddesses. This is because their grief set them apart from the immortals. Demeter grieved as men and women grieve for those they love, not because her daughter had been transformed into a bush, or a tree, or a planet, or into a white heifer, but because she had quite simply died, as men and women and their children die." *And now I must have the candor to speak her name.* But in sudden bewilderment she asked herself: *What is her name? For God's sake, what is her name?* "She—yes, Persephone," she said, making herself pronounce it in a clear, untroubled voice, and she could see the syllables of the name moving like light across the room, "Persephone came back from the dead every spring, and all the new flowers, the violets and crocuses and iris and hyacinths, sprang up in her footprints as she walked."

The papers you write, she wanted to say to them, the elaborate subterfuges for reality that you invent, all this is not your fault. These things were asked of you sometime, somewhere, asked by people who told you this was the way to put it across. You did not invent the answers to the questions that were put to you; you were provided with the formula, and you followed it, and it prepared you for nothing at all. The common experience has been banished somewhere, intentionally and craftily withheld from your understanding, she either said or did not say to them, and now I am asking you to try to give other answers. If Callisto were here, she would sing to you, "Be not too hard when he tells lies, for his heart is sometimes like a stone," and that would be one way of saying it; and if Calliope were here she would ask why the timid and the uncertain in this room are the outcasts in our midst, and that would be another way; and if Virginia Woolf were here, Athena said, hesitating to pronounce still another name they would not know, she would say in a proud but uneasy voice: "For we have to ask ourselves, here and now, do we wish to join that procession, or don't we? On what terms shall we join that procession? Above all, where is it leading us, the procession of educated men?"

"For next week," Athena said, "I would like to give you a quite different assignment. I would like you to write an essay on why we accept to meet in this classroom, and in other classrooms of the humanities, using every possible means to contrive an education that will blind us to the simplicities of life. No, not blind us," she amended it, "but protect us from having to choose between the humble admonitions of the conscience and the substitutes that are offered us in its place."

The Orientals remained as silent as their ancestral tombs, not for any lack of words, but in mistrust of those who dwelt untroubled in their pure white skins. But a young man with viking eyes spoke from the center of the room.

"I'm halfway through my paper on Zeus," he said. "Are you giving us *two* assignments for next week?"

"Perhaps combine them," Athena said. "Couldn't Zeus enter this classroom and speak his mind pretty strongly to us all?"

"You mean, make him a real man?" asked the girl in the front row.

"Well, he was—he is," Athena said.

There were two other classes in the afternoon that day, one in Irish literature, and one that went by the name of "Literature in Society," and before Athena left the college late in the day another note had been placed on her desk. It read: "Please sign these withdrawal forms in triplicate and forward them as quickly as possible to the registrar's office. It is necessary for me to drop out of college for this semester. I am going through an emotional crisis and have to conserve my energies in order to be able to survive as a rational human being." A postscript to the note said: "This should be done *at once* so that my scholastic record will not be adversely affected." *So one more casualty in the fierce battle,* Athena said to the three slips of paper, and she signed them, and found an envelope and put them in, and dropped it in the campus mailbox as she left.

XVII

THERE WAS A FIGURE wrapped in a black cape lying in the shelter of the alcove formed by the tall Corinthian columns. Those passing below in the street would not have noticed it lying there to the right of the green front door where the Vietnamese peasants worked still in the quiet of their rice paddies, and the cruising bird of death hung overhead. Only when she had mounted the steps did Athena see the figure, and she dropped her books and papers beside the soiled bare feet that lay as if discarded under the broadcloth cape's dusty hem. The face was concealed by the high collar, as if to keep the sight of life away, but, kneeling there, Athena could see the crown of the head, and the blond, matted hair that covered it, and her hands began to tremble. *Melanie, Melanie,* the words ran in panic; *I didn't want you to come back like this! I didn't want you to come back defeated! And the children, my God, the children!* Melanie would not have left them, this much she knew; and in the present wildly unhinged moment, she saw them setting out on foot with Melanie from the eastern city, from the darkness of the Underworld, and perishing, first one and then the other, on the way.

It was only when she had laid the collar back, and lifted the girl's head onto her lap, that she saw there was nothing about this stranger that resembled Melanie. The hair had been bleached, and it was growing out, dark brown at the roots, the

full cheeks were mottled, the eyelids inflamed and sore, and the
lashes gone from the encrusted rims. The small, bulbous nose
was reddened and pinched as if from the cold, turned up like a
clown's in the girl's lost face. *And one day I'll come home from
work and find a man lying in the gutter with an empty half-pint
beside him,* Athena told herself impatiently, *and I'll decide right
off that it's Rory.* "Be realistic, practical," she whispered, and
with her fingertips she felt the strong, steady pulse in the girl's
wrist. She put the parched hair back from the square forehead
and listened to the quiet breathing. There were dry flakes of
lipstick on the girl's lips, and after a moment the lips moved,
and the head tossed gently from one side to the other and the
eyes threshed behind the fallen lids.

"I'm waiting for my friends," the girl murmured.

"You can watch for them inside by the bay windows,"
Athena said, her hand smoothing back the faded hair.

The weariness in the girl's face was like a crumpled mask, and
it had made an old woman of her, this ancient weariness of the
flesh, as if every promise made so far by life had been betrayed.
In a low voice that floated rudderless, without direction, the
girl said that the cargo boat for Sweden had left without her.
She hadn't been able to find the dock, but now seamen from
another freighter would be coming for her. She said they were
going to smuggle her on their ship, the words retrieved slowly,
slowly, as if from waters that lapped against a wharf. "It's my
last chance to get home," she said.

"To Sweden?" Athena asked. "Do you come from Sweden?"

"No. My mother, she's buried there," the girl said, speaking
barely aloud. "Charlie Chaplin, he was in love with her once,"
she whispered, and now her eyes opened, small and pale blue
and aged between the sore, cracked lids, then closed again.

"Your friends won't be able to see you if you lie here," Athena
said, and she thought how far the girl had come, for surely the
accent was saying New York, New York; and she thought she
must get her up from the tiles and from under the black wings of

the imperial eagle poised over Vietnam; and she thought the
moment would come when she would drive her up the hill to the
out-patient clinic at the Medical Center, but not abandon her
there; for when she thought of Ann now, she believed she had
abandoned her, abandoned her to her own people, if this could
be done, and as she touched the girl's hair, the weight of guilt
seemed lessened. "It would be better to wait inside, and when
they come, you can tap on the glass," she said.

She held the girl's head and shoulders close against her, and
edged her up inch by inch, raising her, pulling her upright, until
they stood swaying together, the girl's long black cape concealing
all that she was except for the matted hair, the ancient face,
the squat, soiled feet. And now Athena got her through the
door, and onto the wide sofa in the living room where Ann had
slept the first day (which was yesterday). The girl's eyes were
opened again and she did not lie down, but knelt on the sofa,
the soles of her feet turned toward the room.

"Why did you choose this house of all the others on the
street?" Athena asked from just outside the door, collecting the
books, the student papers, from where she had dropped them on
the tiles. *Pound cake and tea as quickly as possible,* she thought,
*or else Dubonnet on the rocks, with a twist of lemon, to save
humanity.* "How did you happen to pick this house?" she asked
again, and the girl looked slowly over her shoulder, over the
black slope of the cape.

"Because they can tie up their rowboat to the tree. It's the
only one," she said, and, knowing the logic of this could not be
disputed, she turned back again to the bay windows to watch the
street below.

Water had boiled in the kettle, and slices of cake lay moist
and yellow on a platter, while slices of lemons were arranged
like miniature wagon wheels on a silver dish on the tray that
Athena carried in. But no sooner had she set it down on the low
table by the sofa than the doorbell cried out sharply. *And what
if the seamen don't care for tea and cake?* Athena asked herself.

What if they want rum, and I know I haven't any in the house.
But instead of the seamen waiting outside, it was Luchies
McDoniel who came through the door when she opened it, tall
and elegant as a figure stepped out of an African frieze, bouncing
a little, but not ostentatiously, on the balls of his feet. A con-
servative Afro crowned his head, and threads of gray were beginning to show in it and in his Vandyke beard. And exactly
what was his quality? Athena asked herself as he passed her with
his casual, half-bouncing, half-stealthy walk, the movement of
his dark neck in the white, cable-stitch sweater propelling him
out of the hallway and into the living room, and finally down
into the peacock-blue armchair.

"Mrs. Gregory, I am disturbed, very disturbed, about you," he
said, and his full, dark eyes swelled larger with his concern. And
what *was* his quality? Athena asked herself again. Even after two
years of knowing him as a neighbor whom she talked with on
the street, she could not define his contumacy, his essence. Was
he merely a good shop-owner and an active member of the local
merchants' association, calm and articulate at neighborhood
meetings, or was he an uncertain man, uneasy even as an upholsterer, a solvent businessman who longed, despite himself, to
take poetry and painting and music and women, whether black
or white, or any woman who seemed beyond his reach, into the
dark, mysterious yearning of his oddly solitary life? "One of your
students?" he asked, indicating with his chin the girl on the sofa,
and Athena saw that now she was lying down, the black cape
drawn around her again, her face turned toward the shelter of
the sofa cushions as she disappeared in sleep. "You work your
students too hard," Luchies said, sitting there in his forest green,
whipcord trousers, green as the Monterey pine in the garden, and
his sober green socks, and the kind of well-polished shoes that
men of distinction wore in the 1950's, and which no bank executive even now would have declined to wear. His dark eyes, convex
like those of a statue, were fixed grievously on Athena. "Just like
you work yourself too damned hard," he said in pained rebuke.

Since eight o'clock that morning, Athena reflected, no spoken or written words had communicated their intent, and it seemed to her now that the day would stammer and falter in confusion until the very end. She carried Luchies a cup of tea and a slice of cake, but he refused it with a slow, grave gesture of his hand.

"What about a Dubonnet to celebrate?" she asked, and he said "no."

"No, thank you," he said shortly, as if spitting out the taste of the drink. "I come here to talk, not to celebrate. I can't make no sense out of what you do, Mrs. Gregory. Like this business of going to jail. To *jail!*" he repeated, his voice gone incredulous and high. "Everybody inside jail trying to get out, and you working your . . . you working yourself into a lather trying to get in."

"You can say the other word," Athena said. "I truly don't mind it."

"The other word happens to be mine, not yours," he said. "I'm speaking classroom English for your particular benefit."

Athena sat down on the edge of the sofa, close to the sleeping girl in the cocoon of her cape, and she took a swallow of tea.

"Luchies McDoniel," she said, speaking either to the upholsterer, with his shop at the corner of the street, or to the solitary, secret man, with his black, cobra-sleek neck, or to them both in the same breath. "Nothing can ever make me believe we're helpless as individuals, as separate human beings. And if I know that as human beings we cannot accept this war, then I must act. There's an expression you hear in France all the time. When somebody's like a ship adrift, when he seems to be cracking up on the rocks, the French say he's 'lost the north,' because he hasn't been able to follow the needle of the compass any more." She took another quick swallow of tea. "I went to jail without having to persuade myself of the logic of it, without arguing with anyone about it," she said, "because the needle of the compass inside me was pointing straight that way, straight to the north, showing me the course to take. It was the only way for me to go then, at that moment . . ."

"I would say categorically," the man said in an acid voice as he hunched himself in his fine white sweater, "that you lost the north when you walked out of this house and into that jail. The only due north course you took was to enter Alameda County. You thought nothing at all of waltzing right out of here and leaving everything to die, to *die!*" he said, his voice going high again, and he tossed in true misery in the blue-green chair. "So it's up to me, with a business running me ragged, to come along and water the ivy, and water the tree out there on the sidewalk they keep snapping the head off of, and me having to climb over the back fence to make it clear to the garden, out there where the plants and the grass is putting roots down and *trying* to keep on growing—me having to tell them that you've lost your head without anyone taking the trouble to snap it off."

"You climbed over the back fence?" Athena asked him in gratitude, and she set the teacup down.

"Over *two* back fences!" Luchies McDoniel cried out. "You cooling your—your—your heels—"

"You can use the other word," Athena said. "I told you I don't mind."

"That's my language, not yours," he said. "You have no inherent right to my way of talking." And then he asked her if she was going back to jail again, inasmuch as she hadn't stopped the war. "Not so far as I can make out, you ain't stopped it," he said. "Not so far as I noticed anything in the news."

He went on saying that one of the differences between them was that he believed in things you could touch and straighten out with your fingers, things whose value was known to you down to the last cent when you held them in your hands, speaking without inflection now, as if the very matter-of-factness of his voice would bring her down from where she was. The materials he worked with in his business, he said, the brocades, the corduroys, the slipcover linens, or what have you, they were what mattered. If you upholstered a sofa with high-shine satin, and did it well, anybody in his right mind would recognize its elegance, he said, and there wouldn't be any argument, and no going to jail about it.

"But what about the materials inside you?" Athena asked. "Even if you can't touch them with your hands, those silks or satins or linens or sackcloth and ashes inside your skin, and the remnants left over from other times and places, still you know they're there."

"Now you're confusing me," Luchies McDoniel said. "First you're a boat with its compass going haywire, and then you're a fence, or a defense, around some kind of private, retail stock of yard goods. A fence or a defense," he said, pleased with the sound of it, and for the first time there was a flicker of satisfaction in the outrage and yearning of his eyes.

For a moment, the sleeping girl's left hand reached out from the folds of the cape, and groped restlessly, blindly, as if in search of something lost; and then it fumbled the black collar higher and was gone again, the hand itself like a wild, naked creature retreating into its covert lair.

"I'll have to try to make her drink some tea," Athena murmured. "I'll have to try to make her eat."

"What kind of homework you been giving her that she passed out?" Luchies McDoniel asked, but he didn't wait for an answer. "You ain't got nowhere with stopping the war, Mrs. Gregory," he went on saying. "So what're you counting on doing next?"

The sudden ringing of the telephone in the kitchen came as a bright, sweet summons to clarity, and Athena went quickly to answer it. But she was not prepared for Calliope, for Calliope's voice saying that she was leaving in the morning for the East Coast, she and Arion, and Athena sat down by the kitchen table, for the strength had left her knees.

"I wanted to get Melanie's address," Calliope said as naturally and simply as if she had known Melanie all her life and merely wanted to see her once again. "I thought I would just drop in and let you know how things are going," she said, and

Athena spelled out the name of the street, and told her the number of the house, hearing her own voice gone foolish and high with eagerness. "No, not the telephone," Calliope said as Athena began the area code. "I think I'll just go there one afternoon and knock on the door. I'll be back in a week."

Luchies McDoniel passed through the kitchen, a shadow moving across the light of Calliope's words, and Athena heard the back door open as he went into the garden. Calliope was saying in several different ways, with laughter and without, like waltz music and like fire engines crashing down the street, that she was going to see Melanie, to see her hands and eyebrows and hair, to hear Melanie talking about miracles, and mystery, and authority with a certainty before which all refutation could do nothing but wither and die. Calliope was about to visit the netherworld where Melanie dwelt of her own choosing, not imprisoned, not captive, yet held in terrible bondage by the deception of a single truth, a single faith contained in the syllables of one man's fallible name.

"You'll be back in a week," Athena said quickly, and then they both spoke exactly the same words at the same moment, or perhaps it was an illusion that they both said, like a single voice speaking: "It is almost impossible to be with people here in freedom who do not live every moment with the knowledge that a war is taking place."

It may have been that as they walked in the evenings twelve times the quarter mile length they had staked in the prison garden, Calliope had told Athena chapters of her history; but however it was the chapters had somehow been lost, forgotten, or else become confused with dreams, for now the question Athena put to Calliope seemed to astonish her.

"When you come back, will you tell me about the people you've come from, who are still there behind you?" she asked. "I've tried so often to imagine, to visualize, your mother, your father," and Calliope's voice interrupted her.

"But we talked about this once or twice," it said, and out of the half dark of the prison dormitory, or through the rusted scimitars of the iris plants in the prison garden, the bits and pieces of scenes and people took shape, people and scenes that Athena recalled without actual recognition, but with the uneasy awareness that they were the re-play, the echoes, of an earlier moment, but where and when that moment had been she could not say. "We were always talking to ten people at once, so you've probably forgotten," Calliope was saying, and Athena thought, *Perhaps because I didn't want to remember it being like that for her,* for the facts of the history were: Calliope was eleven when her father was offered the post of rector of an Episcopal church next to a huge monster of a house which they were to live in in New Jersey. An Episcopal minister is not supposed to divorce, but her father had, so to make it possible for him to accept the offer, a lie had to be invented. The story they told was that Calliope and her sister had lived with an aunt ever since their mother had died, and now that the father was married again, they were to live together, a joyous reunited family.

"Oh, God, oh, God!" Calliope was saying now or had once said. "I wanted to tell everyone the truth, that our mother had died when I was two and my sister four, died of tuberculosis, wanting to speak the truth not because of morality, but because the truth brings you closer to people. I wanted to tell them that after her death, Father had married Dawn, our trained-nurse–housekeeper with the pretty face. As we grew up, she told us that in the last weeks of our mother's life, the doctor had given her pills to help her breathing, and she had managed to take a few extra ones to make her getaway more quickly. Father and Dawn divorced after five years, and we were sent off to boarding school, to a convent school, God alone knows why *that.* And then came this New Jersey offer after Father had married again, and the lie, and the second stepmother, a wild woman who canoed into the sunset. She made monstrous puppets of Bible characters, and had them act out the Old Testament, and she beat my sister, my father's favorite, until her face was unrecognizable." And they lied about the beatings as they lied about their past lives, although before they'd always been punished for telling lies. "We decided it was because it was all right to lie if you were an adult, and all right for children to repeat adult lies, and therefore all right to lie every day and about everything to all the friendly and kindly parishioners who brought us soups and puddings," the story went on. "It was a church world we lived in and lied to, and our house was a poor man's Castle of Trash. The furniture was a collection of attic and cellar storage pieces, donated by the well-wishing. The only good thing about the place was a cherry tree in the backyard. My sister and I used to climb it on Sunday mornings to watch the Sunday School children in their patent leather shoes and white starched dresses dutifully filing into the Parish Hall, where a whirlwind of Christian activity was taking place. Father never made us go to Sunday School. It was perhaps because we didn't have good enough clothes to wear, or perhaps he was afraid we might be tempted to tell the truth when faced with the threat of hellfire. He was a wise man in some ways, but weak and trapped, and because he was not a brave man, my sister and I decided to be brave when we grew up, and whatever was asked of us as adults, we would not lie."

"Calliope, I've been thinking in some kind of guilt how different we are," Athena said. "You take the weak and the lost into your arms and heart without judgment, while I keep asking strength of everyone. The black prisoners needed you, while I was a stranger to them to the end. I'm always afraid people aren't going to be strong, that they're going to lay down their pride in themselves and be defenseless, and you ask nothing of anyone that it's impossible for them to give."

"I have other ways of protecting myself," Calliope said, and Athena heard her laughter. "I turn as weak as water, and then all the weak around me have to pull themselves together and take care of me. When I come back, we'll take the ferryboat to Angel Island, and walk all day there, and talk. And there's another place, wild and lonely along the sea, gray as Wales when the fog comes in, with reefs curved around it like theater galleries. We can—" But Athena at one end of the wire knew, and Calliope at the other end perhaps knew as well, that they could not go to these places, for they were sentenced and bound to prison still.

Luchies McDoniel had come in from the garden, and he stood behind Athena in the kitchen, and had perhaps been standing for some time there, but only now did she hear the sound of impatience in his throat.

"You're so damned weak yourself," he said in a fierce whisper, "so how're you going to ask other people to be strong?" The telephone was silent, for Calliope had said good-by, and Luchies McDoniel went on saying: "I'll be back early in the morning, before you're up, to spray the trees and that bottlebrush bush. They're covered with Caucasians," he said. "Aphids, white fly. I'll climb back over the fences like I did this past week."

"I'll give you a key," Athena said in an absent, an abstracted voice. "Let me give you a key." And then she remembered all that was asked of her at this instant, and she came abruptly back to life. "I'll get you a key right away, and then I'm going to take the girl up to the out-patient clinic. She's in a daze."

"Maybe worrying about what grade you're going to give her," Luchies McDoniel said.

Athena opened a drawer of the kitchen cabinet and took out two keys clasped together on a small steel ring, and she put the keys and the ring into his lean palm.

"One's for the front door, one for the side door," she said. "In a few days I'll have everything straightened out, and then you won't have to bother. You have enough to do in your own life."

"Yes," he said, tossing the keys gently back and forth in his hand. "Upholstery corduroys making their demands, as well as brocades and high-shine satin. Sure. And then you've got brass upholstery tacks, about as fine as any tacks in the world"; all of it, the jibe at Caucasians too, perhaps as funny as anything that could be said were it not for the grief in his dark, swollen eyes.

"Would you help me get the girl down to the car?" Athena asked. It was dusk now, the early dusk of October, almost night itself that pressed against the windows as they walked together into the living room. Athena touched the light switch by the door, and then they saw that the sofa was empty, and Athena stood stricken beyond all sense and reason, staring at the sofa where the girl had lain asleep. "I didn't hear the front door," she said, guilt turned to panic now. "Perhaps she hasn't gone far. Perhaps we could still find her," she murmured, for the girl who had been Melanie in the first moment she had seen her had now become Melanie again, and the tears of omission and of pity for the self that had failed still another time, were almost there. "I should have taken her at once to the clinic," she said. "I shouldn't have waited. Her mind was wandering."

"Not wandering too much to take the pound cake along. And spoons, didn't you have spoons on the tray?" Luchies McDoniel asked.

"Yes, my mother's spoons. But it doesn't matter. It doesn't," Athena said.

It was only after he was gone that she found what the girl had forgotten to take, or else left in exchange: a copy of *One Flew Over the Cuckoo's Nest* and a small dagger with a piercing spine. So I am again the abandoner, not the abandoned, Athena thought, and at the end of this specific day of jammed broadcasts, of garbled communication, she remembered Isabelita, Isabelita, whom she had not yet failed and would not fail. "It is always, always, a matter of beginning again," she said half aloud, and Isabelita became now the vehicle of redemption. She went back to the kitchen and the telephone and dialed the numbers no longer written on her anklebone, but their sequence almost luminous in her memory. She listed to the bell boring through space, then heard it cease as the receiver was lifted.

"Hi," a child's voice said.

"Hi," Athena said, and her fingers tightened on the telephone they held. "Is your grandma there?"

"Abuelita!" the child's voice called.

This time there was no tittering, no hushed laughter, just the information proffered by another child, the voice older, sadder.

"*Abuela está borracha*," it said, and then Athena heard the slap of a hand across a face, and that was all.

XVIII

IT WAS TWO DAYS LATER, and evening again, and Athena sat at the kitchen table finishing supper, reading as she ate, reading that the Vietnamese who were surviving the war in the greatest numbers were the children. "When the war is over," the printed words said, "Vietnam may well be a democracy of the very young." She saw Isabelita's children then as clearly as if they sat at the table with her, and she thought that after she had eaten she would dial information and ask for the street address of their telephone number, and on Saturday she would drive to wherever they might be. "The Buddhist plan for the eventual rebuilding of the country," she read, "is to bring together the half million orphans and the countless thousands of old people who wander from place to place." She could see Isabelita's children roaming forever the devastated countryside of their lives, without shoes, scarcely speaking the English language; she could hear in the silence of the kitchen the crack of a hand across their heads, first the grandmother's hand and then the hands of an alien society. "The Buddhist Church," the article went on saying, "upholds the traditional Asian and oriental relationship between children and the aged, the commitment of the young to the very old and of the old to the very young. The Church believes it is on this unshaken foundation that the cultural heritage of the Vietnamese can be preserved. Men and women in their seventies and eighties have, like the children of Vietnam, lost

their families either through death or through the disruption of
their society, and they sleep in the alleyways of towns, or in the
open country, and, like the children, eat from the garbage of
the military."

Athena sat reading, and eating her own good food, wanting
to be removed from the indulgence of her life now as finally as
when she looked in a mirror and willed the disappearance of
her reflection from its glass. "The Buddhists will help them in
the rebuilding of their lives, the young taking strength from the
endurance of the old, the old finding renewed hope in the
young," she read; and Athena thought of finding Isabelita's
children and Isabelita's mother, and taking them with her into
the lecture hall at college, a small, modest group that she would
usher in, not Vietnamese, but good facsimiles, authentic enough
for the purpose, credible enough to people a landscape in which
two thirds of the water buffalo and other cattle had been killed
by the bombings, a landscape where the replanting of entire
forests must one day be undertaken by hands exactly as young
and as old as theirs. Isabelita's family would stand shyly and
humbly beside her at the lectern, and Athena the statistician
would tell the assembled students that searches would be made
for the bodies of the missing dead, perhaps 40 per cent of whom
had not been found; searches not for the ancient bones or temples of gods and goddesses, as we are doing in the classroom, she
would say, but for the rotting flesh of simple women and men,
and they would be returned to their villages for burial no matter
which side they had fought for, for only complete reconciliation
of the people could give back to Vietnam the separate pieces of
its broken heart.

But the Buddhists envisaged as well another activity, she
would tell the students, one quite different from the breeding of
farm animals and the redeeming of the rice paddies, but just as
vital to the reviving of their land. "They speak of a place, perhaps no more than a roofed-over garden or a pagoda, perhaps a
rebuilt temple, or one that was not entirely destroyed," Athena

would say, "where poets and painters and philosophers, where writers, composers, theatrical troupes, will, by their presence, make whole again the psyche of their country." And perhaps the question would be asked then, the question that had so far been asked only in silence, as to whether the Greek myths were no more than the biased history of the elite of another time, a record in which the common man, the people, had been permitted to play no part. In the questions and answer interval in the lecture hall, Athena might say in an uncertain voice that it could very well be just the opposite, and that the myths were the life stories of all emotional, non-intellectual, tender, belligerent, doomed, poetic, grasping, rebellious, and quite ordinary humanity. And then, recognizing the complexities of man's role, the students would see in the flesh of Isabelita's mother and of Isabelita's children the actual substance of a people with no defenses except fortitude and pride; and as they took their hands and walked with them from the lecture hall, they would believe for that moment at least that the stories concerning the gods were stories that concerned humble men as well.

Athena sat reading, eating, thinking of these things at the kitchen table, not expecting the ringing of the doorbell or the letter the special-delivery messenger gave her. And even with the letter in her hand, she did not return immediately from the country where she had been, but she sat down again at the table and considered the unfamiliar handwriting on the envelope. The name and address were written in small, upright letters, yet each word seemed almost self-effacing, as if it held back more than it declared. It was nothing evil that was being withheld, Athena thought, but simply a final statement held back out of hesitation. It was the handwriting of someone she liked, even loved, Athena knew; a woman who had written the name and address with an excess of tact, of delicacy, each word more a question asked of the post office rather than a direction given. And then Athena saw the postmark on it, and in her haste to open it, she ripped the envelope sideways, knowing now from whom it came.

Calliope's letter was written on both sides of five sheets of thin blue paper, and it began by saying that if there wasn't the war in Vietnam there probably wouldn't have to be communes, for what were the young doing but huddling together in terror, trying not to see that country over there being wiped from the face of the earth. Callisto and Eric were off on a singing-speaking tour for peace, she wrote, and Melanie was as beautiful as the sunrise, and her children were like harp strings; "not too thin," she added quickly. "I don't mean that, but so vibrant, responding to every breath and breeze like the strings of a harp. I didn't see anybody stoned, not a single glazed eye or faltering step," she wrote, "although it may be different on Saturday nights when the Magic Theatre performs. I thought I saw Steppenwolf slinking about in the shadows, although I could be mistaken about that. A bevy of men were (was?) digging a new sewer, or repairing the old one, because—as Melanie explained it with unerring logic—the city was too long in getting around to it, so the commune men, without benefit of experience or a permit, decided it was the natural thing to do. Another cluster of men was erecting a massive wall around Pete the Redeemer's private retreat, and I seemed to catch a glimpse of marijuana plants through the chinks between the stones, but that could have been a hallucination too. I didn't see The Redeemer himself, and his name wasn't mentioned, which is perhaps the way it is concerning the sacrosanct. The women, including fabulous Melanie, were all tending to strictly womanly duties, which would have troubled Lou, the harbor pilot's daughter, if she had happened along. I told Melanie that you and I had been in a rehabilitation center together being rehabilitated, and she smiled politely—my God, those unbelievable eyes!—but the absorbing topic of conversation was the idea they are working on of starting a West Coast branch of the commune. Which city it will be in hasn't yet been determined, but it occurred to me right away that if they do branch out westward, you and Melanie and the children might quite naturally come together again, and not a rehabilitation, but a reconciliation might be, could be . . ."

Yet Charles Manson's picture was still hanging there, Calliope wrote, and Athena, wanting to hear Melanie's voice speaking in Calliope's words, heard instead Charles Manson explicating: "There is no good and no bad, absolutely none. There is only one truth, and that is what is here and now. It's infinite and it's nothing. It's all there is and *it doesn't matter what you do.*" Had he not written from his cell to Pete the Redeemer, pledging his undying loyalty, the Christ who was Pete and Manson the anti-Christ declaring in unison: "I am whatever you make me. I am your reflection. I am you and you are me"? And was not Melanie their garbled reflection, without either Christ or anti-Christ mirroring the purity of her features, or what she was once, or what she might have been? You never saw her asleep at night, Athena said in silence, with a doll in each arm, or witnessed her grief at the death of her turtles in their Japanese garden with their heads fallen forward like leather thongs from under their softened shells; you did not hear her sobs when she found the white mice fathers had waltzed down their runway and eaten their newborn, leaving the scarlet paws and the pink elastic of their children's tails in orderly rows in the sawdust flooring of the cage.

Where were you, Christ and anti-Christ, when Melanie imitated the cuckoo's call as we walked from mountain to mountain with Rory, Athena asked them in silence, echoed the wild bird's voice so plaintively that it left mate, and nest, and its familiar forest to follow us day after day as we climbed? Were you there at that snorkel swimming time when her mask flooded suddenly with water, and I saw her drowning, saw the gasping, reaching mouth and the marble of her sea-flecked eyes, and Rory swam through the interminable stretch of the Mediterranean to where she was, and ripped the mask off, and brought her back, the two of them laughing hard enough to split their sides, but not mine, not mine, any more than my sides are splitting now! Where were you, Pete the Redeemer and Charles Manson, when Melanie was a ballet dancer, her legs and her ponytail like a colt's, or when she was a folk singer, warbling, "How many times must a man look up before he can see the sky," and nobody minding that she sang off-key because of the fervor and purity of what was there? Did not Manson himself maintain after the Tate massacre that "there can't be any real death, just getting into another situation. Death is a figment of the imagination"? (*Hey, Rory, did you get that,* Athena said, giving Rory a nudge with her elbow, wherever he was.) And did not Pete the Redeemer cry out the same message in his own words, saying: ". . . like what Christ had to do before mounting the cross, he said not my will but thine be done, and then there was no cross, no death . . ."? Where were you the winter night when Paula and I waited at Pennsylvania Station for Melanie to come through the anonymous, extinguishable people, clear as starlight down the steps and across the arena packed with nameless, hastening women and men, coming to tell us that the doctor had said yes, it was so, it was true, and she not knowing if Pete would wish this to take place, and Paula crying out softly, "But it's your child, Melanie, it's your child as well as his!"; and that was the first time they had heard Pete's name. And where were they a year later, Christ and anti-Christ, Athena asked herself, holding fast to Calliope's letter, where were they when the department store detective caught Melanie shoplifting, with one baby in her arms and another inside her, and took her, terrified, shuddering with sobbing, to the business office for interrogation? What was it that the counters of a second-rate department store had to offer as temptation, what riches did the panty hose and the infants' wear bargain tables promise would ease her desperation, but did not ease it, that you, false Christ and blood-drenched anti-Christ, finally gave her in the end?

Athena felt weakened, drained, almost undone, by the anguish of her love for Melanie, and she forced herself into calmness as

she asked the other questions of those who had not heard
Melanie, year after year, inquiring about which way to go. What
were Rory and I and Sybil and Paula doing? her quieted grief
went on with it; we were all there. Rory had not wanted them to
grow up, none of the three, but least of all Melanie, and I, came
the old accusation, asked too much in asking them to grow up
immediately. Sybil and Paula accepted adulthood too young,
and subtly, gracefully, turned things around, and made Rory
their little child. Even if they never said the actual words to him,
still the knowledge was there that he would be wounded if he
glimpsed for a moment how old they really were. When Sybil's
oils were shown in New York, she had asked him to drink
champagne before coming, and drink more during the show,
because then you won't have to take them too seriously, she
had not said aloud, because then you can see them as a child's
crayon scribbles, take them as a joke. In her concern for him,
Sybil would not, could not, embarrass or grieve him by the
realization that she was a woman and a recognized painter, and
was even about to marry. She had succeeded, by some feat of
sleight of hand, to present the Irishman who worked in the
British Foreign Office, and whom she would marry, as an older
brother to Rory, who would sing songs of the French Resistance
with him, and teach him some Irish ballads he wasn't grown up
enough to know. And Paula had combed Rory's hair when he
came home in the evening, as she had once combed Melanie's
hair, and filed his nails, and allowed him to defeat her at chess
because his delight in winning was not like a man's but like a
gleeful child's, devious in their conniving to spare him the terrible news that they themselves were children no longer. Paula
had twice put off her public cello recital, had sought to keep the
reviews of her playing from him, drawing even Leo, the news-
paperman whom she would marry after Rory's death, into the
singular conspiracy. It may have been that Paula had postponed
marrying so that Rory need not be faced a second time with
what his daughters had become. Surely no overt word had been

spoken, no artful looks exchanged, yet Leo knew, without quite knowing, that he must cajole the man of other moments, the man who had crossed glaciers, the long-distance skier, the intrepid rock climber, lure him to ski on water with them. He would teach him to water-ski, not asking of Rory the grievous recognition that Sybil and Paula were women, but implying by the invitation to begin again that Rory was as much a child as they.

It was only Melanie who could not transform him into something else. He was her father, and she could not alter it, so, fearfully and in confusion, she turned her head the other way. As for the painting, and the poetry, and the music which defined and salvaged her sisters' lives, she wanted these things with a painful, desperate longing, but she refused to take part in what she saw as left over from the choices they had made. And this proud gesture of refusal came to include all that had once bound them to one another by blood and name. Mother, sisters, dead father were set aside, the members of a circumscribed family life, from which she sought to free herself. She would exile herself from them, even sit in cruel judgment on them, embracing a larger and constantly changing family that would spread its gospel of miracle and mystery and authority to all people for all time. For did not the redeemer claim that all philosophies were incomplete because he himself was the missing link, and until this truth was recognized the world could not be saved? "From me and from me alone," the redeemer had written to a traveling Hindu student who had read the redeemer's description of his own supernatural powers, "it will be possible for you to learn how to re-awaken the fires sleeping in the souls of your Hindu countrymen." If they whom Melanie had cast aside had had the simplicity and the grace to acknowledge the redeemer, Melanie would have forgiven them for what they had been. She would have welcomed them with rejoicing into the community that would be their salvation, and she, as the redeemer's apostle, would have rescued them from the constrictions

of their poor lives. Until you eat of his flesh and drink of his
blood, you cannot be anointed, her silence, her distance, kept
crying out to them; and if only they had laid down their arms
and gone to where she was, she would have wept with joy because of her undying love for them. Her silence and her distance were saying to them that they should be judged because
they looked with judgment on the one way of life that had
given her power. Her mission was to convert them all to the redeemer's ruthless demand for the surrender of the self, for long,
long ago he had exhorted all who would pay heed, as well as
those who did not: "I don't want you to do your own thing. I
want you to do MY thing. WAKE UP!"

I asked too much of her, Athena said weakly and in silence to
Calliope. But perhaps that's better than asking too little, Calliope said uncertainly.

Calliope's letter ended by saying that she and Arion would be
stopping off in Chicago for a few days on the way back, so she
would be longer in returning than she had thought; and that she
hated Chicago and the people there they would have to see.
"Melanie is *not* by any means in solitary confinement," the last
sentence went, "although I would say she is certainly being detained by the authorities."

And then two nights later, actually early on Sunday morning,
Athena was awakened by the sound of voices calling back and
forth on the first floor. At once, the presence of children came
to her mind, a vision of children running through the downstairs rooms, calling out to one another in elation, and she
opened the bedroom door and crossed the landing. When she
looked over the banister, so bright was the entrance hall below
that it seemed every light in the city had been brought here in
celebration of what was taking place. Her mind groped this way
and that to make sense of it all, but she could find no explanation, nothing but the tenuous hope that this was a dream, the
daze through which she moved, the old dream that the war had
finally come to an end, and that the walls of all houses had

dissolved in innocent rejoicing, and the young and triumphant come dancing in. She went slowly back to the bedroom, saw that the clock on her dressing table said half-past four, and put on a dressing gown and slippers before starting down the stairs. She could see that in the brilliantly lit hall below the deep blue expanse of carpeting had been narrowed to a footpath between a clutter of rucksacks, rolled sleeping bags, record albums, electronic equipment, stacked on either side. By the front door lay a collection of hastily discarded sandals and women's knee boots and ankle boots, none of them new, some with the heels ground sideways with wear. She held with one hand to the banister as she stepped into the forest of stringed instruments standing upright, into the babble of voices from the lighted kitchen beyond. From there she saw Lucky the Disciple, a solitary figure in the living room, his black cowboy boots placed by the doorjamb, the branched chandelier and lamps he had lit throughout the room creating a barrier of light, as footlights barricade an actor on the stage. There he stood, tall, gaunt, stoop-shouldered, wearing a long-sleeved white shirt, faded jeans, ribbed white socks. His thumbs were hooked over his broad, silver-studded cowboy belt, and there was a half-smile on his thin, cramped mouth. He stood as if halted in time, no longer a mere vavasor, but a feudal lord come at last into his own. He turned his head to survey his demense, and he saw Athena standing in the hall, and his lips stiffened into a painful grin. But in this moment of ultimate victory, he had forgotten the lines he was to speak.

"How did you get in?" Athena asked, needing the simple details of the maneuver to give it reality. "Why didn't you ring the bell?"

"We didn't have to. Melanie gave us her key," Lucky said. His high cheekboned face was clean-shaven, diamond-shaped, and his ears stood wide and naked against the backdrop of his dark hair. "As soon as we get things straightened out here in the house, Melanie will be coming out with the children," he said, the grin still tight as wire across his face.

"After more than a year of silence on the part of all of you," Athena said (silence, and the unopened letters to Melanie sent back with "Return to Sender" written boldly and coldly across them, the packages for the children sent back with "Addressee Unknown" stamped on them, the telephone calls refused time after time. Was the silent anger in preparation for this? she did not ask aloud). "After that long time of condemnation," she began, but Lucky interrupted.

"Athena," he said, narrow as a lath behind his barrier of light, "we're here because it's time for us to expand, to reach out, and Pete is willing now to include you in that expansion. We're just beginning to grow. We're going to have centers right across America, and up and down the Coast out here. We'll have communities in other countries, in every country on the map. Pete says your being able to speak French will be an asset. In the end, the whole world is going to be his community." It was his eyes that abrogated the apparent simplicity of all he said, his small, stricken eyes in the angular, diamond-shaped face that kept asking the same questions, asking it over and over: *Am I doing it right? Am I doing it like I was told?*

"How many of you have come?" Athena asked.

"What difference does it make how many we are?" Lucky said, his thumbs hooked casually still in the heavy, nail-studded belt, his elbows in the white shirt sleeves jerking a little with the rhythm of his words. "We're one man or we're twenty women and men, but we're still one. You know that. We're all of us Pete." He spoke gently, agreeably, in his moment of triumph, not for an instant the Lucky who had kneeled down with her before the Vietnamese monk in the church a thousand years ago and wept his helpless, confused tears, but a Lucky who had accomplished the mission Pete had assigned him, gentle and genial with her now because for the first time in his life he could lift his head in pride. "As long as I can be of service to

Pete, I'll be able to stay near him," he said. "I've failed him so often, Athena, but as of tonight I haven't failed him. This is going to be his West Coast community center, this house, and I've taken it over for him, and I feel like a great explorer, like Columbus, maybe, claiming land in the name of his king. We're offering you a future, Athena. We want to include you in the family's life. You'll have to accept that," he said gently, patiently, as if speaking to a child.

"No," Athena said above the sound of the voices in the kitchen, her hands thrust deep in the pockets of her dressing gown. "No, I do not accept it."

"So this is the way you welcome your daughter home?" Lucky said, the voice wonderfully indulgent of her inconsistencies, her whims. "You've always wanted her to come home, haven't you? Isn't that what you've been waiting for?"

"No," said Athena, "that isn't what I've wanted. It's something quite different. I want her to be set free."

"Well, now Melanie wants to come back quite freely, of her own accord," Lucky said, and he unhooked his strong, narrow thumbs from his belt and took a step or two forward, his belly concave in the faded jeans. "Melanie wants to give this place a meaning," he went on saying, "a meaning it has never had. You've been asleep a long time, Athena, asleep in a dream of 'peace and love, peace and love.' We haven't anything against peace and love, Athena, but that isn't the whole trip. Oh, you have your fine qualities, and all of us recognize them, Melanie too, but we want to put them to a wider use. Pete was sent to this planet to wake people up, to jolt them out of their stagnation, their self-satisfaction, and make them realize what life's all about. This is Pete's year," he said in quiet triumph, his eyes no longer asking the panic-stricken question, for now the words were coming out exactly right, exactly as they had been said so many times before. "Pete's autobiography is being published, and it's going to sell like wild fire throughout the world. Pete has the key, the great magic key to the secrets of the universe,

and he can unlock every door for you. Melanie's key opened the
door of this house and let us all in, and Pete has the key that will
open the door to all knowledge and understanding for you. We're
not asking you to leave, Athena," he said. "You can always have
a room here. There's no question about that, if that's what's on
your mind."

"Lucky," Athena said, "it's early morning, it's dark still, and
you've probably come a long way. But as soon as you've had
breakfast and it's light outside, I want you all to go."

"Let me straighten you out, Athena," Lucky said. "We're on
a more basic time schedule, the calendar of the tides. It's evening for us now. The girls are getting supper ready in the kitchen.
Feel free to join us. After we've eaten, we want to get some
sleep. It's evening for us now, but you've been doing the same
thing in the same way for so long that it's hard for you to grasp
new concepts. We're continuously breaking ground, trying everything that Venus asks in order to get closer to the natural
currents of the universe. Like, through our time cycle with the
tides we're getting closer to the movement of the planets. Let us
bring you back from chaos, Athena," he said.

"The basic, natural currents of the universe, the calendar of
the tides, the movement of the planets, everything that Venus
asks of us," a Greek chorus of voices in the kitchen seemed to
be repeating, or perhaps the voices were saying something else
entirely as Athena turned to go up the stairs. She stood on the
first step and looked back at Lucky, and a sudden feeling of
tenderness swept over her, a sense of longing for all that was
lost, and she remembered Lucky once earnestly asking the Ouija
board, his eyes swiftly blinking as he spoke, if when the silver
spaceship came to carry them up to Venus he should take blank
tapes with him and playback equipment; and the Ouija board
had said, yes, there would be room on the ship, and the playback equipment could be plugged into the solar sound waves.
And one more thing he had asked, his voice on the edge of

trembling. "Should I pack up all my tools to go with us," was what he had said, "or just my own small personal kit?"

Athena's hands were held fast in her dressing-gown pockets still, and she told herself, *It's Sunday, I don't have classes, there'll be time to work it out. I'll take a bath and get dressed, and go down and have supper with them, and tell myself I'm having breakfast. The thing is to begin again, and to keep on beginning.* But the underground woman was already being carried by unseen hands on an invisible stretcher up the stairs.

XIX

"BACH KNEW EVERYTHING, experienced everything, even jail," the underground woman said aloud to the radio on which a cantata of Bach's, a cantata of his youth, spoke out eloquently and with humorless sincerity. As she dressed, she listened to the oboe lamenting man's fate, and the violins, as if with bowed heads, echoing with muted voices the oboe's recounting of humanity's pain. When the violins took heart and abruptly had a bar or two to say about rejoicing, the oboe tearfully summoned them back to a sorrow and anguish that could not be assuaged. Bach was there in the room with her, bereft for the moment, but still there, and she knew that as long as he was present there was no need to seek out any other friend. "The royal Prussian court was a kind of commune in itself," she said to herself, "and Bach's Pete the Redeemer was the miserable Frederick the Great." She thought of Bach humbly trying out the new-fangled fortepianos at the palace, as the king had bade him, that king who had once said: "The people may say what they like, and I do what I like," and who had never acknowledged "The Musical Offering" which Bach composed for him and sent him. Once she was dressed, she clipped on the largest pair of the great white earrings Rory had brought back from Paris a long time ago. "Earrings for courage," he had said when they buckled on their armor to go to a Foreign Service cocktail party. "Earrings for courage," he would say, "the way I stick pheasant feathers and Alpine medals on my old felt hat."

And now the music had changed to Bach's *Magnificat*, and the choir joined the three women's voices in a hymn of triumph and jubilation that rose in its joy to symbolize the articulate voices of "All the Generations." The two soprano voices and the alto seemed to hover on tremulous wings over this exultant declaration of hope. But the instant the music had ceased, Athena felt her strength taken from her, and in this moment of failing courage she remembered Bach had named the final chorale of his life "When We Are in Direst Need," but had quickly changed it so that no one would know of his despair. She turned off the radio and crossed the room to the telephone on the dressing table, and dialed a number, her finger confusing the digits so that she had to start again, dialing as urgently, as desperately, as if it were the suicide prevention hot line that she called. But it was nothing more than the number Isabelita had written on her anklebone, and after a long moment of listening to the yearning, beseeching sound of the far ringing, a woman's dispassionate, recorded voice enunciated slowly and distinctly across the wire: "I'm sorry. The number you have dialed is not in service at this time." Even after Athena had put the receiver back in place, she could hear the mechanical voice repeating: ". . . is not in service . . . is not in service . . ." But this doesn't mean I can't still get the address, she told herself; I can always do that. I can offer to pay the telephone bill, if that's what it is. If not today or tomorrow or the next day, I can still find them. Nothing is lost, absolutely nothing; it is only delayed.

She went downstairs in the eight o'clock light of morning, remembering the story of a German poet, a woman refugee from Hitler's Germany, who was caught in the rattrap of Marseilles. Why she thought of this woman now she did not know, except that she found herself descending in unnatural rigidity, as if this would bring equilibrium to the chaos of thoughts in her head. The poet had gone to the American Consulate to apply for an emergency visa to escape the gas chambers, to be on her way on the high seas before the Germans closed in on them all, went there cautioned by her American friends not to be dramatic for once, not to make herself conspicuous, but to go in bowing and scraping, curtsying this way and bobbing that, at least until all the affidavits were in. And when even the application for the visa had been refused, she wrote her friends that she had not been in the slightest dramatic, not made herself conspicuous, but that it had happened to be her birthday, and she had walked into the consular offices with a lighted birthday cake balanced on her head. Except it isn't my birthday, Athena told herself, descending slowly, with the greatest care, as if one breath too many would snuff the candles out; it is simply a Sunday on which some kind of decisive battle has been engaged.

In the downstairs hall, the musical instruments still stood upright in their cases, and the electronic equipment, the stacked record albums, the opened rucksacks, their contents now spilling out, made an even narrower passageway between the encumbered walls. The sleeping bags were gone, put to use beyond the closed glass doors of the sitting room, and Athena could see the figures stretched out asleep in their invented night. The kitchen was empty, and the dishes and silver that had been used were washed and stacked in the dish rack on the drainboard. Early sunlight was coming in through the high kitchen window, its brilliance filtering through the silky lenses of the peacock tail-feathers set, tall as iris, in a vase on the sill. And then she saw Lucky stretched out in sleep on the driftwood bench that ran the length of the side wall, the shadow of the heavy table falling on his gaunt, weary face, his folded arms in the white shirt; Lucky asleep, defenseless, an empty scabbard of a man now that the voice and the will of Pete the Redeemer, the two-edged sword of his redemption, had for a moment been laid aside.

Athena ran water into the percolator, measured ground coffee into the perforated tin of its container, and set it on the stove. Then she took an oblong of sweet butter from the refrigerator, peeled the foil from it, and placed it on a dish in the center of the grass mat on the driftwood table. As she put four slabs of bread into the toaster, the pale liquid in the percolator began turning darker with each leap and splash of water into the glass bubble of its dome. The fragrance of the coffee drifted thinly through the sunlight now, and it may have been this that awakened Lucky, for after a little while he sat up on the bench and looked at the room around him and at Athena with dazed, sleep-extinguished eyes.

"Can I give you some coffee?" Athena asked, and he shook his head.

"You know we don't go in for stimulants," he said, and he went on saying in complaint: "I dream so damned much." He ran his lean fingers through his hair, and his mouth stretched slowly open in a yawn. "Do you ever dream about children being beaten?" he asked Athena when the yawn was done. "I dream a lot about the two kids who got beaten."

"What two kids? Who beat them?" Athena asked in a low voice, and an icy hand closed around her heart.

"Oh, one of the guys," Lucky said, still speaking in the daze of sleep. "The kids took some nails he was using to fix the gutters on the roof of Pete's house. I guess he went berserk or something. He hadn't been with us long enough to get straightened out. He's all right now."

"And what about the kids, what about the children?" Athena's trembling voice asked out of the dryness of her throat, and he went on saying slowly, as if still in the power of the dream:

"He took the two kids down in the cellar because they wouldn't own up to taking the nails, and he beat them. And the funny thing is they didn't yell or anything like that, so nobody knew what was going on. Then somebody walking past the cellar windows, somebody heard one of the kids saying, 'Don't hit us any more, please don't hit us any more,' and if that somebody hadn't happened to walk past the cellar windows—one of the girls, I think it was—nobody would've been the wiser. By the time a couple of us got down there, one kid, he wasn't moving any more. I tell you, their faces were swollen up like balloons. You couldn't see their eyes any more. I was dreaming about them." His voice had begun to clear of sleep now, but there was no sound of emotion in it, as if neither dream nor reality had any lasting interest for him. "Someone started making coffee that afternoon," he went on saying, "and now whenever I smell coffee, it's part of the kids being beaten, like we all sat down and had a cup of coffee that afternoon when they'd taken the kids off to the hospital."

"To the hospital!" Athena said out of the unbearable strangling of her throat and heart. "Melanie's children?" she asked, speaking barely aloud.

"Oh, no, older kids," Lucky said. "One was five, the one that was unconscious, and the other one was eight, and Pete analyzed it right away. What that guy was doing was hitting the memory of himself when he was a kid. He was beating himself to a pulp because he'd always hated his parents, and he hadn't dared break away from them. Pete worked it all out in something like five minutes while the rest of us were just standing around trying to make some sense of what the guy had done. That's the way Pete is. All we could think of was the two kids taking the nails, and then this guy going off his nut, but Pete got hold of the *reason* for what had happened, and then we saw it differently. He saw it was the parents' pressure on this guy when he was still a kid, and because of what they'd done to him you could see the guy's reflexes were *logical* and that he couldn't have acted any other way. Maybe I'll have a cup of coffee now," he said.

Athena filled the two cups, and her hand was shaking as she set the plate of toast before him.

"And he's still there, back there where all the children are?" she asked.

"Oh, no, he's with us. He's asleep in there," Lucky said. He had taken the first swallow of coffee, and now he began to grin again. "He's straightened out. You'll meet him and the others when they wake up tomorrow morning."

Athena sat down facing him across the table, her hands pressed tightly between her knees.

"Lucky, I think I made it clear three hours ago," she said. "Now that it's morning, you and the others will all have to get your things together and move on."

"It's night for us. We're on another time cycle," Lucky said. "I already told you that." His tone was casual enough as he buttered a square of toast, and then the motion of his hands stopped and he leaned across the table, his eyes, bold, masterful, obsessed, looking straight into her eyes. It was as if he would force her from the chair and down, down upon her knees, with the terrible power of his cold gaze. "But day or night, we're not getting out, Athena," he said through his thin, barely moving lips. "We're offering you life," he said, his eyes not releasing hers. "We're going to make you see what you're becoming: house, job, bank account."

"Yes, there is that danger," Athena said. "I know there is. But I'll have to solve it in some other way." Her eyes did not move from his as she said: "I want you to wake the others up and go."

"Listen," he said quickly, and his eyes did not swerve. "There's another alternative, Athena. Melanie has always said that Sybil and Paula would like you to live closer to them, wherever they are, you know, and maybe that's what you should do." Some of the old fear had come back into his gaunt face now, but not yet acutely. Nothing is decided, nothing is lost, his eyes were saying to Athena; just don't speak, don't pronounce the words that will be my death sentence as the bearer of Pete's will. "You could get teaching jobs near either one of them, the way you have a teaching job here, maybe even a better one. You know that, Athena," he said. "And Pete would understand if you couldn't afford to give the house, this house, outright to Melanie, or at least not right away, so we'd make an arrangement so that you'd get some kind of compensation, like taking care of the garden for nothing, or even helping you out with the taxes." Surely there was hope still that this single triumph of his life would not be taken from him, surely there were ways and means still untried. "We have something good going, like the beginning of the world," he said, "and it's going to get better every year we live."

"Lucky, there isn't any way to work it out," Athena said. She took her hands from between her knees, and her eyes away from his, and she stood up from the table. "All of you, please go."

Lucky was instantly on his feet, his narrow lips, his rigid jaw, clenched like a fist. Then he reached both arms above his head and his stiff, quivering hands clawed the air in wild summons to the gods to bring down their judgment on her. Once this first speechless moment was past, he began shouting out the imprecations loudly enough to wake the sleeping or the dead, but neither the sleeping nor the dead awoke.

"Your daughter wants to come home and you slam the door in her face!" he cried out, and Athena felt her breathing falter and nearly cease. "Don't do this to yourself, Athena!" he cried, his eyes and voice threshing in panic for the shape and the name of some greater power, greater than either of them in the sunlit kitchen, who would save him from annihilation as the redeemer's trusted and anointed man. "This is the end of your life if you put us out!" he shouted.

"Then it will have to be the end," Athena said in a low voice, and she believed that in some still undetermined way this might be true.

Lucky dropped his arms and took a step toward her, freeing himself of the encumbrance of the table standing between them. He ran his tongue along his lips, and when he spoke now his voice was lower, but the stricken eyes had seized her eyes again.

"Wake up and *feel!*" he said. "Wake up and *recognize* that you're nothing, *nothing*, except as you can perform Pete's will."

"No," said Athena, speaking barely above a whisper. "A thousand times, no."

"Wake up!" he cried out, and he took another step toward her. "You refuse to feel a goddamn thing, Athena! You're a killer, a cold-blooded killer of the spirit! You refuse me as a person and you refuse Pete as a person! You're out to kill the holy ghost in us, in me and Pete and in anyone who's trying to do anything in this world! But you're not going to get away with it because we're going to fight you, and we're going to win!" The words had become now the piercing cries of the mortally wounded, of the brutally and hideously emasculated; they had become the flow of his lifeblood gushing out. But it was not his intention to go down in defeat and death alone. Whatever it cost, he would take the living with him, down, down, in the reeling swoon of death. He stood close to Athena now, and he raised his right hand and struck her hard across the face, and the great white earring was slapped from her ear and broke in two on the kitchen tiles. "Wake up and see yourself for what you are!" he shouted. He struck her twice with his open palm and she stumbled back against the sink. "We'll have this house if we have to burn it down to get it!" he shouted, and he took the last two steps to where she was, his hand lifted to strike again.

But he did not strike again, for now Luchies McDoniel stood suddenly in the doorway, a dark presence in corduroy slacks, the turtleneck sweater deep gold this time, his beard well trimmed, his Afro as ornamental as a meticulously carved and polished headdress crowning his skull.

"So you're having your students sleeping here now!" he said in bewildered outrage. "You've got them lying in there all over the floor!" And then he either saw the mark of the blows and the tears on her face, or the unspent rage in Lucky's, or else the broken pieces of the earring on the floor, and he stopped speaking. He stooped and picked up the broken earring and he slipped the pieces of it into the pocket of his black corduroys. "I can stick it together again. That's no problem," he said, and while Athena held to the sink with her hands behind her, he went on saying to Lucky: "I drop in every now and then to spray the trees and plants back there in the garden." She could barely see him now because of the rush of tears that blinded her, was numb to his presence because of the pain that was like hot iron in her breast. "Mrs. Gregory and me, we were planning on going out to the country today," he said, making up the lines of it as he went along. "We been neighbors for a good many years, and we manage to go out in the country every other week, or something to that effect," he said, maybe not caring if anyone believed him or didn't believe him, having simply made a choice between the savage and the civilized alternatives that were there. "So just get ready now, Mrs. Gregory," he said.

She left them together, and went upstairs and washed her face and combed her hair without looking into the glass. In ten minutes, she was in the front hall and out the door, walking quickly down the street with Luchies McDoniel.

"Where are we going?" she asked, the words like ashes in her mouth.

"To the store," he said. "We can talk there."

"Maybe there's nothing to talk about, nothing to say," she said, not adding the histrionics of *now that my life has come to an end.*

Luchies McDoniel made an impatient gesture with one elegant, dark hand, but he did not speak again until they had reached the plate glass door. Then he took a key ring from his pocket, and his nimble fingertips selected a key from among the others crowded on it.

"Maybe you'd care to begin by telling me the story of your entire life," he said. He held the door open for her, and followed her in from the sunshine of the street into the shadowy assemblage of armchairs and sofas that waited silently inside, some in the tattered finery of worn-out satins, some with springs uncoiling to the floor, others in the neat linen of foundation garments, waiting to be refurbished, their curved mahogany arms naked and empty, their ornate bow-legs polished high. Luchies McDoniel locked the door and led the way past stacked bolts of violet velveteen, of coffee-colored brocades, of flowered cretonnes piled one on the other on the tiers of shelves along the wall. He moved ahead of her, his legs long in the fine corduroys, the gold of his sweater fitting snug as the jacket of a wasp above his narrow hips, past glass-topped counters strewn with outsized books of samples, their disordered pages as delicate in coloring as a Corot painting or else as vulgar as a canvas of Gauguin's. In the cubicle of his office, he gathered up a pile of silky remnants from the chair inside the door, and gestured with his chin for Athena to sit down. Then, holding the armful of shimmering silks, he flung himself into the swivel chair behind the clutter and turmoil of papers on his desk. "Mrs. Gregory, you get yourself into situations," he said, his swollen eyes on her. "The man told me you weren't letting your youngest daughter come home."

She began speaking to him in uncertain, rambling sentences, telling a part at least of the story of the commune, and of Lucky the Disciple, who had once knelt down before a Vietnamese monk on hunger strike in a church, knelt down in acknowledgment of another man's gentleness and faith. But a year later the redeemer had perhaps recommended better weapons, and Lucky and the others had begun to talk of guns instead.

"Lucky wanted my husband's hunting rifles, and a Luger he'd brought back from Germany," she said, not looking at the black man's willfully remote face, his seemingly invulnerable dark throat. "He wanted them to protect the commune people from spades, *spades*," she said, feeling the tears she didn't want returning now. "I dropped the guns and the Luger in the river one terribly cold night. In the East," she said. "Not here. Luchies McDoniel, I cried this morning out of pity for myself, because I had lost my daughter and because Lucky hit me hard."

"Let me ask you one thing," he said abruptly, swinging to one side and the other in the ancient swivel chair. He tossed the bright remnants down in impatience on the desk. "Let me ask you why you didn't hit him back."

"I wasn't angry," she said. "I wasn't holding my anger in." She tried to find him across the pile of silks, to find where he was above the chaos of statements, receipts, the hieroglyphics of measurements of the depth of a sofa, or the length of its arms, or the seat of a chair. "Because I knew it wasn't Lucky's hand striking me. I couldn't bear it any more because it was Melanie's hand."

And now a new wave of despair swept over her, and she closed her fists hard, and turned her head away so as to see nothing at all. If only everything that was remembered could be effaced, she thought; if only the cherished faces and voices and the memory of beloved flesh could be given a final death! She wanted to lose even the knowledge of memory in some bottomless gorge, some crevasse sealed over with impenetrable ice, in order to give herself to a life that would annihilate all that had gone before. She wanted to be held like a child against the stamping of this man's heart, and hear no voices calling out in her blood about things that had happened in other places, other years. *Simply to begin again!* she cried out in silence; *no Rory, no Melanie, and myself newly born, remembering nothing because life will not yet have begun!* But the moment of surrender passed as quickly as it had come, and when Luchies McDoniel jumped up from where he sat, and took her face in his long, cool hands, she turned away in a kind of agony she had not known before.

"No, look at me, look at me," he said, and gently his hands brought her face back to his. "Open your eyes," he said, urging her as a lover urges, and she opened her eyes and saw for the first time the devastated landscape of his life. "Look at me," he repeated, asking for nothing except her recognition that his eyes were swollen with the grief of his own indelible memories, with the outrages to flesh and spirit that had shaped his life, swollen in perpetual mourning for the shackles, the irons, that had been put on him by the time and the place in which he had lived, by the final loneliness that locked him in solitary now. "Look at me," he said again, while behind them in the store the savagely patterned materials still sought to mask the indignities of his history, but could no longer mask them, and she held him close in her arms as he fiercely kissed her mouth.

XX

IT WAS HE who sought to fling aside the flesh of the others that clamored between them, to wipe out by abrupt decisions the other moments, other seasons, stamp out the other streets and cities they had known without each other. It was his impatience with the taste of other mouths, the tenderness of other hands, that drove him to action. Without warning, he released Athena's arms from around him, and on the edge of anger he made the decisions of what to do.

"We got to straighten our lives out," he said. "Make what we got clear and right." He was pacing up and down and tossing and turning in the crowded, dusty office. "I wish we were twenty or twenty-one—no, younger, younger," he said. "That way we'd be starting out in life without nothing behind us, because nothing had time to happen to us before. You only got one earring on," he said, behind the desk now, pulling open a drawer. "While I'm putting the other one back together, you can be calling the po-lice."

"You mean, to put them out?" Athena asked in a low voice.

She sat there bewildered, abandoned, her hands pressed between her knees, not knowing which act to turn to.

"Sure, to put them out," he said. He had taken the pieces of the shattered white earring from the pocket of his slacks, and he held them on his strong, mauve palm and studied them a moment. But even as he ran his fingertip along their edges, it was clear there was something more urgent in his mind. "The telephone's somewhere on the desk," he said, and he jerked his bearded chin toward it without looking in that direction. "Maybe under the remnants I threw down. The number's 553-9111," he went on saying, but there in his voice was the sound of the crucial question he was not putting to her, although the look of life itself depended on the answer that she gave.

"No," Athena said. "I won't do that. I won't call the police. There has to be another way."

"That's a nice little point on your forehead where your hair grows out of," he said. He stood behind the desk still, not looking at her, a tube of Duco in one hand. "Right there in the middle," he said, pleased with the words she had spoken.

"I've been told it's lucky," Athena said, hearing her own voice far and despairing. "They call it a widow's peak," she said, and she lifted her hand, with Rory's wedding band on her finger, and touched the arrowhead of still dark hair.

"I don't know about widows being lucky," Luchies McDoniel said. He placed one piece and then another of the earring carefully down on the clutter of papers. "I got a lawyer friend across the bay. He'll know how to get them out without hassling with the pigs," he said. She watched his fingertip urging the jagged pieces of the earring into place, saw the hairs of his beard alive and tense as he leaned above the desk and gently pressed the filament of glue from the pinhole opening in the sleek nozzle of the tube. For an instant it hung in a silver thread on the quiet air, then drifted down, leaving a trace like a snail's track across the bills and the receipts and the jottings of measurements of backs, and arms, and cushioned seats. "We got to straighten our lives out for sure," he said again, seeming scarcely to breathe as the tips of his fingers wooed the pieces into the suave curve of the earring's broken wing. "There's always going to be little lines running through it, scars like," he said. "But that don't matter. The important thing is to start numbering the things we got to do. Number one's the earring, and I'm getting that done—"

"While I sit here doing nothing, absolutely nothing!" Athena suddenly cried out. "Luchies McDoniel, I don't want to think! I want to stop thinking! Give me something, anything, for me to do!"

"Number two's like this," he said. "I was coming to it." He lifted with care the bed of papers that lay beneath the earring, and carried it to the glass counter, and set it down carefully, carefully, beside the sample books. "While I'm getting legal advice across the bay, I was about to ask you to start stitching up on the machine a pile of slipcovers I got to get done by tomorrow. I already basted them up. Like that we'd be taking care of our solemn obligations to each other." He came back into the little office again, and reached his hand out and touched her cheek and hair. "Number three," he said, "I'll go up the street and pick you up a sandwich, the best they got, and something to drink."

"Just milk," she said. "That will be enough. The slipcovers—"

He led her to the opposite rear corner of the store, where the sewing machine stood, and switched on the machine's small, hooded light.

"You know how to work it?" he asked.

"I learned in prison," Athena said, and she picked up a slipcover from the neat pile of them on the table just beyond.

When he came back with the food, he looked at the earring again, and as he spoke, she halted the humming of the machine.

"It'll be dry by evening. Don't touch it, hear?" he said, and without ever having thought of it before she suddenly knew that he was a father, that he had children, and that he was stern with them. He came to her and took her face in his two hands again. "We're going to straighten things out," he said, but his voice seemed drained of hope now; it had faded and gone hoarse in his throat, as if he had been calling out too long for succor from the lonely place where he was.

He locked her in for safety, and then he was gone, and Athena set the sewing machine into motion again, and with her back turned to the sofas and chairs assembled between her and the plate glass windows and the street, she wiped her mind clear of everything except the work there was to do. There were three slipcovers of St. Malo blue, and a love seat cover patterned with unfading roses of a gloss and a tint that no living flower had ever seen. Against a background of highly polished cream, the hairy, emerald stems reached and writhed, and as the strong, bright needle plunged and soared and plunged again along the chalked line of basting stitches, Athena pled with the roses to shed their armor of gloss and decorative thorns, and become humble enough to wither on the vine. There were pinstriped sofa and chair covers, neat as crew cuts, and these Athena did not address a word to, knowing that they, in their precision, would never lend their rigid ears. But whatever she said aloud or did not say, the gleaming machine, with its pointed forefinger, hummed a smooth accompaniment. Late in the afternoon she ate the turkey sandwich and drank the milk Luchies McDoniel had brought, and then she began work on the wine-colored armchair cover. The stuff of its little skirt had been reinforced by buckram to the substance of cardboard, and its color was that of Dubonnet. As she bent in something like tenderness above it, the sound of the sewing machine was like the muted voices of a thousand bees seeking honey in the store.

It was close to the end of the day when the two bearded black men appeared at the street door, the shorter of the two carrying a brief case, both dressed in printed silk dashikis. It was not until the taller man had unlocked the door and held it open for the other man to enter that Athena was certain who they were. She had never before sensed anything of triumph in Luchies McDoniel, and here he was with his teeth showing white in the mesh of his beard as he introduced the lawyer to her. She sat in the swivel chair at his desk, the bits and pieces of the records of his business dealings held almost guiltily in her hands.

"I was trying to straighten out the papers on your desk," she said in apology, but he did not seem to hear her speak.

"Here's our attorney," he said, elation turning him into someone else entirely.

The lawyer's hair was an intricate and stiff, black lacy cap that had somehow slipped backwards on his gleaming skull, and been caught in the nick of time at the level of his ears before it had gone so far as to leave him entirely bald. His full, bronze face was given length by his pointed beard and his high brow, and his softly fleshed body in the royal blue and orange and crimson silk African dress had the quiet presence of the Buddha. The serenity of his eyes, the untroubled stillness of his being, said quite simply that he knew why he had been given life and what tongue he was intended to speak. He gave a slight bow of deference to Athena, and she saw then that his naked skull had been so sensitively modeled that the contour of the brain itself seemed outlined there. He set the brief case on the desk and snapped the locks open, and Luchies McDoniel took the papers from it.

"Listen to this, Mrs. Gregory," he said, and she understood as he read that there was good reason for their satisfaction, for here in their hands was the solution already drawn up in official language and handsomely sealed in red and gold. The lawyer had prepared on the proper legal form a bill of sale that transferred the property from one name to another, and made ready a deed by which Athena sold her house and garden to one Luchies McDoniel ("known hereafter herein as the vendee"), sold it on paper, in writing, for the sum of one dollar. "And here's the dollar," the vendee said, come alive with jubilation, and he took his wallet out with a flourish from under the purple and sky-blue and silvery folds of his flamboyant robe, and laid the dollar bill before her on the desk.

"If you would put your name here, Mrs. Gregory," the lawyer said. His right forefinger, with its wide rosy nail, indicated the place, and as he leaned beside her the scent of All Spice drifted from his African dress. His bared brown arm was smooth as satin and quite hairless, and his brow, so close to her now, sloped higher and higher to the smoothly sculptured casing of his brain. "Mr. McDoniel has spoken about you for a number of years," he said, his voice subdued, the accent almost British. His dark, Buddha-wide and Buddha-becalmed eyes moved to her face as he handed her the pen, and in them was the gift of respect, not pressed upon her, but offered tactfully, as if seeking to restore her pride to her again. "These papers have no legal value," he said. "They have not been and will not be filed. It might even be questioned in a court of law if papers drawn up on a Sunday were binding on either vendor or vendee."

Then he straightened up, contained in his aura of tranquillity as if within a stained glass temple. And once she had obediently written her name twice on the documents, her fingers and mind numb, Athena got uncertainly up from the swivel chair. She could see no action left for her to take, no work that she could seize upon for direction, and she looked in helplessness from one to the other of the two men, knowing with awful finality that the power to command will, the grace of choice, had for the first time and perhaps forever ebbed from her. From now on until whatever end would come, it would be Luchies McDoniel and the lawyer who would instruct her what to do.

"Number one on the agenda is eviction," Luchies McDoniel said. He had picked up the mended earring from the litter of papers on the glass top of the counter, and he held it out to her on his flattened palm. "Put it on and we'll get going," he said.

"No, no, let me stay here!" Athena cried out softly. She heard the words coming almost in panic, as if from the lips of a subjected woman, and her heart was filled with fear. "There must be some more sewing I could do, or I could go on straightening up your papers—"

But Luchies McDoniel interrupted her. "You ain't being offered no choice," he said, the father's voice speaking again, the father watching her as she tried to clip the earring on.

"Here," he said. She stood submissively before him, her eyes lowered, as his dark fingers clipped it to her ear. "My friend and me here, we're just the onlookers, the witnesses. Now that you got your second earring on, you know what you got to do."

The half-light of early evening lay fragile outside the door, and it gently widened around them as they walked up the street. The air was as warm as if the month was April instead of November, and the first stars could be seen, tentative but steadfast, in the crystal curve of sky above the roofs. The sloping roofs, indigo-dark now, and the chimneys with their tilted chimney pots, were outlined with knifelike clarity against the sky. On Athena's left, Luchies McDoniel held her arm close to his side, and the lawyer walked on her right, his polished brow, his skull, catching the blue of the streetlights hanging between them and the coming night. In silence, they passed two camper buses parked by the curb, their gray sides lettered with slogans, stenciled with outsized floral designs, their licenses from out of state. And then the lawyer began to speak in his quiet voice, with the British accent echoing in it, of a man named Marcus Garvey, who had been a countryman of his.

"Marcus liked to make use of titles and elaborate uniforms, and such," he was saying, and it might have been a friend he spoke of whom he had been exchanging the time of day with just five minutes before. "He did that, at least in my view, to call world attention to the unity that is the most worthy aspect of our situation, the black situation." They passed the little tree with the eloquent exchange of messages nailed to its trunk, and he went on saying: "Mr. McDoniel and I are doing no more than affirming the identity and the dignity of our race, upholding our identity and our dignity as you see us, and as Marcus would like to see us, by the clothes we have put on our backs and the symbolic chains we've hung around our necks. To that extent, we're following in his footsteps, but his feet have made deeper imprints than ours have, and he walked a longer way."

"I don't know as I want to keep walking far in Mr. Garvey's

shoes," Luchies McDoniel said. "Didn't those footsteps you're referring to lead straight to the jail?"

They were mounting the steps to the front door now, and the lawyer asked without rancor: "Are you going to judge a man for that?"

To the three of them it was evening, but to the commune people inside the house it was barely dawn. Luchies McDoniel turned his key in the lock and opened the door, and there in the cold blue angle of light that the streetlamp cast upon the floor, the accumulation of equipment, the open rucksacks, the discarded sandals and ankle and knee boots, the tangled forest of musical instruments, waited still. The three who had come stepped inside, and the lawyer closed the door behind them. It was he, quicker of eye and ear, perhaps because of the total serenity that enveloped him, who first heard the whisper of voices rustling across the hall, and who put his finger to his lips for silence. For no sooner had Luchies McDoniel touched the switch by the door, and the clusters of wall candles sprung to light under their little parchment shades, than the tide of whispers began to run.

"Take your shoes off!" the voices were saying. "Take your shoes off before you come in!" It might have been the sleeping bags themselves, stretched in the darkness of the rooms beyond, that gave them the whispered warning that an alien spirit was in possession of the house. "Take your shoes off!" came the rustle of voices in impatience. "Take your shoes off! Leave them in the hall!"

"Shoes or no shoes, the place has been sold," Luchies McDoniel announced to the open glass doors. "You got half an hour to pack up and go. In thirty minutes the new tenant is moving in."

"Take your shoes off!" Lucky cried loudly out from the kitchen, and immediately the rush of whispering died. "Haven't you any consideration for the lives and the sleep of other people?" he demanded. He had turned on the light in the kitchen, and he stood in the doorway now, his silhouette wild as a scarecrow's, and then the sermon of rage and outrage, of blame and fury and invective began. "Don't you ever *feel* anything, don't you know what it is to *feel?*" he shouted out, his voice tight in his throat with righteous wrath. "You've been put on this planet to *feel*, but you're not capable of emotion! You need to be purified by *truth*. Pete *lives* and *breathes* and *triumphs* in truth, but you can't accept the salvation he offers you!" As he spoke, Lucky kept moving toward them down the entrance hall, punctuating every sentence with a step, then a pause, then another step. "You're *blind*, and *dumb*, and *deaf* to everything Pete is trying to say to you!" he cried out, his voice rising thinner and thinner. "You're full of *vanity* and *pride* and sick ideas about yourselves, and the garbage of your ideas is stinking up the world! Pete could educate you to *understand* and *purify* yourselves, but you've set yourselves up against him. You need to be *humbled!* Pete is *not* a man, he is the *truth*, not the *embodiment* of truth, as you might put it in your *ignorance*, but truth *itself!* But you can't accept that, you aren't humble enough to recognize the *infinite* leader! That's because you're *dead*, all three of you! There's no need for anyone to *kill* you, because you're already *stinking* in your graves, you with your *filthy* shoes on your *filthy* feet!" Now he was as close to them as he could come in the lighted hall, but even though they stood near enough to touch one another, they could not touch, broken apart as they were by the four separate areas of their differences. "Athena with her *hippie* college students and her *hippie* peaceniks, all of them *junkies*, high, freaked out!" He focused his blazing eyes directly on Athena's eyes, then on Luchies McDoniel's, then on the lawyer's, his fierce, accusing, sustained gaze boring and boring, seeking to penetrate the separate visions of life that he could not make them yield up to him. "And you two rigged out like tribal chiefs!" he cried, his lips thin as wire and flecked with foam now, his eyes pressing, pressing first on one and then the other of them in torment. "Are you *pushers?* Is that what you are, the two of you?" he cried out.

The lawyer shook back the sleeve of his silk garment, and his right hand reached up and fell lightly on Lucky's shoulder, the small, smooth, dark hand falling weightless as a leaf on the hard white of Lucky's shirt.

"If I take off my shoes, will you allow me to put a question to you?" the lawyer asked, and it was as if the soft, small, certain hand with its rosy nails had stopped a panic-stricken swimmer in midstream, had for a moment halted him in the deeply twisting, sucking current that must in the end sweep him away.

"What question could you ask that would relate to the loftiest form of government humanity?" Lucky said, repeating in scorn and bitterness to the seemingly humble black man who stood before him words that he and the others must have said over and over, sleeping or waking, to themselves or to those who stood in their way. "Pete has described it like that," he said, and he did not shake the lawyer's hand from his shoulder. "That is the experiment we're engaged in—the loftiest form of *government humanity*, and we've made this house a *celestial house* because we've taken it over as our own. We've made it *sanctified territory*," he said, and now his voice was rising again. "Don't you see what we're trying to do? We're trying to show everyone in the world the way to salvation, the *only* way! I don't say *a* way, I say *the* way, because accepting Pete is the *only* way to expand your souls and be resurrected from the living dead!" Athena saw the points of his teeth, animal-sharp between his flecked lips, and she felt the terrible aching and yearning of his jaws, the savage longing in the hinge of his jaws to close on their throats as fiercely as a cat's teeth close on the body of a bird. "The three of you have never *felt* anything, nothing *ever!* You're *parasites* in a world you've never *experienced!*" Although his eyes still blazed into theirs, his panting, his breath faltered in his mouth now, and he looked down into the lawyer's face and said in a quieter voice: "Take off your shoes."

The rosy-nailed hand, with its dimpled knuckles, that had

rested on Lucky's shoulder, now balanced the lawyer's weight against the molding of the living room door, and with his other hand he pulled the ankle-high, fine suede boot from his lifted foot. His sock was forest green, green as the Monterey pine in the garden, and as fresh and new. Then he shifted his weight to the other hand, and he pulled off the second boot and set it with the other by the door. He stood now in his green socks, almost dwarfed, even more vulnerable, before Lucky the Disciple standing tall as a scarecrow in his cowboy clothes.

"If Marcus Garvey anywhere, any time, held his ground in a pair of socks," Luchies McDoniel said in bitter repining, "there ain't no record of it I ever heard of, none at all." But the lawyer did not seem to know his friend had spoken.

"What is Pete's power over you?" he was asking Lucky, and despite the glossy beard, and the slipping cap of hair on his polished skull, he appeared bathed in eager innocence, almost childlike in mien, as he looked the long way up to Lucky's face. "Exactly what is his power?" he asked.

Lucky did not speak at once, but moment by moment, inch by inch, as he waited the steady glaring of his eyes cut the lawyer down.

"If you don't ask questions, but just accept Pete, you'll be saved," Lucky finally said, speaking slowly. "He'll manipulate you, yes, that's true, but he won't manipulate you for evil." The lawyer stood almost dwarfed, almost pigmy-like before him, ruthlessly, steadily, diminished by the slashing of his eyes. "He'll manipulate you out of drugs and out of the ego-shit you're into. When you have Pete, you don't need anything else or anyone else any more. You don't need newspapers or books. He replaces everything. He gets you off whatever you were getting high on before you met him, alcohol, sex, drugs. Maybe in your case false pride, dressing up like a cannibal chief because you're proud of your race. Maybe in Athena's case being an intellectual, knowing a lot about nothing at all. That's his power," he said.

"And when Pete, the mortal man, is gone, then you'll go back to whatever mandragora you had before?" the lawyer asked.

"Any *what?*" Lucky cried out in scathing irritation.

"Any palliative," the lawyer revised it.

"Pete's never going to go! He'll live in us, he'll live with us on Venus!" Lucky took a step back from them, his eyes pressing on Athena in fearful tenacity. "But until we can leave this planet, Pete wants this house, and we're going to purify it and keep it for him. We're going to have this house for Pete if we have to burn it to the ground!"

"Try striking a match," Luchies McDoniel said wearily, "and I'll turn the garden hose on you. I'll have the fire department here in five minutes. Mrs. Gregory and my friend here go in for non-violence, but I'm violent, I've always been a violent, violent man."

"You can't call the fire department or anybody else," Lucky said. He was smiling now, his lips drawn thinner and thinner across the crooked angle of his face. "The telephone wires are cut. We had to take precautions with people like you around."

The lawyer leaned down and carefully pulled on one soft, beige boot and then the other, stamped his feet gently into them, and at once became a taller man. He reached under the silk of his dashiki and took the folded deed and the bill of sale from his hip pocket, and when he opened them out before Lucky, he appeared to have grown another six inches, knowing in gentle humility that this was to be the moment of Lucky's defeat.

"I had not intended to call the police," he said, and now he seemed to tower above them all, but still contained in his aura of tranquillity, with the soft, far, Buddha-serenity that dwelt in him, remote and untroubled, glowing in his dark, liquid eyes. "It's clear to me now that we're faced with criminal vandalism," he said.

Lucky's lips were trembling as he ran his tongue along them, and his Adam's apple jerked in his throat, for, however it might be explained, the lawyer suddenly stood head and shoulders above him.

"If I wake up the others in there, they'll throw you out on your black asses," Lucky said, but the spirit was quailing, the words of the inviolable scripture were slipping from his grasp.

And as he shifted and trembled in his skin, Athena felt the surge of her returning will, saw him as man defeated by other men, and felt the power of choice come alive in her again. Anger and outrage and even grief were replaced by the ability to act, and the force of this poured through her veins like the clearest of unencumbered streams.

"Please go now, Lucky," she said, and she pulled the front door open and held it wide. Luchies McDoniel and the lawyer were there beside her, but they had become now the motion-less, rooted trees in the background of the landscape, the immovable mountains rising along the rim of her immediate world. "Please go. Go right away, Lucky," she said, her voice quiet as breathing, and her heart beating slowly and strongly in her breast. She looked into Lucky's face and remembered sheepherding dogs she had seen in high mountain places, wild-eyed dogs that circled, and raced, and nipped, as they corralled the errant sheep. But once shepherd or peasant or whoever he might be spoke out his orders to them, the eyes of the dogs went sick and craven, and they sank to their bellies as the presence of man demanded of them. "Get out quickly, Lucky," she said again, and Luchies McDoniel and the lawyer began lifting the paraphernalia from the entrance hall and moving it out on the front steps. Then Lucky, his head lowered, ran past them out the door. For one bleak moment, the underground woman saw Melanie fleeing hand in hand with him, her long hair flying behind her on the mild night air. But the vision faded instantly and Athena turned to the two men. "Here, let me help you," she said. "It's really my problem . . ."; and if she heard the underground woman crying out, *Come back, Melanie! Lucky, come back! Let us talk about things! Please let us talk,* she gave no sign. Instead, she began carrying the musical instruments in their cases from the hall and placing them upright under the slender white pillars, while, below, Lucky could be seen hastening down the sidewalk toward the camper vans. Fleshless as a skeleton he was now, stripped of his substance by defeat. Athena watched him unlock the rear doors of the first camper parked beyond the tree whose glossy leaves, under the high streetlight, shone darkly, richly, as if drenched in oil. Then she walked back into the house alone and into the living room, stepping around and over the sleeping people, and she lit the two floor lamps that stood tall and ungainly on their Victorian brass stems. "It's time to wake up and go," she said to the sleepers and to those who sat up in their blankets or on the soft wadding of their mattress rolls and looked at her with blinded eyes. "It's time to go. Lucky's already loading the cars," she said to the long-haired girls, and to the one sleep-dazed young man, who fumbled their way back to waking.

She moved into the dining room then and switched the light on, and the books on the shelves that reached from floor to ceiling came to sudden and almost articulate life. There were ten girls in all, some slender, some (despite their youth) bloated with fat. Some had ponytails, others had straight lengths of hair, and still others had wide aureoles of gold or red, and in all of them was the same defenseless and fruitless penitence as they obeyed the word of command. So warm-fleshed and womanly they were that the three men among them seemed little more than boys, thinner even than Lucky, but without his bony resistance; soft and broken and perishable, they seemed to Athena, in their pallor and emaciation. All of them, all, rose obediently, their faces turned from her, and folded their blankets, rolled up their sleeping bags, found their shoes in the clutter of them in the entrance hall, and put them on in silence. But not all of them, for Athena came upon two last girls kneeling on the rug in the dining room, groping numbly for their possessions. One of them, heavy-lidded, green-eyed, white-skinned, with tendrils of carrot-colored hair pressed to her cheeks and neck, lovely as a flower, looked up at Athena with the same fierce, hypnotic intensity of Lucky's practiced gaze, and defied the silence of the others.

"You bitch," she said, her sullen voice low and musical. "Last night the Ouija board said you'd die soon, very soon, and that Pete will win in the end."

Then they were gone, and Luchies McDoniel instructed the lawyer to bolt the front door once he had left, and to wait while he got his locksmith friend from up the street.

"Number one is to get the lock changed on the door," he said. "Number two, you'd better have a Dubonnet, Mrs. Gregory. I'll join you in that when I get back."

Athena and the lawyer went into the kitchen, and they sat down with the gray of the driftwood table between them. She could not speak; she could not move to take an ice tray from the refrigerator, to walk to the cupboard and select the glasses, to peel the rind of a lemon from its opalescent flesh, or take out the bottle of ruby wine. All these small, habitual things she could no longer do.

"Mr. McDoniel is a man of action," the lawyer said at last. He sat in his bright, silky dress across from her, his deferential eyes watching, yet not seeming to see, the tears that had begun running down her face. He asked then about the courses she taught, speaking courteously, almost impersonally, as if to give her confidence. "Mr. McDoniel says you've written some books," he said.

"Only two," Athena tried to say, but she could not put the broken pieces of her voice together. "One about Irish fairy stories . . . one about the Greeks . . . their myths . . . the things they believed . . ."

"Yes," the lawyer said quietly, and he did not take his eyes from her weeping face.

"Mythology—you see, mythology transcends the individual," Athena heard herself saying, repeating words that someone else had said sometime, somewhere, a long time before. "The Greek word, *mythologia*, means more than . . . more than a simple collection of stories," she said, and she could not stop the tears from falling. "It also means the . . . the telling of the story." She was speaking in a whisper now, for pain was twisting her voice thin in her throat. "So the narrator . . . and the audience . . . and the whole of humanity," she tried to say without faltering, to say it as she had said it in classroom so many times before, "they come together as part . . . as a part of the echo-awakening process which . . . which is the echoing of history . . ."

"I have heard," the lawyer said so quietly, so courteously, "that if you understand the images of Greek mythology, you will have reached an understanding of all women and men."

"Then I have not understood the images," Athena whispered, and the underground woman gave a silent groan. *Oh, for God's sake, what an orgy of self-pity!* she murmured as Athena's tears ran down her face.

XXI

It was two weeks later when Athena told Calliope the story of the eviction, and the only humor in it was that she had been locked in the upholstery store all one Sunday, stitching slip-covers on Luchies McDoniel's sewing machine. They were ready to laugh aloud at almost any memory at any moment now, for they were at last accomplishing what they had believed they would never be able to do: they were climbing together up the unfolding hills of Angel Island on a late November afternoon. The tall, still, vine-hung trees and the tangled undergrowth mounted step by step with them the couloirs of this green, primordial world, while far above the summits of the trees, through the leafy tree-arms, they could see the rocky heights of another place entirely, the stone towers carved bleakly by the centuries of wind that had passed over the island and the sea, the high, abandoned recording of the slow shifting and tossing and settling of the earth.

"I'm sure Luchies McDoniel is a man of many gifts," Calliope said, "but, *quand même*, I wouldn't like to see you bent over a sewing machine for the rest of your days," and in their elation the two of them burst into laughter again, and lost their breath, and stopped a moment in the climb.

"It might be better, actually, than dealing with things you can't touch with your hands," Athena said, but they did not say the other things that were on their minds. Calliope did not ask if Luchies McDoniel would be Athena's love now, and Athena did not cry out in answer that she could not find the way to begin with love again; and neither spoke Melanie's name. But as they again began to climb, Athena kept a step or two behind Calliope so that she could say more easily: "Luchies McDoniel has a wife and four children. It was when he came back with the locksmith that it was mentioned. The locksmith had a Dubonnet with us, and he asked him how they were."

"I've warned you time and again about the perils of Dubonnet," Calliope said, and they tried to laugh, but when Calliope paused again in the climb and looked back at Athena, their eyes met for only an uncertain instant, as if they could not acknowledge to each other the sight of one man's pain.

"Luchies McDoniel wouldn't take the duplicate key to the new lock," Athena said. Once more they were climbing the steep path, their feet slipping on the loose, gray fragments of rock, on the naked, writhing roots of cedar and spruce and birch. "He said he didn't want to walk in on any future situations," Athena said, "that he didn't have the time to waste."

"That was his pride speaking," Calliope said, not looking back, and Athena repeated in a low voice: "Yes, that was his pride."

"Enough of tragedy!" Calliope suddenly cried out. "This is the one day in our lives we have away from everyone! Athena, Athena, can't we do some mild rejoicing for a change?"

"Yes," Athena said. "We can start by rejoicing that we're free"; and at once the shadow of guilt fell on their hearts.

They walked side by side now, for the path had widened, and they were climbing free of the forest, following the grass-choked ruts of an old wagon road, where military equipment, mule-drawn, had perhaps once passed. The perilously blue sky soared above them, its uncanny color a sign to them that such perfection could not endure, and already the stone turrets of the island high above were swathed in fragile wisps of mist. They were approaching a fine brick building now, a building that even in abandonment was as strong and beautiful as a cannery of the century before. Its wide doors were boarded over, the shingles of its roof torn apart and blackened as if by fire, but it was the fury of rain and wind that had charred it, decade after decade, with the smoldering flame of weather. There it stood in shocked amazement at its rejection, its tall, cathedral windows, empty of glass and heavily barred, asking the reproachful question of them as they passed. It would have been here that Chinese immigrants seeking work on the mainland were detained, Athena knew, and as they passed the broad, broken steps, the sagging porches, of the abandoned place, she could see as plain as day itself the men without papers, without identity, who had stood in line year after year, their names and their faces changing, waiting for a star of hope to appear in the heavens, waiting for justice to be done.

The two women descended in silence the nearly obliterated path toward the long deserted harbor with its crumbling breakwater, and suddenly the scene was altered. Before them lay countless hundreds of gulls, packed close, wings folded, spread in a motionless white cloak across the crazily tilted pilings of the ancient landing pier. As they walked down through the tall grass, Athena put her arm through Calliope's arm in the beloved emerald velveteen sleeve, and at the sight or sound of them, the gulls raised their heads like periscopes, and then the entire white coverlet rose up in separate flakes, the feathered stillness and softness transformed in one instant to a shrill-voiced, hard-beaked, sharp-clawed condemnation of the two women approaching the rotting wharf. They halted to watch the gulls curve divergently away over the bright waters of the bay, wheeling and cawing in paroxysms of hate for all humanity, and in fierce celebration of wave and spume and all that swam and flourished in the sea.

As they stood together before the lonely harbor, watching the movement of the gulls and listening to their hideous cries, Athena knew, as she must always have known, that a veil hung between her and Calliope, the thinnest of veils, and even when they touched each other's hands, the gossamer paling was still there. This had not been true when they worked in prison together, but the time might come even in freedom, Athena thought, when it would no longer be true. They turned now and climbed through the underbrush into the forest again, and as they moved under the trees, a group of the half-tame, gray-coated deer who had taken over the wild island followed at a little distance, their wet noses bright as black patent leather scenting the remains of bread and fruit that the two women carried in their shoulder bags. Yet if one of these deer, just one, should be felled by an illicit hunter, Athena pictured how she and Calliope would turn as one person, inseparable in its passionate defense. Its own kind would wheel and crash away through the forest, but she and Calliope would stanch its wound with strips torn from their own clothing, and one of them would run the long way back to the ferry landing for help while the other held the fallen gray head on her knees, stroking the ears that no longer flickered to sound, asking, *willing* that the black-lashed, brilliant eyes not film over in death. Or if the occasion was something quite different—say, if the ferryboat on which they would leave should be split in two by the prow of a cargo vessel in the deep, rough waters of the bay, she and Calliope would, as one woman, gather the panic-stricken children in their arms, break the skin of their own knuckles as they fought to get the lifeboats free, buckle preservers around the aged, hold the chins of the sinking above the water; only then, as they took action, would the veil that hung between them be dispelled like early morning or early evening mist.

"One year when the children were very young, Arion taught at the University of Baghdad," Calliope was saying now, "and there were ancient, beautiful brick buildings there, too, but made of topaz-colored brick. And what did I learn in Baghdad but that in the total view of history and mankind I wasn't of any particular importance, and nothing that has happened since has changed my mind." She stopped speaking for a moment to laugh. "To be saved from that," she went on saying, "I had to believe in other people, so that's probably how we happened to meet in jail." She said there were certain Days of Protest in Iraq, days when the Moslems took out their wrath on the Jews, and on one of these days the students at the university told Arion there might be violence, and not to hold classes, and so Arion—always the constructive one, she said—got them all into a rather decrepit, chauffeured car and they drove across the desert. "Would it have been an actual desert?" she asked. "I'm hopelessly vague about geography." But there had been endless dunes, and hot winds had blown, and sand gritted hour after hour between their teeth, and now and again, far ahead, the expanse of whatever it was would be broken by the sight of a small tree shimmering like a mirage in the blinding sun.

"A palm tree?" Athena asked as they climbed, and the deer followed on soft feet behind.

"Oh, I don't want to know the names of things! I don't know what kind of tree!" Calliope cried out, but she was proud that she knew Iraq had once been a caliphate. "That means it was ruled by a caliph," she said. Then the rickety car began climbing a rise in the wastes of sand, a hill crowned by an immense stone wall, she went on saying, and rattled them up to a gate, and there an old man collected the entrance fee, a relic of a man who had no teeth, and whose skin was cracked like parchment. "Is parchment cracked?" she asked Athena uncertainly. And he had handed them directions printed in four languages: they were not to take any of the marvelously colored, broken pottery that lay scattered on the ground, for these solid, curved bits and pieces dated back a thousand years or so B.C.; and they were not to go near the jackals, who were likely to become vicious if you approached their pups. So they had wandered somewhat gingerly through the dust-covered Hanging Gardens of Hammurabi, and looked down into the bottomless pits of the dungeons far below. "The hot wind blew, and the dust rose in clouds to the burning sun," Calliope said, "and the only sounds were the sound of the wind in the old stones and the jackals in their caves snarling at the mere thought of us. And we left Babylon rather hurriedly, lost Babylon, carrying on our shoulders the awful burden of that ancient time." And in a few hours they were back in Baghdad again, and it was evening, and the sky cool and immensely turquoise along the horizon, and the university halls were a shambles of broken windows, and in Rashid Street, she said, protesters on this designated day of protest were still shouting and hurling stones. In the North Gate marketplace, four dead men were hanging. "That's when I knew I didn't matter to history, except to speak in a low, scarcely audible voice about violence. That was perhaps what differentiated me from the jackals," she said.

They stopped for a moment then to feed the deer the remains of food from their rucksacks, and as they sat on the carpet of leaves that were still fresh, still green as springtime, Athena began telling Calliope the story about the day, a week before, when she had driven to San Mateo to find Isabelita's mother and Isabelita's children. She had paid the telephone company the six dollars and eighty cents for the September-October bill, and they had given her the family's address. It was an old-fashioned, two-story cottage that she finally came to, not only the faded, sloping roof needing repair but the whole house asking mutely for help as it stood in a block of similarly neglected houses in the run-down outskirts of the town. A weathered fence had collapsed in its effort to enclose the uncut grass of the front yard, and a gate hung sideways on one rusted hinge. Athena had walked up the rotting wood of the steps, crossed the trembling stoop, and it was like approaching a catafalque, she told Calliope, a gray house of the ghostly dead, for there was no stir behind the torn curtains at the windows, no sign of children's discarded toys either among the cattails of the grass, or on the mildewed, faded boards. There was no bell to ring.

"It was the woman next door who told me they had gone,"

Athena said. "She told me the old Spanish grandmother had moved out with her grandchildren the week before, but where they had gone she didn't know. She said the grandmother was taking care of her daughter's children, and perhaps the daughter had found a place for them to move in with her in the city, and I said, yes, maybe that was it."

"Either into lock-up or into solitary," Calliope murmured, "whichever they preferred." And then she got suddenly up from the soft covering of leaves, and as the deer scattered in panic, she cried out: "We must go back to them, Athena! You know that! We're out of our minds visiting abandoned islands like tourists! In another week or two we'll be taking up Bridge! We've forgotten about the others, all the others—"

"We cannot win the war," Senator Gruening was saying in black lettering on printed leaflets that December. "We can continue to pour more troops into Southeast Asia, blast its villages with bombs and napalm, kill more tens of thousands of people, but the problems of Asia cannot be settled by us. Many of our fellow citizens hold the view that it is our patriotic duty to support the Administration, and thus every day dissent and protest become increasingly perilous. Yet it is at just such a time that speaking out is more than ever essential."

Some of the demonstrators still held these leaflets in their hands as they climbed into the paddy wagons, for this time the arrests were being made with greater dispatch. The men and women had sat no more than half an hour in the three doorways of the Induction Center, the streetlights still burning in the dark of early day, when the police read the order to them to disperse, then placed them under arrest. It was as inexorable as the coming and going of the tide, the ebbing of people from the wide doorways toward the waiting vans, and the flow of other men and women to take their places against the plate glass doors. Endlessly, endlessly, went the silent moving out of the tide, and the silent moving in, and, endlessly, patrol wagon after patrol wagon bore the demonstrators away. In one of the moments of flux, Athena stopped short in amazement on the paddy wagon steps, for there was Ann, Ann with her glossy braids and her mini-dress not on a trip from military post to post around the world, but taking her place in the chill of dawn at the Induction Center main door.

"Ann, Ann!" she called out, but Ann did not hear, and the policewoman standing on the cobbles prodded Athena in. "So she didn't go around the world with her father! So it didn't happen," Athena said. "We're beginning all over again!"

"We'll see her soon, any minute now," said Calliope in her green velveteen suit. She sat facing Athena, a barely discernible smile twitching at her lips. "She'll be in the next chariot-full," she said.

Beside Calliope sat Lou, the harbor pilot's daughter, with no cast on her leg this time, but her voice as loud as, or louder than, a cheerleader's shouting:

"There're a thousand people, fifteen hundred maybe this time! I'm pleading *nolo*, so I'll be in for Christmas with the rest of you."

Beyond sat Lydia, the ear trumpet offered this way and that in simple delight, and next to her St. Theresa, looking down at her own small, folded hands. Far in the corner, behind where the driver must be, Callisto had begun to sing, softly at first, but with each line, each voice that joined hers, singing more strongly, with greater clarity.

> *We've got that opposition to conscription* (she sang)
> *Down in our hearts,*
> *Down in our hearts, down in our hearts.*
> *We've got that opposition to conscription*
> *Down in our hearts,*
> *Down in our hearts to stay.*

"Oh, we know that General Hershey doesn't like it, down in his heart!" sang Lydia, and Lou roared aloud: "Down in his heart, down in his heart!"

The purity and the fervor of the *Jongleur de Notre Dame* was in Callisto's voice again as she sang:

> *We've got that old revulsion to compulsion*
> *Down in our hearts,*
> *Down in our hearts, down in our hearts.*

And Calliope's voice followed where Callisto led, singing:

> *We've got that liberation inspiration*
> *Down in our hearts,*
> *Down in our hearts, down in our hearts,*
> *Down in our hearts to stay.*

As they filed through the underground door into the jail, Athena saw Martha for one brief instant. She was being guided in by a police officer, a cop a beefy man, with beadlike eyes sharp as a weasel's above his solid, rosy cheeks. But even with his arm through hers, Martha could not toe the line as a lady was supposed to. There was dried blood on one side of her face, and her left eye was bruised purple from whatever stairway she had careened down the night before, or whatever gutter she had fallen into. When Martha recognized the lot of them, the wreck of her face capsized and she turned it quickly from them so that they would not see.

The demonstrators walked single file down the long, underground hall, a deputy before them and a deputy behind, and Athena told herself that Sybil and Paula would write, but Melanie and Rory were gone forever, somewhere far, far away. *Oh, reality, hold me close, hold me close,* the underground woman asked in silence of the barren walls.

Stand Alone Novel

the Sidekicks